DOWN A COUNTRY ROAD

INGLATH COOPER

FENCE FREE ENTERTAINMENT, LLC

Contents

Books by Inglath Cooper

Swerve

The Heart That Breaks

My Italian Lover

Fences – Book Three – Smith Mountain Lake Series

Dragonfly Summer – Book Two – Smith Mountain
Lake Series

Blue Wide Sky – Book One – Smith Mountain Lake
Series

That Month in Tuscany

And Then You Loved Me

Down a Country Road

Good Guys Love Dogs

Truths and Roses

Nashville – Part Ten – Not Without You

Nashville – Book Nine – You, Me and a Palm Tree

Nashville – Book Eight – R U Serious

Nashville – Book Seven – Commit

Nashville – Book Six – Sweet Tea and Me

Reviews

"If you like your romance in New Adult flavor, with plenty of ups and downs, oh-my, oh-yes, oh-no, love at first sight, trouble, happiness, difficulty, and follow-your-dreams, look no further than extraordinary prolific author Inglath Cooper. Ms. Cooper understands that the romance genre deserves good writing, great characterization, and true-to-life settings and situations, no matter the setting. I recommend you turn off the phone and ignore the doorbell, as you're not going to want to miss a moment of this saga of the girl who headed for Nashville with only a guitar, a hound, and a Dream in her heart." – **Mallory Heart Reviews**

"Truths and Roses . . . so sweet and adorable, I didn't want to stop reading it. I could have put it down and picked it up again in the morning, but I didn't want to." – Kirkusreviews.com

On Truths and Roses: "I adored this book...what romance should be, entwined with real feelings, real life and roses blooming. Hats off to the author, best book I have read in a while." – Rachel Dove, FrustratedYukkyMommyBlog

"I am a sucker for sweet love stories! This is definitely one of those! It was a very easy, well written, book. It was easy to follow, detailed, and didn't leave me hanging without answers." – www.layfieldbaby.blogspot.com

"I don't give it often, but I am giving it here – the sacred 10. Why? Inglath Cooper's A GIFT OF GRACE mesmerized me; I consumed it in one sitting. When I turned the last page, it was three in the morning." – MaryGrace Meloche, Contemporary Romance Writers

5 Blue Ribbon Rating! ". . .More a work of art than a story. . .Tragedies affect entire families as well as close loved ones, and this story portrays that beautifully as well as giving the reader hope that somewhere out there is A GIFT OF GRACE for all of us." — Chrissy Dionne, Romance Junkies 5 Stars

"A warm contemporary family drama, starring likable people coping with tragedy and triumph." 4 1/2 Stars. — Harriet Klausner

"A GIFT OF GRACE is a beautiful, intense, and superbly written novel about grief and letting go, second chances and coming alive again after devastating adversity. Warning!! A GIFT OF GRACE is a three-hanky read...better make that a BIG box of tissues read! Wowsers, I haven't cried so much while reading a book in a long long time...Ms. Cooper's skill makes A GIFT OF

GRACE totally believable, totally absorbing...and makes Laney Tucker vibrantly alive. This book will get into your heart and it will NOT let go. A GIFT OF GRACE is simply stunning in every way—brava, Ms. Cooper! Highly, highly recommended!" – 4 1/2 Hearts — Romance Readers Connection

"...A WOMAN WITH SECRETS...a powerful love story laced with treachery, deceit and old wounds that will not heal...enchanting tale...weaved with passion, humor, broken hearts and a commanding love that will have your heart soaring and cheering for a happily-ever-after love. Kate is strong-willed, passionate and suffers a bruised heart. Cole is sexy, stubborn and also suffers a bruised heart...gripping plot. I look forward to reading more of Ms. Cooper's work!" – www.freshfiction.com

Copyright

Prologue

"Is there a girl out there who doesn't want to be looked at the way Mr. Darcy looked at Elizabeth?"
— *Grier McAllister – Blog at Jane Austen Girl*

The morning had started out typical enough, and might have remained so, if it hadn't been for the eagle flying just above traffic on Park and Sixty-fifth.

From the back seat of a Lincoln Town Car, Grier McAllister removed her sunglasses, lowered the window and stuck her head out for a better look. Surely, she'd been mistaken. But there it was, soaring in a left-to-right pattern, no higher than the top of the street lamps. An eagle? In Manhattan? What in the world?

She remembered then something she'd once heard her mother say when she was a child. Eagle sightings hadn't been so unusual around Timbell Creek, although it was still something to make a person stop and look. Grier had been six or so the day she and her mama had taken a picnic out to the pasture behind her grandparents' house. Her grandpa had an old mule named Lloyd who was willing to act as their shade tree in exchange for the carrots she kept stuffed in her pockets. It was actually a good memory of her mama, and maybe one of the last Grier could actually recall.

They'd spotted the eagle at the same moment that day, watching the majestic bird swoop low out of the sky, like an airplane guided by radar.

"What's he doing, Mama?" Grier had asked.

"Looking," she'd said.

"For what?"

"Most likely his next meal. But my daddy once told me that whenever you see an eagle, it's a sign that maybe you need to pay closer attention to what's happening in your life. Or even what's not happening."

Grier had frowned and asked, "Why?"

"Some people believe eagles are messengers and that they appear when there's something we need to do in our lives."

"Is he trying to tell us something?"

"Maybe."

"Like what?"

"I guess that's the part we're supposed to figure out."

Even at that age, Grier had wondered if the eagle might be trying to warn her mama about the glass bottle she kept hidden in her nightstand. Sometimes, the bottle would disappear, and their life seemed almost normal. No men Grier didn't know coming into the house late at night. No hearing her mama throw up in the toilet in the morning. But then, the bottle always reappeared again, and those were the days Grier wished she could be somebody else, anybody else. The days when she would disappear inside a book, the only escape hatch she could find at the time.

"Did you see that?" she said to Jason, the twenty-something driver maneuvering her through the rush-hour traffic to her office on Madison and Sixty-first.

He looked up, blue eyes locking on hers in the rearview mirror.

"What?"

"That eagle," she said, pointing at the sky.

"An eagle? Really?"

"Yes," she said. "It was right there."

He opened the sunroof and looked upward, shrugging. "You sure?"

"Positive," she said, peering up again only to realize it had now completely disappeared.

"Not too many of those in Manhattan," Jason said, the twinkle in his voice suggesting she might have added a little shot of something to her morning o.j.

"No," she said, feeling silly now and wondering if she had indeed imagined it. "I guess not."

Jason slid the car into a spot in front of a Starbucks green awning. "Same as usual?"

"Yes, thanks," she said, watching as he got out and jogged inside the store. She leaned forward again and searched the strip of sky between the buildings on either side of the car. She couldn't seem to shake the uneasy feeling that she'd seen that eagle for a reason.

Resolving to put it and any unintended symbolism from her mind, she pulled her phone from her purse and began checking e-mail. Twenty-five new messages since she'd gone to bed at midnight. Several new client requests. Seriously needed. A few pleas for last-minute appointments. Would see what she could do.

Jason arrived with her coffee and passed it to her over the seat. "One sugar. Shot of half and half," he said.

"Thanks," she said, returning his smile.

He held her gaze for an extra moment, and then said, "No problem, Ms. McAllister," before pulling back into the traffic.

This wasn't the first time Jason had given her the look, or the first time she'd decided to ignore it. Aside from the obvious, at thirty-seven, the only thing she was likely to have in common with a barely twenty-something guy was an unfortunate weakness for pizza.

And besides, she had recently decided to excuse herself from the predictable course of events that disguised itself as dating in Manhattan. Attraction. Pursuit. Greener-grass-syndrome. She'd just experienced the third phase of this sequence, a nice way of saying she'd recently been dumped.

Carter Mathers – fresh off the divorce train, eyes glazed by the sudden buffet of available women – hadn't actually put it like that. His wording was more along the lines of, "Grier. We're at different places just now. I don't want to lead you to think I have something more to offer you than I do. That wouldn't be fair, would it?"

Fairness being his personal life mantra, of course.

Dating in New York City was its own basic training boot camp. After a while, Grier developed an ear for the subtext and knew that what he really meant was: "Grier. I think you're getting too serious. I like you, but it's only fun as long as no one cares. Besides, there's a great-looking blonde at the table by the window. I'd really like to ask for her number."

Grier had decided long ago that the key was to make expectation parallel with reality. If you knew that, for the most part, Manhattan was full of men who didn't want to see the same face two nights in a row, then expecting to find one who did was simply unrealistic, like hoping your tricep jiggle would completely disappear after two workouts with Gunar at Fitness House.

But if you decided that settling down probably wasn't everything it had been touted to be, then a nice dinner could be had with no hard feelings when he didn't call the next day. Of course, in the case of cute-driver Jason, she would be the one buying the dinner. But even that might have its upside. At least neither of them would foster any unrealistic expectations.

For the next ten minutes, they crept along with the rest of the traffic toward Madison. She lowered her window a few inches, letting in the sounds and smells of the city. Manhattan had its own rhythm, its own heartbeat. Even after nineteen years of living here, it somehow still managed to surprise her. She'd grown up in a different kind of place — a place where the pulse of life beat at a very different rate.

She'd left that place behind at the age of eighteen, catching a bus out of downtown Roanoke for New York City, where she'd been offered a job as a prostitute within twenty-four hours of arriving.

For the first few days, she wandered the streets with her small suitcase, sleeping on benches in Central Park, wondering if someone like her could ever make it in a place like this. She decided then that one of two things could happen. She could let the city run right over her, or she could breathe in the heady power of the place and let it fuel her ambitions. She chose the latter, and she'd never looked back.

At exactly 8:30, Jason pulled over in front of her office building on Madison. He got out and opened her door, again leveling her with a steamy gaze she felt certain he'd used to great effect numerous times before now.

"Good luck with the audition this afternoon," she said, slipping out with her briefcase and purse in one hand, coffee in the other.

He smiled the smile that would surely win him the role.

"If I don't get it," he said, "I'm going to come see you about that image redo."

She laughed, shook her head. "I don't think you'll be needing it, Jason."

"Have a great day, Ms. McAllister," he said. As she walked away, she felt his gaze on her backside. In Timbell Creek, they'd had names for guys brazen enough to cop a feel or leer behind a girl's back. It was just plain bad manners, like talking with your mouth full of potato salad at the church picnic, and would have earned the offender a cuff to the head from Somebody's Daddy. Those of them who had a daddy, anyway.

But with forty in the headlights, Grier decided to take it as a compliment.

Franklin, the doorman, smiled as she approached the building. "Notice anything different about me today, Ms. McAllister?" he asked, with an exaggerated smile.

She stopped, gave him a surmising look. By Manhattan standards, she wouldn't call herself tall, but Franklin stood a good foot below her. He was seventy if a day and had worked the eight-to-four shift in this building for nearly thirty years. He had a book's worth of short stories he could tell about the people he'd seen come and go through its doors. "That's a new suit, isn't it?" she said.

He straightened, lifted his chin a little, and then smoothed his hands down the center of the navy jacket. "What do you think?"

"Smashing."

He flashed another big grin. "Anything else?"

She smiled. "Why, Franklin, look at your teeth. They're beautiful."

"Who knew I still had these under all those years of smoking? Thanks for telling me about that dentist. Nice guy. And the whitening thing didn't hurt a bit."

"I'm glad," she said. "You look great."

"Remember I told you about Marla, the lady who works in the Macy's shoe department?"

"I do," she said. "Any luck?"

"I haven't asked her out yet. She's taller than I am," he said, sounding suddenly worried. "Think that matters?"

"With that smile? No way."

He ducked his head, embarrassed. "I wanted to get your okay on the changes first."

"Franklin, she'd be crazy not to go out with you."

"You think so?"

"I absolutely do."

He nodded hard. "I'll keep you posted."

"I'm counting on it," she said, and headed for the elevator.

On the third floor, she stepped through the glossy red door of Jane Austen Girl, Inc., to find her assistant, Amy Langley, hovering by her desk. As always, Grier felt a little surge of pride for this office she'd worked her way up to. Literally, worked her way up to. The early days of her business had been conducted in an apartment approximately the size of a walk-in closet. A small one at that.

"I thought you'd never get here," Amy said, her voice a near squeak of excitement. She pressed one hand to her cheek, the other waving wildly in front of her like one of those wind up toys kids get in their Easter baskets. A huge fan of old movies, she changed her style according to whatever was currently in her DVD player. Judging from the leggings, the off-the-shoulder sweatshirt and ringlets in her normally straight hair, Grier guessed last night's showing had been *Flashdance*.

"Very Jennifer Beale," she said.

"Thanks!" Amy said, obviously pleased that she got it. She clapped her hands together, her voice catapulting to another pitch. "Oh, my gosh, Grier. You are *so not* going to *believe* this."

Amy talked this way. Emphasis on every two or three words, her eyebrows rising with the intonation so it was easy to get distracted and end up with no idea of what she'd just said.

"Try me," Grier said, heading for her office where she dropped her briefcase and purse onto a leather chair by the window.

"So-an-Irish-duke-is-coming-to-New-York-and-you've-been-chosen—"

Even though Grier was dying to hear the rest, she held up a hand to keep Amy from hyperventilating. This happened to Amy with overstimulation of any sort. The last incident involved a drop-in visit a few weeks before from an A-list movie star who Grier had worked with in the early days of both their careers. Jess Mercer had been her first real transformation, a guy born with true physical beauty and not even a modicum of style. The day he'd come to her then-pitiful excuse for an office, he'd been wearing a horizontal striped rugby shirt with plaid pants and shoes that could only be described as a close cousin to those most often used for bowling.

Apparently, a drama teacher at Juilliard had told him he could be the next big thing if he'd hook himself up with an image consultant who could teach him how to dress. He'd found her in the Yellow Pages, confessing he'd picked her ad because it was the smallest, and he figured he could afford her. No great boost to the ego, but Grier liked to think it worked out for both of them.

At the sight of him in a black Armani jacket and Lucky jeans, Amy had simply lost the ability to breathe. The three of them ended up at the Mount Sinai Medical Center emergency department where she was treated for a panic attack and earned the eternal gratitude of the on-duty nurses who got autographs from Grier's former client.

Thinking they might be headed that way again now, Grier pulled a paper bag from the stack in the bottom of her desk drawer, popped it open and handed it to Amy. She took a few deep breaths, and when she spoke again, her voice was back in its normal range. "Thanks," she said.

"So tell me."

"Okay. George Fitzgerald, Irish Duke of Iberlorn is coming to Manhattan next month for a charity fundraiser ball. The KT Network is doing an episode on it for their show, *Dream Date*."

Grier sat down at her desk, flipped open the lid to her MacBook and turned it on. "Are we being asked to do one of the makeovers?"

"Noooo," Amy said, all but shaking with excitement. "It's even better than that! They want to use the name Jane Austen Girl for the episode and the ball. They also want you to hold a contest in your hometown to pick ten girls for the show."

At this, Grier sat back in her chair, feeling the color drain from her face. "What?"

"Isn't it *great*?" Amy went on without noticing that Grier had just choked out that last word. "To be able to go back to where you grew up and pick some lucky girl who might end up on a date with a duke? How *cool* is that?"

"Why my hometown?"

"Apparently, they want a small-town girl makes good story. Like your own, I guess."

Quiet for a moment, Grier said, "Is that part optional?"

"Which part?

"The hometown part."

Amy looked at her, blinking as if she could not imagine where the question came from. "I don't think so. It sounded like part of the setup."

"Could you call and check?" she asked, trying for nonchalance and hearing her own failure.

"Why?" Amy asked, blue-shadowed eyes widening. "Is that a problem?"

"Ah, yes, actually, it is," Grier said. An understatement, if there ever was one.

"But things have been kind of slow," Amy reasoned. "This could keep us busy, like, *forever*."

"You might be right, but I haven't been home in nineteen years. Going back to Timbell Creek isn't even a possibility. Not for a duke. Not for anyone."

"Oh," Amy said, all of the enthusiasm draining from her face almost instantly. She worried her lower lip with her front teeth, looking at Grier with uncertainty, as if she wanted to say something but wasn't sure she should.

"You can call me an idiot for turning it down, if you like," Grier said. "Most likely you'd be right."

"It's just that—"

"Just that what?"

"Mr. Goshen from the bank also called this morning. He asked me to let you know they can't give you an extension on the remainder of your loan. He said the balance would be due at the end of the month as originally scheduled."

Grier sat back in her chair. "Why? He was just here yesterday and agreed to it."

"I know," Amy interrupted. "He said to let you know it was out of his hands."

Grier turned to stare out the window, trying to remind

herself that she had been in tight spots before. She wasn't unfamiliar with the discomfort. But paying off the loan at this point would wipe out any cushion she had.

"Did I tell you how much the KT Network is willing to offer you?" Amy wheedled.

"No, you didn't," Grier said, not sure she wanted to know.

"Twenty thousand," Amy said. "To set it up, do an initial cattle call, narrow the choices down to ten, at which point they will send in some of their people for the final decision making."

"Did you say twenty thousand?"

"I did," Amy said, her tone making it clear that she couldn't see how Grier had any choice but to accept the offer.

Twenty thousand dollars. Pay off the balance of her last loan and be debt free. In exchange for something she said she would never do. Go back to Timbell Creek.

She thought then of the eagle she'd seen earlier, so conspicuously out of place. Was this its message? *Alert: life-changing decision ahead. You'll have to think long and hard about this one.*

She didn't need an eagle to tell her that.

*

"It's one way in, it's one way out
it's a one stop, one cop, one bar town
where its eight-ball winner breaks, loser racks
it's the same old cars and the same old trucks
the same old coach with the same bad luck
but on friday nights the home team side is packed
it's every reason I left and every reason I go back"
Every Reason I Go Back– Jake Owen

I

_____

*Never, ever, wear open-toe sandals without a
fresh pedicure. Chipped polish is the first thing a
man will notice, even if the rest of you is picture
perfect. Think* Boomerang *with Eddie Murphy.*
— *Grier McAllister – Blog at* Jane Austen Girl

Grier had long envisioned the day she rode back into her
past on a white charger, swiping the muck from every bad
memory with an industrial-size mop until there wasn't a
single marred image left.

But as she drove into Timbell Creek at noon on a
beautiful Virginia May day, her white charger had begun
to limp and the landscape of her childhood appeared
distressingly familiar.

The oil light on the BMW's control panel had begun to

flash a few miles back. Now, the engine made a startling sputtering sound, and then cut off completely. Grier glanced in the rear view mirror, gave the wheel a sharp yank to the right, managing to land two tires on the shoulder before the engine died altogether, and the steering locked.

Sebbie, the twelve-pound ball of poodle fluff who had declared himself hers three years ago by following her home from a run in Central Park, cocked an ear at her.

"Don't ask," she said. "When was the last time I drove the thing?"

Sebbie barked once, now facing her on the leather seat. If he was a man, the translation would be, "So when was the last time you checked the oil?"

"It's not my fault," Grier said. "Isn't that what they're supposed to do when the car's taken in for service?"

Sebbie whined and plopped down on the seat, head on his paws, as if he found the question unworthy of an answer.

Not once in all the times Grier had designed her return-to-the-past stories had they ever contained a scene where she let her car run out of oil. Nonetheless, here she was. She tried the engine again, only to be met with a low groaning sound that signaled nothing more than a complete lack of cooperation. She sat for a moment, her head against the back of the seat, staring through the sunroof at a swipe of vivid blue sky.

How exactly had she let herself be talked into returning to Timbell Creek?

She reached for her phone, swiped the screen and tapped in 411. Nothing. No signal.

Great. Sebbie emitted another low whine, as if this, too, could be blamed on her.

"Looks like we're walking, buddy."

At this new development, he hopped up and wagged his tail.

Grier opened the door and slid out, glancing down at the strappy Via Spiga heels she'd paired with a Donna Karan sleeveless wrap dress this morning. The car had decided to have its oil crisis ten or so miles from the town limits of Timbell Creek, and she did a mental calculation now of how long it would take her to walk that far in these shoes.

She snapped on Sebbie's leash, and he leaped from the car, his opinion on the status of their day clearly having changed.

"Maybe we can pick up a signal down the road a bit," Grier said.

Another bark of agreement, and Sebbie tugged at the leash.

"Hold on," Grier chided, grabbing her purse from the back seat and hitting the remote lock.

They headed down the two-lane road, Grier's heels clicking on the asphalt, Sebbie bouncing along on the end of the leash. The sun glared against her shoulders, its burn

3

reminding her that she didn't have on sunscreen. She flipped the cell phone open and held it up, waving it left and right like a compass in search of true north. Nothing. Nada.

Sebbie pranced along with his head and tail high, as if the two of them were headed for an appointment with the queen of England. Not for the first time it occurred to Grier that it would be nice to have a dog's perspective of the world. Nothing to worry about beyond the immediately visible.

To their right, a herd of black-and-white cows had called a halt to their grazing, staring at them with big, blinking brown eyes. With a snort, a younger calf broke rank and trotted over to the fence for a closer look. Sebbie barked a greeting. The cow lowered its head and let out a long *mooooooo*. Grier wondered what they'd just said to each other. Probably something along the lines of — *wonder what she was thinking when she picked out those shoes this morning.*

The whole herd of cows followed the younger one's lead, and they meandered along the fence until they reached the end, where the cows stood in a group and stared after them. Grier wished for a box of sugar cubes, a bag of carrots or something cows might like. The half-empty container of Tic Tacs hunkering in a corner of her purse wasn't likely to impress them.

Just ahead to the left lay a sprawling cornfield, row on row of short green stalks sprouting from the tilled earth.

The musty scent of clay and fertilizer hurled her back to her childhood and the spring mornings she'd stood waiting for the school bus, watching as Mr. Brooks, who lived across the road, maneuvered his tractor up and down his long field, turning the dirt over for planting.

Uncanny how a memory could send a person straight back to the past. A place she hadn't let herself visit, even in thought, for a long time.

She glanced down at her clothes, aware that the shoes and dress alone cost more than her mama had ever made in three months of working at the sewing factory in town.

She readjusted her sunglasses and blinked the thought away, holding the phone up again to see if it had changed its mind yet. Nope. Sebbie barked and trotted on a little faster, pulling her along with him.

"Hold up there," she said. "I'm getting a blister."

Sebbie actually looked at the shoes and, clearly unimpressed, forged on as if they were the lead contender in a bobsled contest.

A vehicle sounded in the distance, and sudden relief washed over her. She stopped and turned around to glance back, urging Sebbie off the asphalt into the tall grass on the side of the road. Was it tick season yet? She reached down and scratched the side of one leg, the very thought making her itch.

A truck appeared at the edge of what she could see of the long, straight road. The engine sounded like a mad lion, roaring even louder as it grew nearer, and Grier moved the two of them farther into the grass.

The smell arrived a good ten seconds ahead of the mud-green truck. If the stench surrounding it had a color, it would be that exact same shade of mud green. Grier pinched her nose together. Sebbie yelped and made a low-throated protest, before barking in all-out earnest.

As the truck rumbled closer, she read the banner inscribed across the front of the hood. What must have once been white letters had long since succumbed to a dingy brown. **Horace and Son Septik Tanc Cleaning.** Hard to say whether the spelling was intentional in the vein of cute advertising or just an honest case of illiteracy.

To Grier's dismay, the truck began to slow down. Sebbie looked up at her with a pitiful plea in his eyes, wrinkling his nose. She put her hand over her own nose and mouth and blinked hard, her eyes beginning to sting.

The driver hit the brakes and came to a tire-smoking stop fifteen yards in front of them. Just as she considered ducking into the cow pasture, the reverse lights popped on, and the truck began to roll backward. The smell now hit her full force, and she caught a glimpse of the hose hanging from one side, trying not to imagine where it had last been used.

"Hey, there, ma'am!"

Grier lifted her gaze to the lowered window on the truck's passenger side. A young man in his late twenties grinned out at her, his bill cap boasting the same company logo as the front of the truck. "You need some help there, ma'am?"

Sebbie began to bark, as though he'd suddenly realized it was his duty. Grier rubbed his back, saying, "Ah, no, actually, we're fine." She waved her cell phone as if that explained why she was walking this road in her unfortunate choice of footwear.

The driver leaned forward. If the guy on the passenger side was the son in Horace and Son, this could only be Horace.

"That yer BMW back yonder?" he asked. A front middle tooth had gone missing, accounting for the audible whistle between each word.

"Yes, I seem to have a little oil problem."

"Funny how these fancy cars won't cooperate without it," he said, chuckling. "Y'all hop on in here, and we'll give you a ride up to the Exxon."

"Oh, thank you so much," she said quickly, "but it's such a nice day, we're fine to walk."

Son looked at her as if the top of her head had just sprung a worrisome leak. "Shoot now, it's gotta be five miles or more."

Sebbie barked again and started to pull her toward the truck, obviously in agreement with Son.

"Nothing like a good walk on a spring day," she said, painting the words with a big smile.

This time, Horace delivered the look. "If you say so, ma'am."

"Thank you for stopping, though."

Both men nodded, and then the truck ground off one gear to the next, until it turned to a blip in the distance.

The smell, however, lingered.

Grier glanced down at Sebbie, unable to resist scolding him. "You were just going to hop right in there with them?"

He cocked his head to one side and started walking, forcing her to follow.

She teetered after him. "What made you decide you could live with the smell?"

Sebbie barked once and glanced back at her shoes.

"Yeah, well, I can hardly roll back into Timbell Creek reeking of someone's septic tank, can I?"

Sebbie pranced on, head high.

Her blister now raged in protest, and she wished for the first-aid kit in the glove compartment of her car. They walked another half mile or so in silence, the sun raising more red splotches on her skin.

Sebbie started to pant, and sweat stains bloomed in the armholes of Grier's sleeveless dress. Lovely.

She had started to seriously regret her rejection of Horace and Son when another vehicle rounded the curve behind them. She glanced at her swelling feet – her pedicured red toes were starting to look like cherry tomatoes. This time, she wouldn't be so picky.

A red Chevrolet truck roared toward them, the body of which had been jacked a good foot higher than its original intended position above the tires. The chrome bumpers and side runner gleamed as if maintained by someone who cleaned royal silver for a living.

The horn on this one played "I Wish I Was in Dixie." Sebbie's bark now hit a few notes of uncertainty before evolving into a low *rrrrrrr*. The truck stopped, and the driver leaned over, rolling down the passenger side window. "You need some—"

The question ended there, and they recognized each other at the same moment. The sound of his voice flung her back nineteen years to a place she had never imagined again finding herself. First thought? He still looked like Bradley Cooper.

Whoever said life always turned out fair never spent nearly two decades wishing in vain for an old boyfriend to develop a paunch and chin warts.

"Darryl Lee?"

"Is that really you, Grier?" he asked, disbelieving.

"I—yes," she said, hearing the shock in her own voice.

He lowered his dark sunglasses and gave her a long look, following it up with a whistle. "Good gracious, girl, who woulda guessed you'd turn out this fine?"

Should she be flattered or offended? Considering their past, she latched onto the latter.

"Now that's a compliment," he assured her, as if he'd read her decision.

"Thanks," she said, failing to disguise her sarcasm.

"That your car I passed a couple miles back, or are you

on some kind of marathon walking tour?" His chuckle had Southern-boy charm.

"That was my car," she said, forcing the words out through a fixed smile.

"You need some help?"

She kept the smile pasted in place, trying hard not to compare his offer to jumping into a pit of vipers. She'd have sacrificed manicures for a year to have another option, but her feet throbbed, and the possibility of being forced to wear bedroom slippers in front of the cameras tomorrow morning prodded the answer from her. "A ride to the next gas station would be great."

He opened the door and patted the seat. "Sure thing, baby."

"So not your baby," she said, climbing in with Sebbie under her arm.

Darryl Lee grinned an infuriating grin.

The seats had been slicked in silicone spray, and she slid backward with a mortifying lack of grace. Sebbie grappled for footing, too, before giving up altogether and plopping down, legs spread-eagled.

She remembered then that the seats in the Chevelle that Darryl Lee had driven in high school had a similar sliding-board effect. Some unsettling memories of making out in the back seat of that car floated up to the soundtrack of the two of them giggling wildly and slipping around like two fools greased with shortening.

A speaker hung in either corner of the truck's interior, and the low twang of bluegrass filled the awkward silence.

"Thanks for the ride," she said. "If you don't mind, I've got somewhere to be."

His gaze lingered at the neckline of her dress before he slapped a hand on the steering wheel. "No problem," he said, gunning the truck back onto the road, gravel spitting out behind them.

Darryl Lee reached over and patted Sebbie's head, only to receive a low rumble of complaint in return. "He looks like something the cat spit out."

She sliced him a glare.

"Nice leash though. Is that Louis Vuitton?"

"Like you would know Louis Vuitton from Walmart."

Darryl Lee laughed. "Girl, I've had a little polish since you knew me."

Grier pulled Sebbie onto her lap just as Darryl Lee gave his fingers a sniff and then drew back with an astonished, "Whew. What is that smell? You two get into something out there?"

Immediately defensive, she said, "This truck drove by and we. . .never mind." If mortification needed a poster girl, she'd be a shoo-in. Of the many reunion scenarios with Darryl Lee she'd envisioned over the years, this wasn't one of them.

Darryl Lee draped his arm across the seat, steering with his left hand and pinning her with an assessing look.

"Shouldn't you be watching the road?" she asked.

He grinned and wolf-whistled through his teeth. "Damn, girl. You do look good."

"Thanks," she said, aiming for a note of indifference. "You look the same."

"That good or bad?"

"Neither. Just a statement of fact."

"What's it been? Seventeen, eighteen years since we saw each other?"

"Nineteen," she said a little too quickly.

"Ah. Nineteen years. Now, that's hard to believe. I'd hoped I was reason enough to make you stay."

Did she hear real regret in his voice? She turned then to glare at him. "Let's not rewrite history, shall we?"

"What's that supposed to mean?"

"My shadow hadn't left town before you took up with Marta."

He had the decency to look sheepish. "Only because you broke my heart."

"As I said, you haven't changed."

He let that one go, watched the road for a bit. "You married, Grier?"

"No," she said, and then curious despite her declared indifference, "You?"

"Not so much anymore."

She folded her arms across her chest, set her gaze outside the window, unable to keep the sarcasm from her reply. "I'm shocked."

"Hey, now, do I really deserve this kind of grief?" he asked with a smile she remembered only too well.

"If I didn't think you'd kick me out of the truck, I'd say yes."

Darryl Lee laughed. The sound shimmered through her. Unfair that old chords could be so easily strummed.

"Darryl Lee. I appreciate the ride, but let's not pretend there's any love lost between us. As far as I'm concerned, I've seen your true colors, and you don't need to bother with the pretense."

He gave this a moment of consideration before saying, "Does New York City do this to everybody who ends up there?"

"What?" she asked with reluctance.

"Steal their softness."

She absorbed the statement, feeling as if she'd been sucker punched. Not what she'd expected him to say. Accuse her of deserting her beginnings, okay, she could live with that. But he had no idea why she'd left here, and her hand itched with the need to give him a ringing reminder that, of all people, he had no right to judge her.

"How far is the gas station?"

"Half mile or so."

"I can walk the rest of the way. Just pull over, please."

"Hold on, now, Grier," he said on a half-laugh. "Don't you think we're letting this get a little out of hand?"

"Actually, no. The mistake was getting in here in the first place."

"Dang woman, you do know how to hold a grudge."

"Don't flatter yourself. Holding a grudge would mean I've given you a second thought in all these years, and I assure you that's not the case."

He lowered his sunglasses and lasered her with a look that labeled her soliloquy a load of cow manure.

She didn't bother to deny it. The Exxon sign had popped into sight, and with any luck at all, this conversation had gasped its last breath.

"If you say so, sugar."

They veered into the station as if there was an impending shortage on brake pads, and Darryl Lee was conserving. She gripped the door handle and held onto Sebbie's collar to keep him from taking a nosedive onto the floorboard. A white Ford truck pulled away from one of the gas pumps, forcing Darryl Lee to give in and siphon off some of his brake supply. At the same time, he hit the horn, sending out another round of "Dixie."

He lowered his window and waved for the driver to stop. "Hey," he yelled, "I've been lookin' for you! Pull over!"

She got a glimpse of the man in the other truck and the distinct impression that he wasn't as happy to see Darryl Lee as Darryl Lee was to see him. Darryl Lee cut the engine and put a hand on her arm. "Can you wait a minute?"

"As a matter of fact, no," she said, glancing at her watch. "I really need to get going."

"Nineteen years, and you can't wait two minutes?"

She failed to hide her astonishment. "You're not really suggesting that I owe you something, are you?"

He glanced down at her feet, now threatening to burst free from the flimsy straps of her Italian sandals.

"Two minutes," she conceded.

He hopped out of the truck, walked over to the Ford.

Sebbie took his place in the driver's seat, paws planted on the window ledge, staring at the two men as if he'd been given a front-row seat at a catfight.

The truck's passenger side window lowered, and a large black and tan hound stuck its head out the window, greeting Darryl Lee with a tongue-lolling smile.

Sebbie started yipping full blast.

Grier picked him up and shushed him. To no avail. He did a happy dance on her lap, wagging his whole body at the hound, who was, of course, paying no attention to him.

The Ford's driver got out and walked around to where Darryl Lee stood rubbing the dog's head.

Grier tried not to stare, but curiosity got the better of her, and she squinted at the man's face. With a start, she recognized him as Darryl Lee's older brother, the resemblance impossible to miss.

Bobby Jack Randall. The name came instantly to her, even though she'd barely met him once when she and Darryl Lee came back to his house to watch TV, high school code for making out. Bobby Jack had been home from college for the weekend, and she remembered now the way he'd looked at her with what she'd later realized – too late, actually – was pity and even later on discovered the reason for.

If Darryl Lee looked like Bradley Cooper, Bobby Jack could pass for a slightly more serious, slightly taller version. He had the same dark hair and startling green eyes. Amazingly enough, he was even better looking than Darryl Lee.

"You're a rat's ass, you know it, son?" Bobby Jack said, glancing her way with clear disapproval, his voice carrying through Darryl Lee's rolled-down window.

"Hey, man, I wish, but it's not what you're thinkin'," Darryl Lee said.

"Right. I thought you and Dreama were trying to work things out."

Darryl Lee glanced back at Grier, and she decided his two minutes were up.

"Come on, Sebbie." She picked up his leash, opened the door and slid out, waiting for Sebbie to jump down beside her.

He did, jerking the leash from her hand and shooting across the parking lot toward the truck, the hound now barking at him in a very large hound dog bark.

Grier ran after him, her feet again screaming in the hateful heels. "Sebbie!"

"Looks like he's got a little crush on Florence," Darryl Lee drawled, smiling at her.

Grier's face turned three shades of red. She scooped

Sebbie up and without giving either man another glance, teetered toward the inside of the station.

The girl up front studied her as if Grier had fallen out of the sky. She had a tablespoon size wad of gum in her right cheek. Each time she chewed, the gum made a sharp popping sound, the art of which must have taken some practice.

"Is there anyone here who can give me a ride back to my car with some oil?" Grier asked, while Sebbie struggled into a position where he could look back at the truck over her shoulder.

"We don't really allow no dawgs in here," the girl said. "Bobby Jack don't even bring his Florence in, and if anybody was allowed to bring a dawg in, it would be Bobby Jack."

"Sebbie's really not very much like a dog," Grier said.

The girl narrowed her gaze at the back of Sebbie's head. "Looks like a dawg to me. Maybe he could pass for a shrimp." She chuckled at her own joke, then sobered with a reluctant, "You don't look like you're from around here."

"My car broke down a few miles back," Grier said. "It just needs oil."

The girl popped her gum again, watching Grier as though she thought she might grab a pack of the Redman tobacco gracing the rack in front of her and make a run for it. She picked up the phone on the wall, punched a button and snapped out, "Marty, come to the front, please."

She turned back to Grier and said, "I guess we'll make a one time exception for your . . .dawg."

"Thank you so much," Grier said, trying to sound grateful even as she heard the sarcasm in her voice.

Grier glanced out at the parking lot and saw the white Ford pulling away from the station, the hound's head hanging out the window, ears flying back with the wind.

Darryl Lee headed her way. He arrived at the door at the same time as a guy dressed in grease-spotted coveralls, a bandana covering his head.

Gum Girl hitched a thumb at Grier and said, "She needs a tow, Marty."

Marty smiled a brown-toothed smile that made Grier wonder if he'd been dipping into the store's Redman stash. "Not a problem. Let me get the truck, and you can meet me out front."

"Thanks," Grier said.

Darryl Lee waited until Marty headed out the door before saying, semi-hurt, "I could've given you a ride back."

"That's okay," she said. "Dreama's probably expecting you somewhere."

Darryl Lee grinned. "That jealousy I hear in your voice?"

She rolled her eyes and gave him a look that would have humbled most men. Except Darryl Lee, of course.

From the corner of her eye, she could see Gum Girl watching the two of them as if she'd just flipped the channel to a steamy soap. With Sebbie now deflated and whimpering in her arms, Grier cut short the entertainment and headed out the door to wait for Marty and the tow truck.

"Hey, whoa, now." Darryl Lee pulled her to a stop with a hand at her elbow. "How long you gonna be in town, Grier?"

"No longer than I have to be."

"How long's that?"

She rounded on him then, the aggravations of this day suddenly getting the better of her. "What difference does it make to you, Darryl Lee?"

"It makes a lot of difference," he said, his voice soft in a way she had once found completely impossible to resist. "Come on, Grier. You know it'd be good to catch up."

"Isn't that what we just did?"

"It was a start."

"And a finish, as far as I'm concerned."

Marty pulled up in the tow truck, rolling down the window to call out, "You ready, ma'am?"

She nodded and signaled she'd be there in a moment. "Thanks for the help, Darryl Lee. It was good to see you," she said, aiming for a note of graciousness and falling several decibels short.

"Can I call you while you're here?"

"What point would there be in that?"

He dropped his gaze down the length of her, the look in

his eyes answering her question. "Exactly," she said. "You take care, Darryl Lee."

She climbed into the truck, placing Sebbie on the seat next to her. She lifted her hand in a small wave.

"You haven't seen the last of me, Grier," he called out, as the truck pulled away.

She rolled up the window and forced herself not to look back.

2

_____

If it looks too good to be true. . .it is.
— From the Calendar-to-Live-By on Bobby Jack
Randall's desk

Bobby Jack Randall wasn't a suspicious man. But he did pay attention to the daily dollops of wisdom doled out by the desktop planner on which he kept track of his work schedule. He'd long ago learned that the man upstairs handed a guy signs along the way, and if he chose to ignore them, then he had nobody but himself to blame for the consequences.

He'd ignored enough of them in the past to qualify as an expert on the subject.

He leaned back in his chair and opened up the newspaper he hadn't taken time to read this morning. He turned to the sports page, thinking about his brother and the hot number he'd just seen him with out at the filling station, then immediately shoved away the image. If Darryl Lee wanted to flush his marriage down the toilet with an affair, there wasn't much he could do to stop him.

A less-than-pleasant odor wafted up and hit him in the nose. "Aw, Flo," Bobby Jack said, waving the newspaper in front of his face.

The hound curled up next to his chair raised her head and looked at him with practiced innocence.

"What the heck did you get into this time?"

She dropped her chin onto her outstretched paws and sighed as if to say she was admitting to nothing.

The front door of the office burst open, bringing with it a shot of warm spring air. Bobby Jack loved this time of year and only tolerated the sometimes too-long and too-lonely Timbell Creek winter because of its eventual yielding to his favorite season.

"Daddy! You're not going to believe this!"

The whirlwind blowing into his office was his sixteen-year-old daughter, Andersen. Andy for short. Waving a blue flyer in her right hand, she picked up his to-go cup of iced tea and took a sip, making an instant gag face. "Needs sugar," she said.

"Ruin your own tea," he said with amused affection. "I like mine how I like it."

She plopped down on the floor next to Flo, rubbed the

dog's silky ears and rolled her eyes. "Even if you're wrong?" And then to Florence, "Shoo, Flo."

Florence didn't even raise her head this time, content to sleep through the ridicule.

"You need to get her some probiotics, Daddy," Andy said, waving her hand in front of her nose.

"She needs to stay out of Harvey Larson's cow pasture."

"In her defense, Kyle and I used to pretend to eat cow pies when we were little—"

"Andy," he said quickly, cutting her short.

Andy laughed. "I did say pretend."

Bobby Jack smiled in spite of himself. He loved to hear his daughter laugh. It was one of his favorite things in life. He adored her with a fierceness that couldn't lay claim to a single ounce of objectivity. He figured that was how it should be, since parenting sometimes required the dredging up of skills a man didn't know he had. That love did not, however, completely blind him to his daughter's shortcomings. Including the fact that she would argue with a fence post if she had even the remotest chance of bringing it around to her way of thinking. She'd come by that stubbornness honestly.

"What's with the flyer?" he asked.

She put it on the desk where he could read it. He scanned it once, quickly, laughed and shook his head. "Where did you find this?"

"Mama left it on my windshield."

"That should answer any questions you have about it

right there," he said, all the amusement evaporating from his voice.

"She thinks I ought to enter."

"News shocker of the day," Bobby Jack said.

Andy's eyes narrowed, and she folded her arms across her chest. "This isn't a hoax, Daddy. It's true. I Googled it."

Bobby Jack glanced at the calendar on his desk, pointed at the day's quote to live by. "Too good to be true?"

Andy leaned forward and read it, and this time, she laughed. "You really believe those things, don't you?"

"I have some personal experience on this particular tidbit. Your mama being exhibit number one if you're looking for evidence."

"Who said I was looking?"

He glanced at the flyer again.

Win a Date With a Duke!!

Auditions Held at the Mockingbird Inn

May 5th at 9 a.m.

"Andy, what on earth would you want to enter something like that for? As smart as you are, you don't need—"

"Mama thinks it would be good for me."

"How the heck does she figure?" His voice rose with the end of the question, the way it almost always did on any subject involving Priscilla.

"You don't think they'd pick me, do you?"

He got up from his chair, opened a filing cabinet drawer

and started sticking papers inside. "I didn't say any such thing."

"You're thinking it, though," she said, hurt threading her voice.

He turned and looked at her. "No. I'm not. It just seems—"

"Beneath me?"

"Well, yeah. Exactly."

She waved a hand at her surroundings, her gaze sweeping the small but neat office, a desk at each wall, a row of windows on the front that looked out onto Main Street. "How could a date with a duke be beneath me?"

Bobby Jack blinked once, hard, reminded himself that sixteen year olds said things they didn't mean.

Florence lifted her head and studied them both.

Andy stomped to the door, yanked it open, then swung back around.

"You like that I'm not as pretty as Mama, don't you? That way you can be sure I'll hang around a little longer than she did."

Bobby Jack stood silent while she slammed the door behind her. He heard the Ford truck he'd given her on her sixteenth birthday roar to life, tires squealing once as she popped the clutch and peeled out of the parking place.

He sat down in his chair, picked up his iced tea and then tossed it in the trashcan. He'd be getting Dad-of-the-Year for this one.

Florence put her head back on her paws and sighed as if she agreed with him.

The door opened again, and Alice Marshall bustled in from her lunch hour, carrying a pocketbook as big as a mail sack. Alice was nearly as wide as she was tall. Thanks to a monthly dose of Miss Clairol, her hair had remained nearly the same bright red in the past three decades of her life as it had the first three. She had a deep dimple on both cheeks and green eyes that could bathe a person in approval or dress them down with equal effectiveness.

"Was that Andy I saw tearing off down the street?" she asked, her voice cracking under the remains of a cold.

"Yeah," Bobby Jack said, unable to keep the defeat from his response. He crossed the office and helped her unload, placing her things on her desk.

"Hey, now," Alice said, patting his shoulder with a hand that arthritis was starting to get the better of. "They don't know what they're saying at that age. Their brain's been temporarily taken hostage by hormones."

"Isn't there something a doctor can prescribe for that?"

Alice laughed, picking up her purse and putting it behind her desk, then walking over to give Florence a pat on the head. "If there was, I don't know a parent who wouldn't be lining up at Doc Barker's door. Unfortunately, it's one of those things you just have to swim through to get to the other side."

Bobby Jack sat down at his own desk, leaned back with his hands laced behind his head. "Why can't they stay like they were when they were ten? Before all the puberty crap? At ten, you can have an honest conversation with them, and yet they still look at you like you might know a thing or two."

Alice lifted her shoulders in a shrug. "That, you'll have to ask the man upstairs. So what was the upset between you, anyway?"

"She wants to enter some ridiculous contest to win a date with a duke."

Alice raised penciled-in eyebrows. "Really, now?"

"Like there's even a remote possibility the thing is on the up and up."

"And? What's the worst that can happen if it's not?"

He considered this, then shook his head. "She'll end up feeling foolish."

"So let her."

"Let her?" Bobby Jack shot back. "What kind of advice is that?"

"The only kind that's going to get you out of the doghouse."

"If it keeps her from making a mistake, I'm willing to stay there a while."

"Bobby Jack. You've got to let that girl start making some of her own mistakes. For the child's whole life, you've been throwing yourself in front of her every time she gets ready to fall. How's she ever going to learn what it's like to have to pick herself back up when you're no longer there to act as a mattress?"

"You got plans for her to go somewhere or something?"

"The last I checked you're as human as the rest of us. At some point, you have to let them grow up, Bobby Jack."

He glanced out the window, saw Priscilla's banana yellow Corvette pull into a parking space across the street. "Yeah, maybe. But first there's something else I've got to do."

Florence at his heels, he stepped outside of the office onto the sidewalk, then jaywalked in front of Pete Thompson's old clunker farm-use truck. Pete, almost as ancient in appearance as the truck itself, shook a finger out his rolled-down window and honked the horn.

Bobby Jack just smiled and waved, as if he couldn't hear Pete's grumbling through the lowered window.

Most days, Bobby Jack went to great lengths to avoid run-ins with his ex-wife, succeeding largely even though their respective businesses were right across the street from each other. When she'd sailed back into town a few years ago and opened up her Well-Kept Woman Day Spa and Salon right across the street from him, he'd considered moving. But he liked his office. As a matter of principle, if anyone moved, it should be Priscilla.

In the parking lot, he stopped just short of her car, shoving his hands in his pockets to keep from giving in to the temptation to strangle her.

"What the devil kind of nonsense are you trying to fill my daughter's head with now?"

"You mean our daughter." Priscilla Randall leaned

forward to check her hair and lipstick in the rearview mirror before opening the door and giving him a look of concern. "And Bobby Jack, you better watch that temper of yours. High blood pressure can certainly become an issue at your age. I mean who would take care of poor Florence if you up and left us?"

"I'll worry about my own damn blood pressure," he said, even as he felt his face redden. "Try and stick to the subject if you can."

"And what was the subject again?" she asked, sliding one curvy leg from the car and then the other, before closing the door and executing a supermodel catwalk to the beauty salon, not even bothering to check to make sure he was following. Men had been following Priscilla since she'd first learned how to blink her big baby-blue eyes, and she'd never once questioned the continuing success of her efforts. Certainly not where Bobby Jack was concerned.

"Our daughter. See if you can hang onto that thought for the next ten seconds."

"Now, see, Bobby Jack, that's where you get your backward reputation. It's hardly politically correct to make fun of those of us afflicted with ADD."

Bobby Jack resisted the impulse to roll his eyes. Somewhere along the way, Priscilla had found a doctor who had diagnosed her inability to stick with one man, one project, one interest as symptoms that fell under the latest disorder umbrella. He didn't doubt that for some people the problem actually existed. But for Priscilla, it made a handy hat rack on which to hang a lifetime worth of excuses.

Having been married to her, Bobby Jack would have fine-tuned the diagnosis to a severe case of bored-too-easily, aggravated by a never-ceasing need for the new and different. New shoes. New car. New husband. But then nobody had asked him.

"All aspersions to your affliction aside, why can't you encourage Andy to put her efforts into something that might actually lead somewhere?"

Priscilla turned the key in the lock and pushed the door open, flicking on a light and dropping her purse on the receptionist's desk. "Well, I think a shot at becoming royalty would qualify as somewhere, don't you?"

Florence plopped down on the tile floor, as if she thought this might take a while.

Bobby Jack stared at his ex-wife for several long moments, completely at a loss as to where to take the conversation from here. How he had ever imagined the two of them compatible enough to actually marry was beyond him. But then he'd had a different rating scale back then, the basis of which had little to do with lifelong compatibility.

"Do you for one minute actually think that hoax is for real?"

"Why, yes," she said, splaying a hand on one hip. "Yes, I do."

"Are you still trying to tell her the tooth fairy's for real, too?"

This got him a look of real annoyance. "Don't be ridiculous, Bobby Jack."

"The tooth fairy's ridiculous, but this isn't?"

"Not when it has an honest-to-God TV network and a well-known image consultant backing it."

She made the pronouncement as if the president himself had signed off on the whole proposal. Bobby Jack shook his head, speechless. "She's a straight-A student, Priscilla. She could go to any Ivy League school of her choosing if she keeps her grades where they are now, and you think this is how she should be spending her time?"

Priscilla circled the salon, flipping on lights. "She's also a girl, Bobby Jack. Something I think you'd do well to notice once in a while."

"What's that supposed to mean?"

"Exactly what it sounds like. You take her out working with that obnoxious crew of yours like she's just another redneck with a hammer."

"That 'obnoxious' crew of mine happens to be a good bunch of guys, so I'd appreciate it if you'd table the slander. And Andy helps out because she wants to."

Priscilla picked up a brush, began pulling out excess hair and dropping it in a trashcan. "Maybe when she was twelve. In case you haven't noticed, that's no longer true."

"Did she say something to you?"

"She didn't have to."

"Oh, you're a mind reader now?"

"A mother senses these things."

That statement alone was enough to send Bobby Jack off on a tangent. "I advise you not to go there, Priscilla."

Her blue eyes narrowed. "I know what kind of mother you think I am, Bobby Jack. But Andy is my daughter. And I do love her. Whether you like it or not."

"Since when do loving mothers run off and leave their baby?"

Priscilla made a sound that was half laugh, half disbelief. "You cannot let it go, can you?"

"Actually, no, I can't. I don't see why I should have to. You're the one who made the choices you made, Priscilla. Nobody forced you to leave and spend the next eleven years pretending you were still a teenager."

"People get divorced every day," she said, her voice heating up. "And people find a way to make it work. But not you, Bobby Jack! You're so all-fired convinced that you've been wronged, you let that bitterness eat away at you a little more each day. Pretty soon, there's not going to be anything even recognizable of the old you left. You're just going to be this dried up old fart who rides around with a hound in the front seat of his truck instead of a woman!"

"I didn't come over here to rehash our history," he cut her off in a sharp voice. "I came over to tell you to quit filling Andy's head with nonsense!"

"First of all, I don't take orders from you. And second of

all, she doesn't see it as nonsense. Did you ever think she might want to know that you believe in her, Bobby Jack?"

"I do believe in her. I believe she can do great things with her life. And that's what I want for her."

"As long as those things fall under your definition of great, right?"

He started to answer, then stopped. He didn't have to listen to this crap from the woman who had conveniently dropped him and their daughter three years into their marriage, as if they were yesterday's old newspapers. "You know what, Priscilla? This was a complete waste of time. As talking to you always is."

Flo got up and trotted after Bobby Jack just as Priscilla threw out, "Come on back again when you don't have such a bee in your bonnet. You could use a good hair cut!"

3

---

*The state of your closet is a direct indicator of the
state of your life. Trousers mixed in with dresses?
Summer clothes mixed with winter? A shoe
missing in action? If this sounds familiar, it's a
good bet chaos is ruling outside the closet as well.*
— *Grier McAllister – Blog at Jane Austen Girl*

By the time Marty towed Grier's car into the garage, she'd
all but wilted from the events of the afternoon. Even
Sebbie drooped and showed definite signs of needing a
nap.

Amy had reserved a room for her at the Mockingbird
Inn where the selection process would take place. The
ever-accommodating Marty drove them over in the tow
truck and dropped them at the front with a promise to

have Grier's car up and running again by tomorrow. He'd recommended giving it a check-up just to be safe.

With Sebbie at her side, she rolled her suitcase into the small lobby and headed for the registration desk. A friendly young man with slightly buck teeth checked them in, the name Beaner Purdy stitched across the pocket of his burgundy uniform.

"I believe you're here for the Jane Austen Girl auditions, aren't you, ma'am?" he asked, smiling a big blinding smile.

"Yes," she said, following along with Sebbie as Beaner pulled her suitcase to the elevator.

"It's got the whole town buzzin'."

"I hope that means we'll have a good turnout for the auditions then."

"Oh, yes, ma'am. I expect you'll fill the place up. My sister, Edith? She's a shoo-in for your makeover. If it weren't for the wart on her chin, she'd look just like that actress with the tattoo on her shoulder. The one who adopted all the children?"

"Really?" Grier said.

"I keep tellin' her she oughta get one of them laser doctors to take that thing off. But she just gets on her high horse and starts sayin' how men are all about the superficial."

"Hmmm," Grier said, not sure what to add that would be anything remotely resembling diplomatic.

The elevator dinged, and the doors slid open.

Beaner stepped out and beckoned for Sebbie and her

to follow. "You and your buddy are right down this way, Ms. McAllister." At her door, he took the card and slid it into the lock. She stepped inside, removing Sebbie's leash. He made a beeline for the king-size bed, hopping up and making himself at home among the quartet of pillows propped at the headboard.

Beaner pointed out the room's amenities, mini-bar, TV, and pullout couch should she need it for any reason. "If you want anything at all now, you just buzz the front desk and ask for me."

"Thank you so much," she said, handing him a five.

He nodded, grinned and then ducked his head once before letting himself out of the room. As soon as the door closed behind him, Grier collapsed onto the bed next to Sebbie.

Her feet literally throbbed, and she held one foot in the air, managing to gingerly remove the strappy sandals before letting them drop to the floor. "Ah," she said, thinking she might actually cry with the relief.

Sebbie cracked one eye as if to make sure she was all right, then buried his nose beneath a pillow and resumed his nap.

Her cell phone rang. She considered not answering it, then grabbed her purse off the floor and fumbled through the outside pocket until she found it.

Amy's number flashed on the screen. "Hey," Grier said.

"You're there," Amy said, with what sounded like a sigh of relief. "I've been calling for hours."

"The service here seems to be somewhat intermittent," Grier said, collapsing onto the bed again.

"You sound funny. Are you all right?"

"I had a little car trouble. Sebbie and I both are out of gas."

"Tell him I miss him terribly."

"I will," Grier said, smiling.

"Is your car fixed?"

"It's in the shop."

"Should I get you a rental?"

"If it's not ready by tomorrow. I won't need it tonight."

"How does it feel to be back home?"

"Strange."

"Everything look the same?"

"Yes and no."

"Seen any old boyfriends yet?" Amy asked, cheeky.

"Unfortunately." She immediately regretted the admission, not wanting to get Amy started on her find-a-man-for-Grier campaign.

"Really?"

"It was no big deal."

"High school flame?"

"Sort of."

"Ah. Is he married?"

"It doesn't matter," Grier said, eager to change the subject. "I won't be seeing him again."

"Too bad," Amy said. "I thought for a second there you might be ending your dating drought."

"I like my dating drought."

"Grier, they're not all like. . ."

"My last ten dates?"

Amy laughed. "They weren't all bad."

"Bad enough."

"You just haven't met the right one."

"And I'm not looking."

"Well, it's been like ages since you went out with anyone."

"Have you heard me complaining?"

"No, but. . ."

"All right then. Gotta go. Busy here."

"It's not normal!" Amy managed to get in before Grier ended the call. She flopped back on the bed and folded herself around a pillow. She wasn't lonely. She'd turn herself into the Sahara Desert of loneliness before she ever gave Darryl Lee Randall the satisfaction of knowing she'd given him a second thought in the years since she'd last been home.

When the rumbling of her stomach began to disturb Sebbie, who made his displeasure known with breathing sounds that could only be equated to a heavy sigh, she got up and headed for the shower. She stood under the warm spray for a good twenty minutes, her feet finally coming back to life along with the rest of her.

She dug some running clothes out of her suitcase, opting for comfort over style, and then left Sebbie still sleeping while she went in search of food, heading out of the Inn and walking the two blocks that led to Main Street. At almost four o'clock, the sun was still hot so she pulled off her running shirt and tied it around her waist, the white tank top she'd put on underneath much more pleasant.

She dropped her head back and breathed deeply. Amazing that a place could have its own scent, Timbell Creek's signature blend of freshly mowed grass and honeysuckle. She thought she could identify it anywhere. These streets were familiar to her too. She'd once known them as well as she now knew Manhattan. Better, actually.

Maple led to Sycamore. Sycamore to Hampton. And then across to Main where she turned right and headed toward the center of town, hoping Angell's Bakery still sat in the same place. With the smell of fresh baked bread, she grew hopeful. But the name had changed. It was now the Maple Leaf Bread Company. The aroma promised good things though, so she went inside and stood at the front counter, reading the menu behind the register.

A teenage boy with a nice smile popped out of the back, wiping his hands on his white apron. "Can I help you, ma'am?"

"Yes," she said. "I'll have a tomato and Havarti on rye with a little mustard."

"Anything to drink?"

"Iced tea, please."

"Sweet tea?"

"Why not?" she conceded.

The front door opened, the bell hanging above it jangling once. Grier glanced over her shoulder at the tall blonde woman who'd just come in.

"Earnest," she said, "you got any more of that cinnamon raisin bread y'all made up yesterday?"

"Just baked some fresh loaves, Ms. Randall."

At the name, Grier's ears perked up, and she gave the woman a sideways assessment. Darryl Lee's Ms. Randall?

The woman turned and looked at Grier, her smile wide and white. Grier smiled back, trying not to show her curiosity, then glanced away.

But she reached out to press a hand to Grier's arm. "Oh. My. Goodness. Are you the lady doing auditions for that show tomorrow?"

"Ah, yes," Grier said. "I am."

"Well I sure never expected to run into you here." She stuck out a hand that featured perfectly manicured nails. "I'm Priscilla Randall."

"Grier McAllister."

"So nice to meet you." She leaned in and lowered her voice to a whisper. "My daughter is auditioning. Poor baby, her daddy is just dead set against it. I've been tellin' him what an exceptional opportunity this is for her. She's always been a bit of a wallflower, and to tell you the truth, I was more than a little surprised when she agreed to put herself in the running."

"Ah, well," Grier said, not sure what else to say.

"Any tips you could throw her way?" she asked, sounding hopeful.

Grier shrugged, forced a smile. "I'm sure everything will be covered tomorrow."

Earnest returned from the back with her toasted tomato and Havarti sandwich. She pulled some money from her pocket and paid him, a little uncomfortable under Priscilla Randall's continuing stare.

"I own the beauty shop just across the street," Priscilla said. "Not to be nosy, but there was a rumor circulatin' there today that your mama is Maxine McAllister. I said a woman who looks like you couldn't possibly have a mama who. . ." She stopped there, as if suddenly thinking better of the remainder of her comment.

For a moment, Grier could think of absolutely nothing to say, her mind a complete blank. She had forced herself not to think about her mama on the drive down since she had no intention of seeing her while she was here. A wave of shame rose up inside her for the fact that her mother had chosen men and booze over her.

On the heels of that old shame, though, came another feeling. An unexpected desire to defend her mother. But as quickly as it had appeared, it was gone again. After all, if Priscilla Randall knew her, any defense Grier had to offer would be so much smoke.

"My cousin Emma-Ann works out there where your mama's stayin'. Somebody like you coming in there would sure cheer everybody up."

"What place?" Grier asked before she could stop herself.

"The Sunset Years Retirement Home over on 38." Priscilla Randall made the pronouncement with careful enunciation, as if Grier's ability to process the information had suddenly become suspect.

"Oh," Grier said, her face flaming with instant mortification.

Priscilla cocked her head and said, "You didn't know she was there?"

"I—of course," she stammered, hearing the lack of conviction in her own voice.

"I'm sorry," Priscilla said. "I shouldn't have said anything."

Picking up her sandwich, Grier turned to leave. "Nice to meet you, Ms. Randall. Wish your daughter luck for me."

"I certainly will!" Priscilla called out.

Grier walked back to the inn as quickly as she could, her hunger gone, and in its place, an absolute certainty that she never should have come back to Timbell Creek. Eagle be damned. Her decision to do so had been about nothing more than pride and a false sense of being so far beyond what she'd left behind that it could never hurt her again.

On that, however, she didn't suppose she could have been more wrong.

4

_____

*This baby will be special. I've always believed
that unexpected things usually are. I'll be a good
mother. Who's to say we have to follow the
example we've been given? I'll give my baby what
I never had. I'll do better than my own parents
did. I will.*
— First entry written in the baby book given to
Maxine McAllister for her daughter Grier

For a long time, Maxine McAllister counted the number of
days. Then she counted weeks. Months. And finally, years.
Nineteen, now.

Nineteen since Grier had left Timbell Creek.

Maxine stared at the newspaper photo, a glamorous
headshot with a photographer's credit in the lower right-

hand corner. She studied her daughter's features. Wide green eyes, full lips so like hers, clear, unlined skin that spoke of a care she'd never given her own.

Grier. What a beautiful woman she'd grown up to be. In a way, Maxine felt as though she were looking at a stranger, even as she saw remnants of the little girl she'd once rocked to sleep at night.

An ache set up in the center of Maxine's chest, a painful throb of remorse and regret. She let the newspaper collapse onto her lap, her right hand gripping the arm of her wheelchair in an attempt to steady against the sudden dizziness swamping her like an ocean wave.

She closed her eyes and fought it back.

"That must be your young'un."

Maxine stayed as she was for a few moments, not answering. When she finally opened her eyes, Hatcher Morris stared at her from the seat of a wheelchair exactly like hers, arthritic hands laced together in his lap, his fingers so gnarled with the disease they were painful to look at. "Yeah," she said, surprised. "How'd you guess?"

"McAllister's not the most common name around," he said, his voice coarse evidence of the decades of cigarettes to which it had been subjected. "And one of the nurses mentioned she thought you had a girl named Grier."

"Had," Maxine agreed, putting her gaze back on the picture.

"Don't you ever see her?"

"Not for a very long time."

"Mind if I ask why?"

Maxine shook her head, unable to answer. Hatcher Morris was about the only friend she had in this place. On the first day they'd met, he'd read her history in the lines of her face the same as she'd read his in the yellowed whites of his eyes and the distended stomach beneath his faded flannel robe.

"Well, I don't expect it's any of my business, anyway," Hatcher said.

"It's not that," she finally managed, lifting a hand and waving it once.

Hatcher reached for the newspaper, looked at the article, and then in his gravelly voice, read, "Image Consultant Comes Home to Find Date for a Duke. Sounds like a big undertaking."

"I would imagine," Maxine said.

"She's made it pretty big then, huh?" He lifted an eyebrow, looking impressed.

"Yes," she said, pride etching her voice despite the realization that she had absolutely no claim to any credit for it. "She has."

He glanced at the paper again. "She resembles you, you know."

"No," she said, unable to see any current resemblance between herself and the beautiful young woman pictured in today's paper. "You angling for my chocolate pudding again tonight, Hatcher?"

He chuckled. "Naw. I wouldn't fool you on something like that. Anybody could see she's yours."

Maxine could have hugged him then and there. Hatch had a good heart. Like her, he'd thrown away some of the best years of his life with nowhere better to go at the end than a place for people who'd made a practice of taking the wrong roads. "Except I'm the rode hard and put up wet version."

Hatcher smiled, lines fanning out from his dark eyes. "She comin' by to see you while she's in town?"

Maxine forced herself to laugh so the tears gathering in her throat wouldn't make their way out as a sob. "I doubt she'll have much extra time. I guess a TV show would have something of a schedule," she said, hearing how pitiful her explanation sounded, and, at the same time, willing him not to pity her for it.

Hatcher nodded as if there were nothing to question. "You two ever talk?"

She could have lied. But she wouldn't fool him. Hatcher was a sharp man. In fact, she'd begun to think he'd probably done more good as a therapist for some of the people in this place than the doctors who worked here. "No," she said, shaking her head. "We don't talk."

He was quiet for a couple of minutes, rotating his thumbs back and forth, one over the over. The TV in the far corner of the room blared Jerry Springer reruns. Maxine had grown to hate the show, but Edna Gardner and Mish Caldwell sat glued in front of it every afternoon as if they might find the answers to their own screwed-up lives on that twenty-seven inch screen. Somewhere along the way, Maxine had realized the only answers to be found anywhere were the ones that nagged low inside her in that place where she'd tucked the truth away so she didn't have to look at it. Better not to look when there wasn't a thing you could do to change any of it.

When Hatcher spoke again, his voice sounded far away, as if he were looking back down the tunnel of his own past and regretting what he saw there. "My kids don't talk to me neither. 'Course I don't blame them. I was nothing but a mean son of a bitch to all three of them."

"You?" she said, disbelieving. "Mean?"

"Nothin' meaner than a drunk lookin' for the next drink. Except maybe an out-of-work drunk. I was both."

"I can't imagine—" she began, then stopped there. Actually, she could imagine. She'd seen the change alcohol could bring over people. For her, it had been little more than a curtain behind which she could hide. A shade to pull when things got too gray.

"I wonder sometimes," he said, "what would have happened if somebody had told me what the doctors are saying now. That some people have a gene that's like a switch being thrown at the first sip. I wonder if I might have left the stuff alone. Never touched it."

"Probably not," she said, uncertain whether that was supposed to make him feel better or worse. She didn't think it would have stopped her. Self-destruction was a powerful force to resist.

"'Bout the only thing I ever did for my kids was write them a letter a couple years ago telling them they might have that same gene I have. That one drink might be all it took to put them on the same path as me." Probably too late, but it made me feel better to know I said it.

"That must have been a hard thing to do."

He lifted a shoulder, glanced off to the side. "Not really," he said. "I was kind of relieved to know a person might actually have a choice if they never touched the stuff at all."

"They listen to you?"

He rubbed a thumb across his whiskered chin. "My oldest son sent me a letter that basically said I was an arrogant s.o.b. for assuming he'd ever make the same choices I'd made. I never heard from the other two."

"I'm sorry, Hatch."

"Hey, don't be. If I were him, I'd hate me, too."

Sad, but she couldn't think of a thing to say to make him feel any better. Not when she could apply the very same sentiment to herself. There were just some roads in this life that could never be retraveled. Some choices that could never be remade. And if she was honest with herself, she'd admit that she didn't want her daughter to come here. Didn't want her to see how she'd ended up. Better to leave it all behind that door Grier had closed nineteen years ago. The only thing Maxine had to offer her daughter was an apology. And what good would that do? An apology didn't change anything. Much as she wished that it could.

She tucked the newspaper between her leg and the side of the chair, then started rolling toward the door. "I think I'll go take a little rest, Hatch," she said.

"You all right?" he called out after her.

"Fine," she said. "I'm just fine."

"I'll come check on you in a bit."

"Thanks, Hatch," she said, without looking back, certain that if she did, the tears she'd been holding in would come spilling out. And once they got started, there was a very good chance they would never stop.

5

This is a place of quiet. If you cannot respect this policy, please choose a spot outside the library where your conversation will not be an imposition to those who do respect it.
— Wall plaque above Andersen Randall's favorite reading spot

"I should have guessed this is where you'd be hiding."

Andy Randall glanced over her shoulder to find Kyle Summers looking down at her with something close to aggravation simmering in his green eyes. She pointed at the sign on the wall and put a finger to her lips.

"Then let's go outside," he said, without bothering to whisper. Andy had known Kyle since preschool, and his lack of concern for rules the rest of the world made an effort to pay attention to was nothing new.

Today, however, it irked her.

She frowned at him and tapped the page of the book she'd been reading.

"Come on. Five minutes," Kyle said.

Andy breathed a disgruntled sigh. Second to his disregard for rules was a streak of stubbornness that had allowed him to lead the Timbell Creek varsity football team to a state championship this past fall, even though they'd started out with a group of guys that easily deserved the mantle of a season-long losing streak.

She marked her place in the book, then slid her chair back and followed Kyle out of the library to the miniature park just down the street, where a bench sat in the shade of a huge oak tree.

"So what is it?" Andy asked, doing a poor job of hiding her irritation.

"You got your period or something?"

Andy beamed him a look and said, "I'm not going to dignify that with an answer."

"So why'd you bag school today?"

"You actually noticed I wasn't there?"

"Of course I noticed."

"Of course."

He frowned at her sarcasm. "Where were you?"

"I just didn't want to go."

Kyle arched a dark eyebrow. "This from Miss Harvard Bound?"

"Did you come all the way over here just to harass me?"

He leaned down, traced a finger in the dirt beneath the bench. "I was worried about you, Andy. That's all."

For a moment, Andy felt the sting of guilt. The note of uncertainty in Kyle's voice reminded her of the old Kyle. The one she'd grown up making mud pies with, the one who'd spent the night at her house on weekends until her daddy said they were too old to be sharing a bed together anymore. That Kyle had been happy to spend an entire afternoon swimming in the creek or helping her build one of the doghouses she'd been selling since she was ten, earning them both money for their college savings accounts.

But the old Kyle didn't come around much anymore. The new Kyle had him way too busy with cheerleaders and weightlifting and more cheerleaders.

She fixed her gaze on the street just beyond the edge of the library and said, "I had an argument with my dad."

Kyle leaned back with a look of surprise. "You two?"

"What's so weird about that?"

"Nothing, except that you both think the other one walks on water."

"That's not true," she said, embarrassed.

"Yeah, it is. What's the rift between you?"

Andy considered not telling him. But by tomorrow, he'd know anyway. It might as well come from her. She reached in her pocket, pulled out the flyer and unfolded it. Kyle took it and began to read. Once he was done, he shook his head and made a noise that fell somewhere between a laugh and a hoot. "You're kidding, right?" he said.

She grabbed for the flyer, but tore off the top half, leaving Kyle holding the rest. "What is so ridiculous about me entering this?"

Kyle started to say something, stopped, then tried again. "A date with a duke? Come on, Andy."

She snatched the other part of the flyer from him and took a step back.

"You're as bad as he is," she said. "You don't think I can win either!"

"I never said that."

"You didn't have to," she said, hating the crack in her voice.

"It just doesn't seem like something you would do," he said.

"More like something one of your cheerleader girlfriends would do?"

Kyle ran a hand up the back of his hair, letting it pause in mid-air for a moment before falling to his side. The gesture was classic Kyle, and for just a moment, something inside her caved with regret for the changes between them this past year.

"It sounds like a scam, Andy. Of all people, I can't imagine you falling for something like that."

"It's not a scam. I checked it out."

"Checked it out where?"

"With the TV network that's sponsoring it."

"And they said it's legit?"

"Yep."

Kyle folded his arms across his chest, causing the muscles of his biceps to flex at the edge of his shirt. Andy felt a dip in her stomach and looked away.

"Are you mad at me or something?" Kyle asked.

She pasted on a look of indifference. "We don't see each other often enough anymore for me to have a reason to be mad at you."

He rolled his eyes. "Every time I call you, Andy, you've got some excuse about why you can't go out. Why couldn't you go to the movies Sunday?"

She looked down at the ground, scuffed the toe of her running shoe in the dirt. "Too much homework. And besides, wouldn't Sheila mind you going to the movies with me?'

"She knows we're—" he stopped there, didn't finish.

"Knows we're what?" Andy asked abruptly, meeting his gaze head on.

"Friends."

"Friends," she said, doubt in her voice, suddenly needing to hurt him as much as he had hurt her.

Kyle stared at her, confusion clouding his eyes. "At least I thought we were."

"People change, Kyle. It's time we both grew up. We're not little kids anymore."

"You wanna tell me exactly what you mean by that?"

"Maybe we ought to quit trying to hold onto something that doesn't work anymore. Admit that we've outgrown each other."

For a moment, something she could almost believe was hurt flashed across his face. He quickly banked it, throwing up a hand and taking a step back. "Hey. If that's what you want, Andy, you won't get any argument from me. You used to be somebody I wanted to hang with, but you know what? Now, you're just a pain in the butt."

He wheeled then and jogged off, jumping into the old Jeep he'd left parked across the street. Andy watched as he popped the clutch and took off, tires squealing.

For a minute or more, she stood completely still, afraid to think about what she'd just done.

When the reality of it began to sink in, she sat down on the bench, staring at the half-torn flyer still clutched in her right hand.

She stifled a scream of frustration. She was just so mad at him.

Not that she'd ever bothered to tell him, pride keeping her silent. Instead, she'd acted as if she thought it was great that he was dating the captain of the cheerleading squad, thought it fine that he had a whole new group of friends she had absolutely nothing in common with.

The truth? Sometimes she missed him so much, she actually ached inside. It was like having an arm or leg removed, knowing it was no longer there, and yet phantom pain throbbed in the place where the limb had once been.

But the simple fact was that Kyle had moved on. Outgrown her. Oh, he tried to touch base with her often enough to keep from ditching their friendship altogether, but the last thing Andy wanted to be to Kyle was a noose around his neck. So maybe it was better for them both that she'd cut him loose. He didn't have to feel obligated to her any longer.

He could get on with his life. And she could get on with hers.

She glanced down at the ripped flyer in her hand. Which was exactly what she intended to do. Starting now.

6

I'm going to make sure my daughter knows what's important and what's not. No cheerleading, no beauty contests. Just the stuff that will actually make a difference in the real world.
— Bobby Jack Randall's famous last words on the day his divorce became final

Bobby Jack had his speech all prepared. Along with it, Andy's favorite supper of veggie burgers sizzled on the grill out back, and crinkle-cut French fries baked in the oven.

It was seven o'clock though, and she still wasn't home. He'd started to get worried about an hour ago. Bobby Jack hated worrying. He'd made a pact with his daughter when she'd turned thirteen and started going more places without him that she would always call if she was going to be late. He'd now tried her cell phone six or seven times, only to have her voice mail pick up.

At seven-fifteen, just as he was considering calling everyone he knew, the front door opened, and Andy breezed in.

He heard Flo jump off the living room sofa and trot out to greet her.

Within a few moments, the two of them appeared in the kitchen doorway.

"Hey," Andy said, dropping her book bag on the kitchen counter and heading for the refrigerator where she pulled out a bottle of water and guzzled a third before saying, "I'm going up for a shower."

Bobby Jack stared at her for a few moments, wondering who this teenager with an attitude was and what she'd done with his daughter. "Hold on a minute," he said to her retreating back.

She turned, arched an eyebrow, took another sip of her water.

"Where've you been?" he asked, trying to insert calm into his voice.

"Just doing stuff," she said, annoyance in her tone.

"I've been trying to get you on the phone for more than an hour. You said you'd be home at six."

She glanced at her watch, lifted a shoulder. "Sor—ry," she said, breaking the word into two syllables.

"What's going on, Andy?" he asked, folding his arms across his chest and leaning against the kitchen doorjamb.

"Nothing, Daddy. Look, I'm tired. And I've got homework."

"Supper's ready."

She glanced at the plate of veggie burgers on the counter, then looked down at her shoes before saying, "I'm not hungry. I'll fix a salad or something later."

"Is this about this morning? Are you angry because I don't think you should waste your time on that ridiculous?—"

She threw up a hand to stop him. "I don't think it's ridiculous!" she cried. "Why can't you be happy that I want to do something different?"

On that, she turned and ran out of the kitchen and up the stairs. A few seconds later, he heard her bedroom door slam.

Flo looked up at him, her big brown eyes worried.

"I know," he said, rubbing the top of her head. "I need to learn when to keep my mouth shut."

He stood in the same place for a long time, trying to decide when life as he knew it had turned inside out, so that he recognized virtually nothing of the current landscape.

The phone rang, jangling him out of his state of stunned shock. He picked it up with a distracted hello.

"Let me speak to Andy."

Priscilla's highhanded demand tipped Bobby Jack right

over the edge. "Why? So you can brainwash her with more of your ideas on how to get ahead in this world?"

"Oh, Bobby Jack, we all know you have the only secret formula available, so why would I bother?"

Her sarcasm ignited him even further. "There's no secret to where hard work and a good college will get her. Where do you think winning a date with a duke will get her?"

"Maybe she'll marry him. Don't they come with country houses and servants?"

"You've got to be kidding me," he said on a choked laugh. "This is your idea of parental guidance? No, wait. Forget I said that. You don't have the slightest idea of what it takes to be a parent. Because you weren't around for eleven years of her life. Now that you've remembered you have a daughter, this is your contribution to her development? Filling her head with garbage?"

"She doesn't think it's garbage. You're the only one who seems to think that. And as a matter of fact, I met the woman who's going to be choosing the makeover candidate. I'd like to give Andy a few tips before her interview tomorrow."

Beneath her breezy arrogance, Bobby Jack broke. "Or why don't you just skip to the part you know best? Maybe you could tell her how to get pregnant and force the guy to marry her. There's some wisdom you could surely pass down to her."

"You are such an asshole, Bobby Jack."

"Because I don't choose to drape our history in pink roses?"

"That's your version of our history," Priscilla said, her voice suddenly flat.

"No, that's the truth."

With that, Bobby Jack clicked off the phone and tossed it on the kitchen counter. He forced in several deep, calming breaths. Hearing a noise, he walked down the hallway, suddenly sorry he'd let temper bring out accusations he'd long ago shelved and catalogued as irrelevant.

Footsteps sounded on the stairs. He reached the bottom of the staircase only to see Andy take off running midway up. "Andy!" he called out.

But she ignored him, again slamming the door to her bedroom. This time, he heard the click of the lock. And along with it came the sickening realization that she'd heard every word he'd said.

7

If you believe in yourself
and what you're doing with your life, stand tall
and don't make excuses for who you are.
— _Grier McAllister – Blog at Jane Austen Girl_

At just after nine o'clock, Grier climbed into the comfortable king-size bed from which Sebbie had only moved when she took him out for a walk to do his business. She tucked his head against her shoulder and rubbed his side with her thumb, taking pleasure in his soft snoring.

Too restless to sleep, she picked up the remote control and flicked through fifty or so channels, not a single one catching her interest.

For the past few hours, she'd immersed herself in work

she'd brought along on her laptop, answered e-mails and reviewed her notes for tomorrow's interviews. All in a futile attempt to avoid thinking about what Priscilla Randall had said about her mother and whether it was true that she was living in the nursing home at the edge of town.

She flicked off the TV and dropped back against the pillows behind her, one arm flung over her eyes. The thought was too horrible to contemplate.

She let herself remember the place now. At Christmas, during her sophomore year in high school, she'd gone there with the choir to visit with the residents and sing carols. They'd taken along hot chocolate and cookies, as well as some gifts she'd quickly realized were the only ones most of them would be getting that holiday. Before leaving they'd sung one last song, "Oh Come, All Ye Faithful," and she'd stood in the back row, looking out at the faces staring up at them with such gratitude. That was the part that humbled her, lifted sobs from deep inside her so that she could only stand there, mute, tears streaming down her cheeks.

She pictured her mother now sitting in that audience of faces, and an actual pain knifed through her chest. Even all those years ago, the place had been a rundown, sad excuse for an ending. Maybe someone had bought it and turned it into something different than what it had been then. But judging from the look on Priscilla Randall's face when she'd mentioned it earlier, that wasn't too likely.

What had she expected, though? For most of Grier's childhood, her mama had lived her life paycheck-to-paycheck, bottle of booze to bottle of booze.

Truthfully, she guessed she'd imagined her finally finding a decent man to love her. She wasn't sure what kind of logic she could possibly attach to this assumption, since a decent man had never once managed to find his way to her mother's door while she'd been living with her.

Guilt nagged low inside her now, even as she determined to push it back. Choices, she reminded herself. Life was all about choices. Every single one mattered somewhere down the line. For the bad ones, there was eventually a price to pay.

And still.

She was her mother.

A knock sounded at the door. She sat straight up on the bed, startled out of her misery. Sebbie woke up and started barking. "Shh," she said. "It's probably just Beaner with some ice." He'd already been up three times, once with a newspaper, once with flowers and the last time with complimentary coffee and dessert.

Sebbie resumed his position, head on his paws, eyes wide open.

She reached for a robe to pull over her cotton pajamas and went to the door. But the man standing outside was not Beaner. The man outside her door was Bobby Jack Randall, Darryl Lee's brother.

She stared at him, at a loss.

He stared back.

"Could I help you with something?" she finally managed, pulling her robe closed at the neck.

He shook his head, blinked hard. "I—you're—"

"Grier McAllister," she finished for him. "We met this afternoon. With Darryl Lee."

"Yeah. I know," he said, running a hand through wavy black hair. "I thought you were—"

"The current wedge in your brother's marriage."

He folded his arms across his expansive chest, giving her a long look. "And you're not?"

"Hardly. Look, Mr. Randall, would you like to tell me how you found my room?"

He hesitated and then admitted, "Beaner Purdy's a sucker for banana splits."

"Ah. Nice to know the security here is of such high standards. Is there something I can do for you, Mr. Randall?"

"You're doing the interviews for that show – *Dream Date*?"

He said the show's name as if it left a bitter taste in his mouth. "I am," she said, bristling a little.

"Could we talk for a minute?"

"Sure," she said, waving a hand for him to continue.

He glanced over his shoulder and then back at her, his green eyes lasering her to the spot. "Somewhere a little more public," he said, his gaze lifting over her shoulder to the room behind her.

She tightened the belt of her robe, cleared her throat. "Mr. Randall, I was about to go to bed. I'm expecting a long day tomorrow."

"It's Bobby Jack. And please, this won't take long."

She glanced back at Sebbie, now studying them both through eyes at half-mast, his chin still resting on his paws. "Why don't I meet you downstairs? Give me a few minutes to change."

"Thanks," he said, taking a step back. "I'd appreciate it."

He turned and headed for the elevator while she stood for a moment, noticing the ways in which he favored Darryl Lee. An athlete's build. Wide shoulders, long legs. And yet, there was a noticeable difference, too. In high school, Darryl Lee's walk had defined confidence. Bobby Jack's took it a step further, and she could imagine that he wasn't used to taking no for an answer.

Maybe he needed some practice.

DOWNSTAIRS, SHE FOUND HIM waiting for her in a sitting area off the main lobby. Lamplight threw soft shadows across the sofa and chairs arranged in the center of the room. On spotting her, he stood, wiping his hands down the front of his blue jeans, as if he was nervous.

"Please," he said. "Sit down."

She took the chair opposite his corner of the couch, crossed her legs and said, "Mr. Randall, what can I do for you?"

He studied her for several long moments, until she

began to feel uncomfortable under his assessing gaze. "I mean you no disrespect, Ms. McAllister, but this thing you're doing here tomorrow. I don't want my daughter to have any part of it."

For a moment, Grier had no idea what to say, the disapproval in his tone impossible to miss. And not a little insulting. "How old is your daughter?"

"Sixteen."

"Well, since she's under eighteen, there's a consent form. It has to be signed by a parent."

"That would be her mother."

"Let me guess. Priscilla."

"I believe you two met this afternoon."

"Yes. We did."

"Priscilla thinks this is a good thing for our daughter. I don't."

Grier sat up in her chair, tugging at the collar of her blouse. She suddenly felt as if she'd arrived in Timbell Creek pulling a trailer full of snake oil. "I'm not sure what you've been told about the show—"

"I know enough," he interrupted. "Andy's a smart girl. She doesn't need something like this."

"And what exactly is this?"

"Frankly?"

"By all means," she said.

"Nonsense."

She managed a short laugh. "That's frank."

"As I said, I mean no disrespect."

"Mr. Randall—"

"Bobby Jack."

"Bobby Jack," she said, attempting to keep her voice even, "I'm obviously an outsider, but it seems to me that the person you're disrespecting here is your daughter."

Heat flared in his eyes, and she could see that she'd overstepped her boundaries.

"You know nothing about my daughter," he said.

"You're right. I don't. And you're also right that there's no Nobel Prize waiting for the winner of this contest. But neither is there a bloody death or a one-way ticket to life-is-over-as-you-know-it."

He sat for a good minute without responding. Grier determined to wait him out. "I'm not criticizing other people's choices," he finally said. "Frankly, I don't care what other people do. But I do care about my daughter and what happens to her. You're not here to watch out for her best interest. You're here to pick some girl who's going to think she's won a fairy tale when the ending will not be happily ever after."

Despite her best efforts at composure, Grier wilted a little beneath the heat of the words. "And how do you know that?" she asked, her voice not as steady as she would have liked.

He stood up abruptly and headed for the door. "Because," he said, turning to glance back at her, "there's no such thing, Ms. McAllister. And that I know for a fact."

8

---

*When I look in the mirror, what I see is someone
I never wanted to be.*
*— Andy Randall in a chat room confession
at LivingSolo.com*

Andy sat in front of her computer screen, staring at the blinking cursor. When the conversations got too personal, the questions too intense, she just backed out. That was the great thing about the Internet. Now you see her. Now you don't. A girl could be her own Houdini.

She closed her eyes, leaned her head against the desk chair. She heard her father's voice, his words pounding at her temples. *Maybe you could tell her how to get pregnant and force the guy to marry her.*

Somewhere deep inside, maybe she'd always known the

truth. She wondered now if this was something a baby could feel, even inside its mother, whether it was wanted or not.

For Andy, hearing the truth was like throwing light across the nagging feeling she'd always had about her parents' marriage. She got up and walked over to the bed, dropping onto the pillows. She rolled over and curled up in a ball, her knees drawn tight against her chest.

From beneath her bed, Tangerine meowed, then shimmied out and jumped up beside her. She rubbed a hand across the back of the orange tabby cat, smiling a little as he arched high, his tail straight in the air.

He meowed again, then leaned down to rub his face against hers. She pulled him close and held him in the curve of her arm while he began to purr, the noise rising in volume until it sounded like the idling engine of a small car.

She'd spotted him on the side of the road one morning when her daddy had been driving her to school. At first, she'd thought it might be a little roll of yarn someone had tossed out the window, but after seeing it move, Andy had pleaded with him to stop. They'd pulled over to the side of the road, and she'd jumped out, running back to the spot where the little orange kitten sat, mewling. As gently as she could, Andy had picked him up, a soft cry of despair erupting from her throat at the sight of his crusted-together eyes and the little body that was nothing but fur and bones.

They'd driven him straight to the vet who'd pronounced him blind from the infection that had gone too far and destroyed vision. With the realization that he would never see, Andy had cupped the tiny kitten to her chest and promised she would take care of him for the rest of his life.

And she had.

He never left her room, his food bowl and water bowl always placed in the same spot where he knew to find them. The same for his litter box. He roamed the room as if he could see every inch of it, napping on the windowsill in the afternoon sun, waiting by the door for her return and pouncing on her shoestrings when she did with absolute joy for the game.

Sometimes, Flo would sleep with them at night, and the cat would curl up on the pillow beside the dog's head, purring them both to sleep.

Andy wished all love could be as simple as her love for Tangerine and his for her. It really wasn't that complicated, was it? Love was just needing and being needed. People made it complicated. Her mom. Her dad. Kyle.

A knock at the door made her jump. "Andy. Honey. Please. Let's talk."

She heard the worry beneath each word in her father's voice and squeezed her eyes shut tight, refusing to let herself care. "I think I've heard about all I need to hear for one night," she said.

"Let's not leave things like this."

"Not now, Daddy. I don't want to talk now."

Silence. And then finally, she heard his footsteps receding down the hallway.

For now, she wasn't going to think about her mother or her father or Kyle. She would focus on what was immediately ahead and nothing else. Winning the Jane Austen Girl contest. She put on her pajamas and climbed into bed. Tangerine curled up next to her, and under his soft roar of contentment, Andy finally closed her eyes and went to sleep.

9

Inner peace has its own stamp of beauty. Settle up with your old issues. Left unresolved, they can fume away inside you like a toxic chemical and eventually make their way to the surface in the form of worry lines and other signs of premature aging.

— Grier McAllister – Blog at Jane Austen Girl

Grier tossed and turned until the clock by the bed blinked a mocking 3:15, after which she fell into a thin, restless sleep that left her groggy and grouchy when the alarm went off at six a.m.

She shrugged into enough clothing to appear decent and then trekked outside with Sebbie to do his morning routine. He sniffed several bushes and a half-acre or so of grass, before finally relenting and taking care of the serious stuff.

Back in the room, a look in the mirror made her wish for a couple more hours under the covers. But the group meeting was scheduled for eight o'clock, and she wanted to be prepared. She stood under the warm spray of the shower, thinking about last night's visit from Bobby Jack Randall, and its ensuing effect on her sleep.

The man had nerve, she'd give him that. She wasn't sure whether to feel sorry for or envious of his daughter. She wondered what it would have been like to have a father like that when she was growing up. Someone to walk along in front of her, not only willing, but insistent on pointing out the hairpin curves as they appeared on his radar.

Was that what she looked like to Bobby Jack Randall? A hairpin curve he was convinced could only throw his daughter off track?

Something about the assumption bothered her.

But then something about the man himself bothered her, too.

Maybe it was the arrogance. It was different from Darryl Lee's cockiness, an attribute that had always been so obvious as to be inoffensive, sort of like Wile E. Coyote and the Road Runner.

Bobby Jack's dismissal of her and the reason she'd come here had nothing to do with surface level interpretations, but with his own gut check that obviously told him she and her sideshow, as he saw it, were bad news.

Standing in front of the mirror with a towel wrapped around her, she considered the fact that from a father's point of view, Jane Austen Girl wasn't the highest of goals to aspire to. With the plethora of reality shows mapping TV channels today, even she could see how he might arrive at that conclusion.

And why was she doing it? For her own gain, of course. The publicity alone would put her business on the radar of women all over the country. She couldn't deny wanting this.

Even so, she hardly qualified for black-hat status. It wasn't as if the girls she ended up picking would be immediately drained of their IQ like the fair-haired victims in those zombie movies that used to be shown in high school during lunch period.

In all fairness, she thought it could be safely said that Bobby Jack Randall had based his opinion on a number of cliché assumptions. Having arrived at that conclusion, she resolved to shelve any lingering feelings of dismay over his surprise late-night visit to her room.

She was fine with what she'd come here to do. And she didn't need to reassess anything based on the accusations of an overprotective father who obviously had some issues of his own to sort through. Especially when that father was a relative of Darryl Lee's.

She blow dried her hair and then quickly got dressed.

From the things she'd brought with her, she chose a slim, black, Max Mara suit she could only wear when she'd been sticking to her veggies and avoiding the Italian restaurant two blocks from her apartment where they served the best Risotto Milanese this side of Milan.

She finished up with lipstick and a spritz of Jo Malone and then leaned across to pick up Sebbie. He whined and looked at the pillow with longing. "You want to stay put?"

He whined again.

"Okay," she said, setting him back onto the bed where he immediately curled up and closed his eyes. "Be good," she said. "I'll be back to check on you in a while."

He licked her cheek in response, and she stood up, rubbing his soft coat. On the lower shelf of the nightstand, she spotted a yellow phone book. On impulse, she reached for it. She kept her hand on the cover for a moment, then quickly opened it to the residential pages and flipped to the B's. She traced her finger down the right-hand column, coming to a stop at McAllister, Maxine. 54 Knolltop Rd. Same number they'd had since she was seven, and they'd moved to the house a few miles outside of town.

She stared at the line of information, something inside her unraveling a little. She dialed quickly before logic could take over and change her mind. A beep sounded, followed by an operator's voice that declared the number no longer in service.

She replaced the receiver with a bang that jangled her arm, then sat there rubbing it for a moment, before picking up the phone book and stuffing it back inside the nightstand. She didn't have time for this.

Where was the sudden guilt coming from anyway? She didn't owe her mother anything. And besides, what would they have to say to each other after nineteen years? Grier: *Sorry I moved away and never called.* Her mother: *Oh, that's all right. I assumed it was the lousy childhood and all.*

And what exactly was she supposed to say other than: *At least you were right about that.*

10

---

*We are pleased to inform you of your acceptance
to the Atlanta School of Design. Your impressive
GPA along with the talent shown in your
drawings make you an ideal candidate for our
fashion design program. We are proud to continue
our tradition of educating some of the country's
finest clothing designers. And we look forward to
hearing from you regarding your decision to
attend ASD.*
*— From the acceptance letter Maxine
McAllister received on the same day she
discovered she was pregnant in the spring of her
senior year of high school*

Maxine had been awake since four. She couldn't
remember the last time she'd slept through the night.

It was funny how people took things for granted, never realizing their value until they were gone. For Maxine, sleep was just one thing on a long list.

She lay on the less than comfortable mattress and stared at the ceiling while light eventually crept into the room. In the bed by the window, April Bower moaned softly and then mumbled a few words in her sleep. Almost always, she called out one of her children's names, followed by something she'd probably said to them often when they were growing up. "Sammy, finish your breakfast. Manny, time for your bath."

In the six months they'd been sharing this room, April's sons had only visited her twice, both of them glancing at their watches most of the time they'd been here. It didn't seem fair that April should have kids like that. Years ago, Maxine had actually known her as a nice woman who worked at the county library. A woman who'd lost her husband too young and worked hard to take care of her children. Only to end up in this place with two sons who begrudged what little time they gave her.

Unlike her own story.

Maxine had never once questioned Grier's leaving Timbell Creek and not coming back. But there were times when she'd missed her so badly she thought it might actually kill her. And like a good night's sleep, she hadn't appreciated her daughter until she was gone.

The knife-sharp pain that had woken her two hours ago renewed its rant, stabbing low in her abdomen. She gasped out loud and bit her lip. She squeezed her eyes shut and tried counting, focusing on getting to twenty, since that was how long it usually took for it to begin to fade. Only this time, she hit thirty-five, and the pain hadn't let up. Tears streamed down her cheeks.

She gave in then and pushed the call button for the nurse.

Five minutes later, Mrs. Marsh waddled into the room, stopping at the side of her bed. "Pain bad this mornin', honey?"

"Pretty bad," Maxine said, wiping the back of her hand across her face.

The nurse patted her leg and clucked with sympathy. "You hold on now. I'll be right back with somethin' for you."

It seemed like an eternity before she returned, even though it was probably only minutes. The pain had become a fog through which Maxine could see nothing beyond the immediate.

"Here, hon," Mrs. Marsh said, handing her the two pills and then holding a cup of water to her lips.

"Thank you," Maxine managed, her voice raw.

"I'll come check on you in a few minutes," the nurse said.

Maxine bit her lip and nodded. It took fifteen minutes for the pain to begin to lessen, finally lowering its intensity to a dull throb. She opened her eyes and found Mrs. Marsh watching her from the doorway.

"Any better?" she asked.

"Yes," Maxine said.

The heavyset woman walked over to her bed. "I could ask the doctor to increase your pain meds. I know you haven't wanted that, but I think it's time, sweetie."

The woman's compassion was almost more than Maxine could take. Hearing it, she could no longer fool herself about the progression of her disease. Which, she supposed, was exactly what she'd been doing. Pretending there was some possibility it could still go away. "I'd like to think about it," she said.

"Okay, honey, you do that," the nurse said, patting her on the leg.

Maxine lay there a long time after she left, letting acceptance creep in degree by degree until there it sat in front of her. Undeniable. Time was running out.

Had she thought she might actually leave this place one day? Maybe that was the way the mind dealt with the unthinkable. Reshaped it into something that could be processed. Something that didn't loom like an axe at the neck. But it was time to face the truth. And if she let herself finally admit as much, it would be a relief to concede to the stronger medications. The battle was beginning to wear her out.

She reached for the call button again, but stopped herself just short of pushing it. Later today. She would tell them later. But first, there was something she had to do.

11

---

*I was hoping you'd come by last night. Give me a
call. I'm missing you. Maggie.*
*— Note left on the windshield of Bobby Jack
Randall's pickup*

Bobby Jack drove the county road to his current job site
with one hand on the steering wheel, the other beating a
distracted rat-a-tat on his knee.

He glanced at the piece of paper he'd tossed on the seat
beside him, guilt nagging low in his gut. He knew he ought
to call her. Decency dictated as much. And yet something
inside him balked at the thought. He was just so bad at this
part. Casual dating, he could handle. But when it started
heading toward something more, that was where he had
trouble.

He didn't want more. Didn't need it. Had no space for it.

And that was hardly fair to a woman like Maggie Morgan who'd done nothing more wrong than send him a couple of signals at a church picnic a few Saturdays ago. Signals he should have ignored, but instead had responded to in a weak moment.

Maggie was a nice woman, divorced, no children. And lonely as all get out.

It was this realization that had convinced him he shouldn't see her again after the first date. But then she'd called him with an invitation to come over for dinner. Caught off guard, he hadn't been able to come up with an excuse that sounded anywhere near convincing. And so he'd gone, immediately ashamed of himself for all the obvious effort she'd gone to. Fresh flowers throughout her house, the smell of homemade bread greeting him at the door that made his mouth water. She was a great cook, preparing a meal for him that he truly would not forget anytime soon.

They'd spent a couple of hours on her sofa with a glass of wine, Maggie asking him a hundred different questions about his business, his life. The conversation had been followed by some pretty intense kissing. But Bobby Jack had been the one to pull back, telling her he had to get home and check on Andy who'd had a bit of a sore throat when he'd left. A tiny white lie. The truth was, Maggie Morgan was a nice woman who needed a nice guy to appreciate her efforts enough to take it somewhere.

Bobby Jack wasn't that guy. It just wasn't a road he wanted to take. He'd been single a long time, and mostly, he liked it that way. Raising Andy while Priscilla played coach from the sidelines didn't leave him with a burning desire to add another female personality to the mix. Even one as nice as Maggie.

Thirty minutes outside the town limits, he pulled into the driveway of a nearly completed spec house he'd built on Clearwater Lake. It was one of four he had under construction on the lake, fast becoming known around the country for its clean water and beautiful shoreline.

The real estate boom here had started out as a trickle a few years before, most recently reaching its current mind-boggling status for every builder in the area. People were moving in from places like New York and California and paying upwards of a million dollars for houses that would have gone for half that not so long ago.

Bobby Jack wasn't complaining. He believed in making hay while the sun was shining. He knew from personal experience that the clouds always came, sooner or later.

He got out of the truck and spotted Darryl Lee at the front door of the house, talking to a painter. About a year ago, he'd brought his brother on board with him when the workload had started keeping him in the office until ten o'clock every night. Darryl Lee had no complaints. He'd spent the past dozen years working for his father-in-law, a situation that had grown less and less attractive with the demise of his marriage to Dreama. And the truth was when Darryl Lee turned his thoughts to something other than chasing skirts, he earned every penny Bobby Jack paid him.

"Mornin'," Bobby Jack said, walking past his brother and Rod Morris, the painter whose business they were keeping busy full-time.

"Whoa, there," Darryl Lee said, clapping him on the shoulder. "We were just going over those last color choices for the house on Bent Tree Road. The main color we've been using is on back order over at the building supply. Want to wait on it or pick something else?"

"How long before it's in?" Bobby Jack asked.

"Week," Rod said, pulling a round tin of tobacco from his back pocket and pinching out a small chunk before inserting it between his lower lip and gum.

"Let's just wait then. That color seems to be the one that makes most people happy."

"Got it," Darryl Lee said.

Rod stepped off the porch, threw them a wave. "I gotta get going then. Catch up with ya later."

"We about to tie things up here?" Bobby Jack asked Darryl Lee once Rod's truck backed out of the driveway.

"Yep. You got a buyer for this one?"

"Not yet."

"The way things have been going, it won't take long."

They talked business for several minutes, going over the things that had to be done that day, before Darryl Lee propped a hand behind his neck and said, "Hey, Bobby Jack, about yesterday."

Bobby Jack looked at his brother, raised an eyebrow. "You don't need to explain anything to me."

"Man, I think you got the wrong idea."

"Did I?"

"You know who that was?"

"Actually, yeah, I found out last night. She's the woman doing interviews over at the Inn today for that reality TV show."

Darryl Lee leaned back, his forehead knit together and said, "Say what?"

For a moment, Bobby Jack figured his brother must be lying. But then he looked as surprised by the news as he had been when Grier McAllister opened the door to her room last night, and he'd realized she was the same woman he'd seen with his brother that afternoon. "So how do you know her?"

"We dated a while in high school. Before she took off and left town."

"When was that?"

"Senior year. Never did know the reason why."

"So what? You two hook back up or something?"

Darryl Lee laughed. "I wish. Hot, isn't she?"

Bobby Jack folded his arms and glanced out at the lake where a Sea-Doo cut across the wake of a ski boat and went airborne. He ignored his brother's assessment and said, "So what's the deal with you and Dreama, anyway?"

"She's not givin' me the time of day. That's pretty much it."

"I thought she'd decided to forgive you."

"Yeah, me too. Apparently, not permanently."

"Cheating's not the easiest thing to forgive a person for," Bobby Jack said, trying to keep his own history out of the assessment.

"No, it's not."

"Proving yourself to someone takes time."

"Yeah, it does," he said, looking down at his boots. "I don't know. Maybe we should just throw in the towel."

Bobby Jack leveled him a look. "That wouldn't have anything to do with your old girlfriend, would it?"

Darryl Lee had the decency to look sheepish. "I knew Grier a long time ago. I was crazy about her then. And I sure as hell never expected to run into her yesterday."

"See though, brother, that's the problem. Commitment is about forgetting what might have been or what might be down the road. You're still looking around, Darryl Lee. Just like our old man, you're still looking." With that, Bobby Jack went inside the house, leaving Darryl Lee out on the porch.

A few minutes later, Bobby Jack stood on the deck off the kitchen, looking out at the lake where a lone fishing boat hovered, and a ski boat roared in the distance. There were times when he could wring his younger brother's neck. He'd been dressing Darryl Lee down for his womanizing since they were teenagers. And obviously, there wasn't a word of it that had sunk in yet.

Growing up, how many times had they walked in on their mama bent over the kitchen counter, her shoulders shaking with silent sobs? Every time it had happened, Bobby Jack had wanted to pound his father to a pulp. But his mother had always forgiven him, and for a while, everything would be all right. Until the itch became too persistent to resist, and his dad would start coming in later and later, some nights not at all.

If possible, Darryl Lee had hated their father's infidelity even more than Bobby Jack. Even after their mother gave him the inevitable next chance and let him back in the house, Darryl Lee would go weeks without speaking to him. And yet, here he was, treating his own wife the same way. The human psyche. Go figure.

Bobby Jack thought about Grier McAllister then and the fact that she'd once dated Darryl Lee. Something about it didn't click. She hardly seemed like the type of woman to go for Darryl Lee's smooth talking. But then Bobby Jack had no idea what he was basing that on. What business of his was it, anyway? Darryl Lee was his brother, and he loved him, despite his shortcomings. But that didn't mean he thought he could ever reform him.

Bobby Jack resolved to wash his hands of the whole deal. Darryl Lee would make his own mistakes, regardless of anything Bobby Jack said. So why waste his breath?

As for Grier, maybe she deserved a warning. But then if

she'd known Darryl Lee in high school, she ought to know what to expect from getting involved with him. It was hardly his place to go waving her a red flag. The cavalry he was not.

Surprisingly, the woman he'd talked to last night didn't seem like anyone he'd ever known Darryl Lee to be involved with. Maybe it didn't count when you were kids. Anyway, she probably dated guys now who paid more for a haircut than Darryl Lee allowed for his monthly truck payment.

Bobby Jack pushed away from the deck railing and told himself he didn't have time to be standing out here thinking about his brother's former conquests or his future mistakes. He had his own drama to deal with, namely a daughter who wasn't speaking to him and an ex-wife who couldn't be more thrilled about it.

12

People look at the outside of a person and assume they know everything there is to know about the inside of that person. The trouble is a few coats of paint and some new shutters can do a lot for the exterior of a house, but tell you nothing about its foundation or its ability to weather life's storms. I would say the same is true of people.
— Grier McAllister – Blog at Jane Austen Girl

To say the turnout exceeded Grier's expectations would have been an understatement.

The conference room at the back of the inn was full to overflowing, girls between the ages of sixteen and eighteen chatting and giggling with nervous anticipation. Grier decided maybe she'd slightly underestimated the appeal of a date with a duke.

Gil Martin, the cameraman sent by the network, wound his way through the center of the room. Mid-twenties with an MTV rock-star kind of appeal, he looked like a bull who'd just wandered into a field full of heifers.

"I have one word for you," Grier said, from her stance behind the speaker's podium.

"What's that?" he asked, the words a little dazed.

"Jailbait."

He grinned. "Look but don't touch, right?"

"Right."

"The estrogen levels in this room must be off the Richter scale."

"Let's hope for your sake it's not contagious," she said, smiling.

"Oh," he said, raising his eyebrows, "I'm a big fan of estrogen."

Gil had a nice way of lightening the atmosphere. He'd arrived late last night, leaving a message for her on the room's voice mail to meet him for breakfast where they'd gone over everything he wanted to film throughout the day, including a clip of each girl's interview in case she ended up winning.

"Shall we get started?" Grier said.

Gil glanced at his watch. "Nine o'clock on the dot."

Grier tapped on the microphone and said, "If everyone could please take a seat."

The girls quickly weaved their way to their chairs, silence settling over the room.

"Good morning," she said. "I'm so glad all of you could be here today. As you know, the KT Network is producing an episode for its show, *Dream Date,* called 'Jane Austen Girl.'"

A nervous round of laughter rose up, followed by a chorus of clapping and a few wolf whistles. Once the group had quieted again, Grier said, "I can see I'm going to have my work cut out for me with so many pretty girls. Timbell Creek must have a secret."

"It's the water," someone called out, inciting another round of giggles.

"Well, you sure don't look like you need any help from me where image is concerned."

"Yes, we do!" A lone voice shot up from the back of the room.

Grier swiped her gaze across the rows, spotting the girl who had thrown out the statement of disagreement. She looked sixteen or so, her straight blonde hair loose about her shoulders, its natural shine one that was hard to achieve even with the priciest of salon products.

The woman sitting next to her Grier recognized instantly. Priscilla Randall from the coffee shop. The girl resembled her, but her style was much simpler and less polished.

Priscilla Randall had clearly made looking good part of her essence, the success of her efforts easy enough to see in the pampered smoothness of her skin and the toned muscles in her long arms.

"Some of us more than others," Priscilla said with a knowing laugh. She took one of her daughter's hands and patted it, as if certain there would be no question as to who would be the eventual winner here. She glanced at the rows of girls in front of them with a barely concealed look of pity for the time they were wasting.

Grier raised an eyebrow, surprised by the woman's audacity.

The girl at her side pulled her hand away, looking uncomfortable.

"So," Grier said, regrouping, "first of all, I'd like to thank each and every one of you for coming out this morning. This is an incredible turnout. I would guess we're in the range of one hundred and twenty-five of you?"

Laughter rippled up and then settled back.

"Well, he is extremely cute, our George," Grier said.

More laughter.

Grier held up a hand. "So, the question is how do we get there? I've been given the task of finding George's dream date, and the first thing I'm going to do is have you girls fill out a questionnaire to determine whether you're compatible with this young man. Because if your favorite sport is sumo wrestling, and his favorite sport is polo, it won't really matter what kind of dress you're wearing once he gets past how beautiful you are."

The room again erupted with nervous laughter.

"Can you tell us what kinds of things he likes?" a young girl with dark hair and bright blue eyes spoke up from the front row.

"Well, that would probably color your answers, wouldn't it?"

"But we might like polo if we had a chance to experience it."

"That's true," Grier said, with a small laugh, "but somehow, someway, I've got to narrow down his choices. The questionnaires are really just basic stuff. We'll take an hour to go through them while you girls mingle and get to know one another."

Grier handed out the forms to the expectant looking girls who took them from her with polite thank-yous.

Most of them finished writing well before the hour was up.

Grier began collecting the papers and once she had them all, directed everyone to the adjoining room where refreshments had been set up.

Priscilla and Andy Randall were the last two to leave the room, the look on Priscilla's face again one of extreme disapproval.

It was then that Grier glimpsed the woman sitting in the very last row. She wore a faded red sweater, and her once blonde hair was completely gray.

Grier stared for a moment, stumbling, and then righting herself with the edge of a chair. She stood frozen, then turned for another look, the room again tilting around her.

Silence swelled for several moments before the older woman said, "Grier. Hello."

Grier opened her mouth to respond, but not a single word would come out. Gil stood beside her, putting a hand on her shoulder. "Are you all right?" he asked.

She shook her head, trying to clear the fog, and then took a lurching step forward through the door.

"Grier!" the suddenly too familiar voice called out.

But Grier kept going, walking faster and faster and then running, certain that if she looked back again, the pain in her chest would swallow her whole.

13

_____

Don't be fooled into thinking there will never be a
day of reckoning. The past always catches up
with us. One way or the other.
– Advice Maxine's grandmother had once given
her.

Maxine sat staring at the closed door. Maybe it was true
then that the piper had to be paid before anyone left this
earth. If so, her tab had definitely come due.

But wasn't that the way it worked? Everything
eventually coming to full circle? And what had she
expected anyway? Open-arm forgiveness?

"Would you like some water, ma'am?"

Maxine glanced up, blinking the young girl standing
before her into focus. "Thank you."

"You look pale," the girl said.

"It's a little warm in here."

"I just came back to get my purse. But I can sit for a minute." The girl took the empty chair next to her, twisting the cap off a bottle of water and handing it to Maxine.

"So how do you know Ms. McAllister?"

Maxine took a sip of the water, rubbed her still-shaking thumb down one side of the bottle, silent.

"I noticed that she looked kind of surprised when she saw you," the girl explained.

"I'm her mom," she said in a low voice. "Guess that's hard to believe, huh?"

The girl looked at her then, her blue-eyed gaze considering. "She looks a little like you."

"Not much similarity now," Maxine said, pressing one hand to her wrinkled cheek. "I'm Maxine, by the way. McAllister."

"Andy Randall."

Maxine rolled the name through her memory and said, "Your daddy is—"

"Bobby Jack," the girl finished for her.

"I see the resemblance," Maxine said.

Andy glanced down at her hands. "People say I look like him."

Maxine nodded. "I haven't seen him in a while, but from what I remember, looking like him would be a good thing."

Andy lifted a shoulder. "No one ever says I look like my mom."

"She's—" Maxine stopped, the name eluding her.

"Beautiful."

"Well, so are you."

Andy glanced up, shook her head. "No, I'm not."

"And what makes you think that?"

She made a face, the kind teenagers make when they think something an adult has said is particularly dumb. "I have a mirror."

Maxine considered this, and then, "Mirrors don't always tell people the same things." "I know what I see."

"What about what others see? Does that count?"

Andy shifted in her chair. "Sometimes people tell you what they think you want to hear."

"That's a lot of cynicism from someone so young," Maxine said.

"It's true, don't you think?"

"Maybe sometimes."

Andy folded her arms across her chest and said, "Why was your daughter surprised to see you?"

"We haven't seen each other in a long time."

"She lives in New York City, doesn't she?"

"That's what I hear," Maxine said.

"Oh. Well, I, ah, guess she must be awfully busy being so successful and all."

"I imagine so."

An awkward silence followed the admission. When

Andy spoke, it was in a careful voice. "Is she mad at you for something?"

Maxine remained quiet for a bit before saying, "She is. And rightly so."

"What happened?"

Maxine sighed, wondering why this girl was talking with her. She had long ago stopped believing in coincidence. Everything happened for a reason. And maybe that included the fact that Andy had found something of interest in an old woman who stood out like a sore thumb in this room full of beautiful young girls. "I wasn't a very good mama," she said.

"Oh," Andy said again. "Why?"

The pain from earlier that morning stabbed across Maxine's abdomen. Maxine drew in a sharp breath and then pressed her lips together.

"Are you all right?" the girl asked, alarm widening her eyes.

"Yes," she said, releasing her breath and praying the pain wouldn't renew its angry tirade. She sat for a moment, eyes closed, resting her head against the wall behind her chair.

The girl put a hand on her arm and said, "Are you sure?"

Maxine nodded, tried to look convincing.

"You don't look all right."

"I will be in a minute."

They sat without talking until the pain had lowered its volume to a throb. Maxine spoke then, her eyes still closed. "What about you and your mama? Are you two close?"

"I guess that depends on what you mean by close," Andy said. "We're pretty different."

"How so?" Maxine asked.

"I don't know," Andy said, lifting her shoulders in a shrug. "Sometimes, I think I'm a disappointment to her."

At this, Maxine forced herself to open her eyes and look at the girl. "Now, I can't imagine there being any truth in that."

"Some things are hard to miss. Even when you don't want to see them."

Maxine felt a swell of tenderness for the girl, along with a dizzying sense of regret for the fact that she had never once sat and talked with her own daughter this way when Grier had been Andy's age.

The door opened, and Andy's mother stuck her head inside. "Andy, what in the world?"

"I'm coming," Andy said, standing.

"Good luck," Maxine said.

"Thanks." Andy straightened the waist of her slim skirt. "Will you be here when I come out?"

"I'm not sure."

"Okay," Andy said. "You're all right though?"

Maxine nodded. "Much better now," she said.

Andy left the room then, but not before glancing over her shoulder to give Maxine one of her pretty smiles.

Maxine sat back again, closing her eyes under the

sudden certainty that she did not belong here. She had been wrong to come. Wrong to think that Grier would want to see her. It was selfish, and she didn't know why she hadn't let herself realize that before now.

This trip to Timbell Creek was about Grier, for Grier. It had nothing to do with her. There was so little she could give her daughter. She had nothing of material value to leave her, even if Grier would have accepted it from her. But what she could do for her daughter was leave her alone. Not stir up a past Grier so obviously wanted to forget.

She could give her that. And she would.

14

_____

_Through the eyes of others, we're very often
significantly off the mark from our own
interpretation. Maybe it's safe to say the truth lies
somewhere in between the two._
— Grier McAllister – Blog at Jane Austen Girl

Grier locked herself in the toilet stall and wilted against the wall, one hand to her chest. What was her mother doing here? How dare she just show up with no warning whatsoever?

Fury replaced the confusion inside her, and she felt her face redden with it. She didn't have to talk to her. She owed her nothing.

She squeezed her eyes shut, seeing her face again, reliving the shock of it after so many years.

She looked. . .so old.

Above all, this shocked Grier the most. Maybe she'd somehow imagined she would be the same. Her vibrant, too-pretty-for-her-own-good-mother. Not this worn-out version of her.

She stood this way for several minutes, aware that she had to get herself together, and fast. But she couldn't seem to make herself move. It was as if, after all this time, she'd finally hit a solid wall of reality that refused to yield to any delusions she might be willing to entertain about her mother finally getting it together and turning her life around. All she'd needed was that single glimpse to tell her it had never happened. And if it had, it was just too little, too late.

With the realization came a dousing wave of regret mingled with sadness. She opened her eyes and clawed her way to the top of it, refusing even for a moment to succumb. Harsh reality number one: we all make choices. Her mother had certainly made hers. Grier's years of therapy had led her to the indisputably logical conclusion that she was not responsible for her mother's choices. She wasn't about to throw a hand grenade in the center of the perfectly manicured lawn of reason that she and her therapist had spent so much time grooming.

She grabbed a tissue and wiped her eyes, then her nose. She had a job to do. And once it was done, she would go back to New York, back to her real life.

WHEN GRIER WALKED into the conference room a few minutes later, it was to the immediate realization that her mother was no longer there.

Undeniable relief washed over her, and she felt as if she could finally breathe again. Shame nipped at the heels of the relief, but she pushed it away, unwilling to give it any pull.

She was grateful when Gil returned to help her with the stack of questionnaires. She had been given extremely specific parameters for an initial elimination. The duke was quite specific in his likes and dislikes. No airheads. GPA 3.4 or above. Dog lovers only. She could like him for that one. No fu-fu girls who disapproved of a few dog hairs, and if they weren't cool with a dog in the house, then they weren't the girl for him. That one alone knocked twenty-five out of the running. And then there was the question about why it was nice to have money.

A: It made getting into clubs easier
B: It was always nice to pamper yourself
C: It gave a person choices

Surprisingly enough, his preferred answer was C. And that eliminated another twelve girls.

The last question: What was the most important thing a guy could give a girl?

A: Flowers

B: A cool ride for dates
C: Respect for his mother

This one really made Grier wonder. What seventeen-year old boy would have written that? Maybe his mother had written it.

That answer knocked out another sixteen girls, leaving the new total at thirty-two.

"Well, that does it," Gil said. "Guess we'll go from here."

Grier felt a little sorry for the ones who would be leaving after this, but the thought of weeding her way through thirty-two determined and likely deserving girls made her wonder if she had been crazy to take this on.

She put the non-eliminated questionnaires in a folder. "Now for the not-so-fun part," she said to Gil. "Shall we bring them back in?"

Gil went to the adjoining room and signaled that they were ready for them.

A few minutes later, the girls were all reseated, staring at Grier with the same look in their eyes she had seen in the eyes of *American Idol* contestants right before their elimination. "Okay, everyone, as I said before, this initial elimination round is based on questions sent by George about the kind of girl he feels he's most compatible with. And while I wish every one of you could be chosen to go to that ball with him, unfortunately, it will only be one of you. If I call your name, please follow Gil outside the room into the lobby area. Jessica Jameson, Holly Munroe, Tara Munson."

And so the names went on for another seventy or so, until the room was left with the girls who had not been eliminated. "You thirty-two young ladies will remain for the next round of consideration."

A cheer erupted in unison, the girls hugging one another and high-fiving. Grier's gaze went to Andy Randall, still sitting beside her mother in the back row. Andy's expression showed no emotion of any kind. Grier wondered whose idea it was for her to be here anyway.

Grier left the room and stepped into the lobby where the seventy plus girls stood looking as if they no longer had anything to live for.

Her heart went out to them, and she wished somehow that she could tell them life would hold joys and wonders far more amazing and wonderful than a date with George. That this letdown was really just a little pothole along the way.

"Girls, I want to thank you for coming out today. I understand that each of you had your hopes up for this. I wish that I didn't have to disappoint any of you. If it were up to me, every single one of you would be the winner."

Half smiles and shrugged shoulders met the statement. Grier watched as they turned and trudged from the lobby through the doors of the inn. Gil looked at Grier. "They'll get over it. At sixteen, everything is life or death."

The two of them rejoined the group of still bubbling

over teenagers, and Grier began the process that would shatter the hopes of yet a second round of eager girls.

The interviews were conducted in a small sitting room off the main lobby. Gil directed each girl in and out and held her to the five-minute time allotment like a German Shepherd holding a suspect in place while the arresting officer questioned him. If it weren't for his careful monitoring of the time Grier spent with each girl, they could be here until midnight.

The difficult thing was that each of the girls had something about them that made them special. Some of them were funny, some serious, some more eager to know about Grier's career than about George.

Andersen Randall was a tough nut to crack though. She walked into the room, wearing a deadpan expression that hid what Grier already knew was a beautiful smile. "Hello, Andersen," Grier said.

"Hi. I prefer Andy."

"Have a seat, please, Andy."

She pulled out a chair, crossing her arms across her chest, looking suddenly awkward and gawky.

"So why are you here today, Andy?"

"I want to go on a date with George, like everybody else here?"

Grier smiled. "Now why don't I believe that?" She looked down at the application Andy had filled out, saw the 4.0 GPA, the interest in historical architecture. "You don't seem like someone who would care an awful lot about that."

"What do I seem like I would care about?" she asked, a little short.

"Meeting someone on your own?"

"Around here?" Andy said.

Grier inclined her head, then said, "So why do you want to go out with him?"

Andy's gaze went wide, as if she felt she was being unfairly prodded as to her motivation. "Does it really matter?"

"Yes, actually, it does," Grier said. "I just kind of have a feeling that you're not here on your own."

"That's not true," Andy said. "I am here on my own."

"And your mother very much wants you to be?"

"And my daddy very much *doesn't* want me to be. But I don't really care what either of them thinks. I'm here because I want to be here."

Grier considered this, doodled on her paper for a minute and then said, "What if he's not what you're expecting?"

"Well, I'm not expecting much. Surely, he'll live up to that."

Grier laughed then, charmed in spite of herself. "He would certainly have his hands full with you."

Andy looked surprised by this. She glanced away, folded her arms across her chest and bit her lower lip.

"Haven't you ever just wanted to go somewhere, do something different, be somebody different?"

"Actually, I have," Grier said.

"Is that why you left here?"

Grier raised an eyebrow. "How did you know?—"

"My daddy said you used to date Uncle Darryl Lee."

Grier had to press her lips together at the sound of uncle and Darryl Lee paired together. "Yes, that was a very long time ago."

"He's not as bad as everyone makes him out to be," Andy said. "He just likes to have fun."

"Nothing wrong with that, as long as no one gets hurt."

Andy considered this. "Daddy thinks he's irresponsible."

"Your daddy could be right."

"I think Daddy would do well to borrow a little of Uncle Darryl Lee's 'live and let live.'"

"Hmmm," Grier said. "So what is your daddy going to say if you win this date with George?"

"There's not a whole lot he can say."

"Actually, you're sixteen. There's a good bit he could say. If there's a chance that he won't allow you to do this, then it's really not fair to take the opportunity away from another girl."

"Don't say that!" Andy erupted with clear indignation. "This is something I want to do. My mom already signed the consent form. It doesn't matter what Daddy thinks."

"Andy—"

"Please," she said. "Don't eliminate me based on that. Give me a chance!"

Grier's heart twisted a little at the pleading in the girl's voice. She wasn't sure of the origin of it, but she knew it was real. She remembered suddenly what it felt like to be sixteen and yearn to be anywhere in the world except where she was. Even if it was just for a day.

Gil entered the room with an abrupt knock and a pointed glance at her watch. "Okay, time's up."

Andy stared at Grier, then stood and in a soft voice said, "Please."

"Thank you, Andy. It was nice talking with you."

While Grier waited for the next interviewee to come in, she thought about the look on Andy's face and wondered about the real truth behind why this was so important to her.

15

Dear Andy,
Will u b my girl?
__Yes __ No
Note from Kyle Summers
Second Grade – Timbell Creek Elementary

Andy didn't bother to wait for her mother.

She stormed out of the inn, click-clacking down the sidewalk in her ridiculously high heels and, waiting until she had rounded the corner out of sight, tossing them in the shrubbery by the sidewalk.

She had never felt so stupid in her entire life. What had she been thinking to enter such a lame-butt contest anyway? It wasn't as if she really gave a pile of cow poop about ever actually going on a date with George, Duke of Wherever. He was probably a total zero anyway.

All she cared about was GETTING OUT OF THIS TOWN. Away from her mom. And her dad. And their infernal fussing over her.

Entering this contest was exactly the kind of thing her mom would have done at age sixteen, according to her dad's recollection, anyway.

Sometimes, Andy wanted to be exactly like her. And others, she wanted to run from the very thought. This was one of those times.

But somewhere down deep in the mess of all this, she wanted to show her dad that she could do the things that her mom did. That she was every bit as pretty. That she was her mother's daughter.

But then that was crazy, wasn't it? Because this morning during every minute of sitting in that room, all she had wanted was to get up and run, as far and as fast as she could from the whole thing.

A horn tooted behind her. She glanced over her shoulder and saw Kyle idling up in his rattly old Jeep. He leaned across the seat and rolled down the window.

"Hey, Andy! What are you doing?"

"Walking. What does it look like?"

"You're in the middle of town. Barefoot. In an evening dress."

"It's not an evening dress," she said.

"Cocktail dress. Whatever. Where have you been?"

"None of your business."

He revved the engine and rolled on ahead, then pulled over at an angle, swinging the door open. "Get in," he said. "We'll go get ice cream."

"I don't want any ice cream."

"You always want ice cream."

"I don't want any now."

"Andy, come on, get in."

She glanced over her shoulder, saw her mother's convertible pulling up behind them, and jumped in, saying, "Go! Go!"

"What is wrong with you?" Kyle said, taking off while eyeing the low neckline of her dress and then jerking his gaze up when she gave him a pointed look. "Where have you been?" he asked.

"At the inn," she said. "Can you just go?"

He gunned the truck, and they took off. "Don't tell me you were there for that stupid George, Duke of—"

"Stop!" she said.

He started to laugh. "You really entered that, Andy?"

"It's none of your business whether I entered it or not."

"Are you kidding me? You? Why in the world would you care about some ridiculous date with a—"

"A date with a duke sounds like a pretty good thing to me right about now," Andy said.

"Since when?" he said.

"Since you became such a jerk?"

"Andy. Ever since I started playing football—"

"You don't have time for anything you used to have time for."

"I lift weights and run track so I don't get out of shape."

"And hang out with the cheerleaders," Andy said.

"You're jealous."

"I'm not jealous."

"Andy, I asked you to come to the games last fall."

"I didn't want to come to the games. I hate football."

"Well, I need a scholarship for college. Unlike you, mine's not paid for."

"That's not fair."

"Life's not fair. You haven't picked up on that yet."

They glared at each other, while Andy swam in a pool of mixed emotions. Fondness for the boy she had known since she was six years old and the first day of kindergarten. Frustration for the jock he had become since school had started in the fall and he'd become such a big football star. Whatever it was they'd been to each other all these years was no longer there. And it was just high time they both accepted it.

A car laid on the horn behind them.

Andy glanced back to see her mother barreling down on them.

"My mom's still behind us. Go! I don't want to talk to her right now."

Kyle swung a right on Cherry Street, hit the gas and the old Jeep shuddered once, then bolted forward. He hung a left on Amherst Way. Andy glanced back. Her mother had missed the turn.

"Yay," she said, sinking back against the seat.

"So why are you running from your mom?"

"Because she makes me crazy," Andy said.

"A person could call you Sybil where she's concerned."

Andy shrugged at this. "It is kind of like that."

"What did your dad say about you going to that thing?"

"What do you think he said?"

"No."

"Doesn't matter what he said."

"Since when?"

"Since I decided it's time I grew up."

He looked at her and then said, "Why don't we go to a movie tomorrow night?"

"I'm sure you already have plans with your cheerleader friends."

"I don't have plans. If I did, I wouldn't have asked you."

"Oh, yeah, sure, now that you think I might be going out with a duke, you're all hot after me."

He laughed. "Who says you're gonna win?"

"I say I'm gonna win. And for your information, I'm busy tomorrow night."

Kyle turned into her driveway. The brakes squeaked. "I'll get out here," Andy said, popping open the door.

"I can drive you up, Andy," Kyle began.

"No need. See you, Kyle," she said, hopping out and

walking barefoot down the paved road. She had to try her very hardest not to look back.

16

"Winners, I am convinced, imagine their dreams first. They want it with all their heart and expect it to come true. There is, I believe, no other way to live."
— *Kyle Summers' favorite Joe Montana quote*

Kyle turned off the engine to the Jeep and let it coast down the gravel driveway, flicking off the headlights just before he rounded the curve to the trailer.

It was late, after eleven now. His dad would have fallen asleep hours ago in the recliner chair where he'd spent every night in front of the TV for as long as Kyle could remember, watching shows guaranteed to rot the brain. He rolled to a stop next to his dad's truck and pushed in the parking brake.

He dropped his head against the back of the seat. He dreaded going inside. Dreaded his dad waking up and asking where he'd been. It was the same question he asked every time Kyle came home. A question they both knew the answer to. It didn't matter where he was as long as it wasn't here.

Blowing out a sigh, he opened the door and slid out, crossing the mostly dirt yard to the trailer door. Through a window, he saw his dad in the chair, wished that for once he could make it to his room without waking him.

He turned the knob and slowly pulled the door open. The hinge squeaked, and his dad sat upright, shaking himself awake. "Kyle. What time is it?"

"Six or so."

His dad stared at him for a moment, then raised the chair to an upright position. "I must have dozed off." He still wore the blue Dickey pants and shirt he wore each day to the textile factory where he'd worked for the past twenty years. His hair, once as dark as Kyle's, had gone mostly gray while Kyle was still in elementary school. It seemed like one day, all of a sudden, his dad had just become old, his shoulders no longer straight, but stooped. His skin wrinkling like balled-up tissue paper.

"You had dinner?"

"I'm not hungry," Kyle said, sure there wasn't anything in the fridge even if he had been.

"All right, then."

"Got some studying to do," Kyle said, catching the scent

of b.o. as he walked by his dad's chair. He wondered how many days it had been since he'd showered. A feeling of disgust rolled up inside him. Kyle pushed it back and headed down the short hallway to his room at the end of the sixty-five-foot trailer.

He closed the thin, fake wood door behind him, flicked on the lamp next to his twin bed. The dark paneled walls were covered with posters of football heroes, Walter Payton, Jerry Rice, Joe Montana and Eli Manning. Today's heroes didn't do much for him. It was the legends who interested him. Because that's what he wanted to be one day. A legend.

On a rectangular table in the far corner of the room sat the trophies he'd won throughout his years of sandlot football, then junior varsity and now varsity.

He stood there against the door, thinking about his dad's apathy. There had never been anything momentous that Kyle could pinpoint as a single cause. Instead, as he'd gotten older, he'd come to see in his dad something that terrified him more than a physical disease ever could have. Defeat. His dad had given up. Let life beat him. Finally admitted that he was never going to get ahead. The hill had gotten too steep, and he'd just stopped trying to climb it altogether.

It was this realization that made Kyle wonder sometimes if he would ever really have another life. If he would struggle like a fish on the end of a hook, until, like his dad, he just one day gave up and accepted his fate.

Not if he could help it. There were things he wanted in this world. Things he intended to have. And at the top of the list was respect. Respect for himself. And the respect of other people. Neither of which he'd ever seen in his dad.

Kyle shoved out of his clothes, then went to the bathroom next to his room and took a hot shower. When he sat down at the desk he'd put together out of milk crates and an old table top, he picked up his cell phone and texted Andy. Don't like it when you're mad at me.

He waited a few moments, and when there was no reply, he tossed the phone on his bed, and opened his science book.

But he couldn't concentrate. He kept thinking about Andy and how great she'd looked in that cocktail dress. . . evening dress. . .whatever the heck it was called. She never wore things like that. And even though he felt like he'd been looking at someone other than Andy, his heart kicked up a notch at the memory of her in it.

Andy was the only real friend he'd ever had. The one person he'd shown all his emotional baggage to, piece by piece, until he'd thought for sure she'd back off big time. Not want anything to do with him.

He thought about her happiness when she'd told him about the interview for that show. He'd been a jerk. There was pretty much no other word for it.

But a date with a duke? How real could that be? Andy was so much better than something like that. He wondered sometimes if she could even see it, though.

All through elementary school and junior high, he and Andy had been best friends. Their friendship was the one thing in his life he knew he could count on, and he valued it above everything else.

But then last year, things had started to change. Andy didn't seem as comfortable around him. He'd started to think maybe she was bored with him. And then this whole dating thing. Part of him felt like he ought to be able to talk to her about the girls he went out with. And part of him didn't think it felt right at all.

With the beginning of this school year, she'd started to pull away from him. Just little things at first. Not meeting him at their lockers in between classes. Not sitting together at lunch. Not studying together after school. And then not having time to get together on the weekend.

It was like they were standing on opposite sides of a canyon that kept moving farther and farther apart. Sometimes, it felt like even if he shouted, she could no longer hear him.

He slapped the book closed and blew out a heavy sigh. He wanted what they used to have back.

He'd start tomorrow with an apology. And as for that stupid show? He'd be her biggest supporter. Because wasn't that what friends did? Supported each other. Even when you didn't always agree on what they were going after.

17

_____

By some accounts, a man gets exactly what he deserves in this life.
— Words of wisdom from Bobby Jack's father on the day he died

Bobby Jack met Andy at the door.

"Where have you been?" he asked, trying to keep his voice level.

Andy refrained from rolling her eyes. "Kyle brought me home, Daddy."

"Can't he actually drive you up to the house?"

"I wanted to walk."

Bobby Jack ignored the sass in her voice. "Why did you leave the inn without telling your mama?"

She gave him a look.

"You should have told her where you were going."

"Sorry," she said, even though her tone clearly said she wasn't.

She started up the steps, but he stopped her with, "So, how did it go?"

"What do you care?" she asked.

"Andy—"

"It went fine. I made the first cut. I don't know about the second yet. Sorry to disappoint you."

"That's not fair. I never said I wanted you to lose."

"All but."

"No, I don't want you getting your hopes up over some silly date with a royal jerk. What kind of duke needs to get a date that way, anyway?"

She didn't answer, disappearing at the top of the stairs.

"Andy," he called out, "did you forget Darryl Lee and the kids are coming over tonight?"

"No, I didn't forget," she tossed back.

"I'm getting the grill started. We need to get some tomatoes and onions cut up for the burgers."

"Yes, Daddy."

Bobby Jack sighed and headed for the kitchen. "Yes, Daddy" used to sound so sweet to him. Now it sounded like "Whatever, Buzz-Kill."

The cookout hadn't been his idea. In fact, it was the last thing he wanted to do, considering his current level of aggravation with his brother. But he'd hoped it might cheer Andy up. She loved her cousins, and they thought she all but walked on water.

He glanced at his watch. And they would be here in fifteen minutes.

He got busy pulling dishes from the cabinets, locating some napkins, forks and knives, pulling a case of Coke from the pantry. The doorbell rang. He frowned. It wasn't like Darryl Lee to be early for anything, but he guessed there could be a first time.

All the way to the front door, he warned himself against getting into it with his brother.

But it wasn't Darryl Lee and the boys standing on his front porch. It was Grier McAllister.

"Hi," she said, holding up a familiar-looking purse and looking awkward in a way he didn't imagine she often did. "Andy left this in the meeting room at the Inn. I thought she might need it."

He took it from her, words tangling on the end of his tongue. "Thanks," he finally managed. "Did you want to see her?"

"That's not necessary. I just thought I would drop it off."

"Okay, then. Thanks again."

Footsteps clattered down the stairs behind him.

Andy bulldozed her way in between him and the doorframe. "Ms. McAllister! What are you doing here?"

Grier smiled. "You left your purse at the inn. I just dropped it off."

Bobby Jack swung the purse in front of Andy.

She smacked at it. "Daddy!"

Grier's smile grew.

"Thank you," Andy said, looking embarrassed.

"You're welcome," Grier said, opening the car door and starting to get in.

"Would you like to stay for dinner?" Andy called after her.

Stunned into silence, Bobby Jack stared first at Andy, then at Grier.

"Oh, that's all right," Grier said. "I better get back."

"No, really. It'll be fun," Andy insisted. "We're cooking out on the grill."

Bobby Jack started to speak, then stopped. This was the first time she'd made any mention of the plans for the night being anything close to resembling fun.

Andy jogged out and took Grier by the arm, tugging her back towards the house. "Come on, really. You could use some good home-cooked food, I bet. You probably don't get that in New York City."

Grier looked at Bobby Jack, as if certain he would axe the idea. But he surprised even himself when he shrugged and said, "We have plenty."

Grier opened her mouth, as if to protest again, then promptly closed it. "Well, then, thanks."

Andy led the way to the kitchen. Flo was stretched out on the rug next to the table. She lifted her head, looked at Grier and thunked her tail once in greeting before promptly going back to sleep.

"Once Flo's called it a night," Andy said, "she doesn't get up for much of anything."

"I never realized hounds were so laid back," Grier said.

"Unless Daddy's heading for the truck. And then you'll never beat her to the front door."

Grier laughed. "Is there anything I can help with?"

"You can cut up the onions," Andy said with an impish grin.

"Sure," Grier said. "They don't make me cry." She began peeling, and then used the cutting board and knife Andy passed to her for slicing.

Watching them, Bobby Jack felt at a loss for what to do with himself so he got busy in the backyard getting the grill going.

He came back a few minutes later to find that Darryl Lee and his three boys, Jake, Joe and Jameson had arrived. He wasn't sure who looked more shell-shocked, Darryl Lee or Grier.

Andy made the introductions with the boys, and they politely shook Grier's hand, each adding on a nice-to-meet-cha.

Watching Grier's reaction to Darryl Lee was like watching a cage door close behind a lioness. She was clearly determined to find a way out. And yet, it was as if Andy had picked up on this, and was heading her off at the pass.

"Grier's staying for dinner, Uncle Darryl Lee."

"Is she now?" Darryl Lee asked, with that woman-snagging smile of his. "Well, surprises never stop around here, do they?"

Grier looked at Andy. "You know, Andy, I really do have to —"

"Are you finished with those onions yet, Ms. McAllister?" Andy interrupted.

Bobby Jack couldn't begin to guess what Andy's agenda was, but it was clear that she had one.

"Darryl Lee," Bobby Jack said.

Darryl Lee looked up and gave Bobby Jack a nod. "Thanks for having us over, brother."

"Hey, boys," Bobby Jack said, ruffling their hair and giving them a hug.

"Hey, Uncle Bobby Jack," each of them chimed in unison.

"Can we go play out back?"

"Sure you can," Bobby Jack said.

"Y'all be careful on those swings," Darryl Lee called out after them as they headed for the door.

"Dreama couldn't make it?" Bobby Jack said pointedly.

"Bobby Jack, you know dang well Dreama and I have been living apart for the past two months."

"Oh, that's right," Bobby Jack said evenly.

"Where's that pretty little nurse you've been seeing after church on Sundays?" Darryl Lee asked, deadpan.

Bobby Jack pinned him with a look. "I would imagine she's at home."

"Well, you should have invited her tonight. Then we

could have coupled things up," he said with a suggestive glance at Grier.

Grier raised her eyebrows. "I don't think so."

Andy stood watching all of this as if she'd just stumbled across a steamy soap channel on the cable box.

Disgusted with himself for participating, Bobby Jack opened the refrigerator door and pulled out a platter of hamburger patties.

Darryl Lee looked at them, then glanced at Grier. "You still vegetarian?"

"Yes, I am, but I'll be fine with tomatoes and onions."

"I'd be happy to fix you something else," Bobby Jack said.

"Actually, I love tomato sandwiches," she said.

"All right then," he said and headed outside for the grill. The boys were romping and playing on the swing set, making enough noise to warrant a pair of earplugs if he'd had them.

A minute later, Grier appeared beside the stone-based grill. "This is really awkward," she said. "Would you mind if I—"

"If you want to go, I totally understand. But don't let him run you off."

The idea seemed to sting because she said, "Don't worry. I wouldn't give him the satisfaction." But something in her tone told Bobby Jack differently.

"I remember when you two dated in high school."

"Some things are better forgotten," she said.

"Darryl Lee's always had a way with the girls."

"Girls plural," she said.

Bobby Jack laughed. "I never did think you seemed like his type."

"You barely ever saw me. How would you know whether I was his type or not?"

He hesitated, and then, "I knew who you were."

The admission seemed to startle her, leaving her at a loss for words. "Oh, I, well, you were older, and I guess I never dreamed you knew I was alive."

"A lot of guys knew you were alive, Grier." He glanced at her face, saw the color staining her cheeks.

"You're making me blush," she said.

He laughed, flipping a burger. "Well, it's true."

They looked at each other, wary, assessing. And maybe that was the moment that it clicked deep inside him. Some little spark of something that he hadn't felt in a very long time. Attraction. Real attraction.

Darryl Lee slapped open the back porch door and took the stairs to the patio two at a time. "Y'all got it going on out here?"

He looked at them both, as if wondering what they'd been up to.

"Just about," Bobby Jack said. He placed another round of burgers on the grill and then closed the lid.

The three boys ran up, Joe tugging at Darryl Lee's sleeve. "Daddy! Will you and Uncle Bobby Jack give us a piggyback fight?"

"Awww, I don't know if we're up to that tonight, son."

"Dadddy, pleaassee!"

"Bobby Jack?" Darryl Lee said.

"Okay."

The two youngest boys went first, Joe hopping on Darryl Lee's back, Jake climbing aboard Bobby Jack's.

Andy came outside and stood beside Jameson while the two boys began jerking Darryl Lee and Bobby Jack all across the yard as one tried to unseat the other.

Grier and Andy laughed, watching them, and Bobby Jack found himself catching Grier's gaze more than once before he and his brother ended up in a heap on the grass, giggling boys piled on top of them.

18

_____

I've decided the kind of man I want in my life doesn't actually exist. Why bother continuing to look?
— Grier to her assistant Amy just last week

Grier was starving by the time they sat down to eat on the stone patio. Andy had covered the wrought-iron table with a beautiful country French tablecloth. The table held plump sour dough buns warmed in the oven, a platter of tomatoes and onions and a roasting pan of sweet potato French fries. The grilled burgers held court in the center.

Bobby Jack said the blessing before they ate, and Grier couldn't be sure, but she thought Andy had deliberately seated her next to him, putting Darryl Lee at the other end of the table, surrounded by his boys. Darryl Lee seemed to have noticed because he was looking at his brother now with a suspicious glare.

"Let's eat," Bobby Jack said, picking up a platter and passing it to Grier.

She took one of the buns and began making her own veggie sandwich, noticing as Andy copied her choices.

"What's it like to live in New York City, Ms. McAllister?" Andy asked.

"Please, call me Grier."

Andy nodded.

"It's exciting, most of the time."

"Isn't there always something new and fun to do?"

"There are a lot of things to do there, that's for sure."

"Do you just meet like the most incredible people every day?"

Grier smiled. "Well, not every day."

"I think it would be an amazing place to live."

"It has its good points and its bad points," Grier conceded.

"Isn't that what you always wanted, Grier?" Darryl Lee piped up. "To live in a big city?"

"I suppose so," she said.

"Or was it that you just wanted to live somewhere other than here?" Darryl Lee added.

"There's some truth to that, too," Grier answered.

"Timbell Creek isn't exactly the most exciting place on Earth," Andy said.

Grier glanced at Bobby Jack who looked as if he wanted

to argue, but restrained himself. "There's a lot to be said for living in a place where you know everybody and somebody's always watching out for you," she said.

"We have another word for that," Andy said. "Busybodies. This town's full of them."

"Now, Andy, is that fair?" Bobby Jack spoke up.

"Well, it's true," Andy said.

"Most of those people just care about you."

"Yeah, well, I could do with a little less caring," Andy answered.

"When you live in a big place like New York," Grier said, "you kind of have to get used to fending for yourself."

"I would like that," Andy said. "What do you do there? What's your typical day like?"

"I doubt if all the men at this table really want to hear about that," Grier said.

"Well, I do," Andy objected.

"Go ahead," Bobby Jack said, "we'd like to hear."

The boys were done with their burgers now, and Jake asked if they could go play.

Darryl Lee said, "Sure, son," and the three bolted up from the table and resumed their wrestling in the middle of the yard.

"I usually work with people interested in refining their look, whether they're pursuing an acting career or applying for a higher-level job and want to go at it with a new level of confidence."

"Have you worked with anyone who's gotten famous?" Andy asked.

"Yeah," Grier said. "I have."

"Who?"

She unraveled a couple of names while Andy sat back, staring at her with her mouth open.

"You're kidding!"

"No," Grier said, laughing. "Everyone has to start somewhere."

"But he's such a great dresser now."

"You should have seen the plaid pants he wore to our first meeting."

Andy laughed.

"So you basically teach people how to dress?" Darryl Lee said.

"Well, it's a little more than that," Grier replied. "It's about feeling good in your own skin, I guess. Being who you are."

"That seems like a good thing to do for people," Andy said.

"Well, sometimes people really do have it figured out. They just haven't let themselves realize it yet," Grier said.

"If you were going to do a makeover of Uncle Darryl Lee or Daddy," Andy said, smiling mischievously, "what would you start with?"

"Well, it ain't easy to improve on perfection," Darryl Lee said.

"Right," Bobby Jack said, shaking his head. "She could

start with taking some of the air out of the tires of your ego."

Again, everyone laughed.

"Well, you know what they say," Darryl Lee said, "if you got it, flaunt it."

"You sure enough do that," Bobby Jack said.

"Grier, you still haven't answered," Andy said.

Grier smiled and shook her head. "I'm not touching that one with a ten foot pole." She glanced at Bobby Jack, feeling his gaze on her, suddenly aware there wasn't a single thing she could think to do to improve that man's effect on anybody. His dark-green eyes had this crazy kind of warmth that rolled over her like a first sip of hot chocolate, leaving her with only the very pointed awareness that she wanted more. The thought jolted through her, and she sat up straight in her chair, as if she had spoken the thought out loud.

"We've got brownies for dessert," Bobby Jack said. "I'll get them."

"Grier, would you mind going in and getting the ice cream?" Andy asked.

By now, Grier was convinced that Andy had a little matchmaking up her sleeve.

"I'll be glad to help with that," Darryl Lee shot out.

"Oh, I'm sure Grier doesn't mind," Andy said. "Do you, Grier?"

"Well, no," Grier said, standing and following Bobby Jack into the kitchen.

He looked at her as soon as the door closed behind them. "Sorry. I have no idea what she's up to."

Grier tried to laugh. "That's okay. Teenagers."

"Teenagers," he agreed.

He pulled a pan of brownies from the oven, the dish still warm. "Vanilla ice cream's in the freezer."

She opened the door and pulled it out. "Do you have a scoop?"

"In that drawer over there."

She retrieved it, then took the lid off the ice cream and stuck the scoop inside.

He turned around with the brownies just as she turned with the ice cream, and their shoulders brushed. They both jumped back as if electricity had jolted through them.

"Sorry," he said.

"Sorry," she said.

They stared at each other for a frozen second, and Grier felt something warm and curious uncurl in the middle of her stomach. Good heavens, he had the most beautiful mouth. She couldn't stop looking at it, even as the moment drew out into something defining, an admission of sorts. *Okay, I find you unbelievably attractive.*

She felt the response from him as well. And knew the moment it revealed itself how utterly crazy it was to even acknowledge it.

"I, we, better get this back out there," she said, making her way for the door.

He didn't answer her, but appeared at the table a few seconds later with the tray of brownies.

"Um, that looks wonderful," Andy said. "Daddy makes the best brownies."

"Doesn't he though?" Darryl Lee said, eyeing his brother knowingly.

"I'll slice them," Andy said. "Hey, boys, y'all better come and get it!"

The three boys came running, and Andy made them each a bowl with a brownie and topped it with ice cream.

They dropped to the grass beside the table and began to eat as if it were the best thing they had ever tasted.

Andy made a bowl for Grier and passed it to her. "Thank you," Grier said.

"Oh, you're welcome," Andy said, meeting her gaze. Grier wondered whether Andy was talking about the brownie or something altogether different.

They had just stood to clear the table when one of Darryl Lee's boys let out a blood-curdling, "Daaad! Joe just threw up! And it's all over my shoes."

"Greeeat," Darryl Lee said, looking first at Bobby Jack and then Andy.

"Don't look at me," Bobby Jack said. "Been there, done that."

"Did not," Andy said, looking horrified.

"Did, too," Darryl Lee said. "I personally witnessed it. You were five."

Andy rolled her eyes.

Darryl Lee crossed the grass to where Joe sat with his knees pulled to his chest, his head tucked low. "Sorry, Daddy," the little boy said.

"Oh, it's all right, son. Did you eat your brother's dessert again?"

"He didn't want it."

"You know your stomach can't handle that much sugar."

"I know," he said, looking miserable.

Darryl Lee leaned down to lift the boy into his arms and kissed him on the forehead. "Let's get you home," he said.

"Want some Pepto Bismol or something?" Bobby Jack asked.

"Naw, he'll be all right," Darryl Lee said. "It's not the first time. Come on boys, get your things," he added.

Andy took Jake and Jameson's hands and followed Darryl Lee to the back door.

On the top step, Darryl Lee swung around and said, "Y'all don't have too much fun now without me, hear?" And it was clear he wasn't joking.

Once they had all disappeared inside, Bobby Jack looked at Grier and said, "I'm sure you'd like to go on, too, after all that interviewing today."

Grier searched for the jab in the words, but didn't find it.

Just then, Andy stuck her head back out the door. "Daddy, Kyle's outside waiting on me. I'll be home a little later."

"Where are you going, Andy?"

"Out with Kyle."

"Since when?"

"Since he texted me during supper."

"Andy, you don't need to go out tonight."

"I won't be too late," she said. "Bye, Grier," she added and disappeared.

By now, it was clear that Andy had an agenda. Bobby Jack looked at Grier and shook his head. "I'm sorry about that."

"It's okay," Grier said, smiling.

She joined Bobby Jack then in carrying the dishes inside the house. He rinsed while she loaded the dishwasher. They said little to nothing until she had placed the last bowl inside and asked, "Want me to start it?"

He nodded. "The detergent's under the sink."

She reached for it, poured a measure and then put it back, pressing the wash button. The machine began its slow buzz.

"You have any coffee?" Grier asked, feeling like she could use the caffeine lift.

The question clearly caught him by surprise. "Ah, yeah," he said. "Would you like a cup?"

He pulled a glass carafe from a nearby cabinet, a bag of coffee from the freezer.

"Dunkin' Donuts," she said. "My favorite."

"Mine, too," he said, measuring four tablespoons into

the carafe and then adding water from the hot dispenser at the sink. "We'll just need to wait a minute."

"Cups?" she asked.

He pointed at the hutch at the far end of the kitchen.

She walked over and reached for two cups and two saucers, bringing them back to the kitchen counter.

"You take cream or sugar?"

"Nope, just black."

He pushed the plunger into the carafe and poured them both a cup of the steaming coffee.

"Smells delicious," she said.

"Wanna have it outside?"

"Sure," she said and led the way, sitting down in the chair at the end of the table.

Bobby Jack sat down across from her, glancing off once and then swinging his gaze back to her. "So what are you really doing here, Grier?"

"Here in Timbell Creek or here at your house?"

"Both, I guess."

"In all honesty, I came back because this was an opportunity to boost my business. One I didn't think I could pass up."

"Even though you didn't want to come back."

She tipped her head to one side. "The reasons for that are complicated."

"They usually are," he said. "And the other part?"

"Here at your house?" she said, stalling.

"Here at my house," he repeated.

"That one, I'm not so sure about."

"You trying to make Darryl Lee jealous?"

"Hardly."

"I think you did, anyway."

"That probably had more to do with you than with me."

"Ordinarily, I might agree, but not in this case. Were you in love with him?"

"In high school?"

He nodded.

"I think I thought I was. Is that so hard to believe?"

"Yeah, actually it is. You two couldn't seem much more different."

"Darryl Lee was. . .fun. That was something I guess I needed at that point in my life."

"He says you broke his heart though, you know that?"

Grier shook her head and laughed self-consciously. "For ten seconds maybe."

Bobby Jack shrugged. "No, I think you were different."

"I don't think so."

"So why did you leave? I mean I get that you would have eventually. You're not the type to stick around a place like this forever. But Darryl Lee says you disappeared in the middle of the night."

The conversation felt as if it had suddenly headed toward a place she didn't really want to go. She set her cup down on the table and stood. "You know, I really should be going. Thanks for the coffee and the supper."

"You're welcome," he said, standing. "Hey, I'm sorry if I overstepped my boundaries."

She held up a hand. "It's okay. It's late. I should go."

"I'll walk you out."

"No. I'm good. Thanks. Tell Andy I'll see her in the morning."

He nodded once. "Good night, Grier."

"Good night," she said, and walked out of the house to the awareness that she had already stayed longer than she should have.

19

Just when you think you've got a game plan in
place, life flips the page and suddenly, what used
to be a pristine white beach is now quicksand.
Any woman who expects to know happiness
should be ready and willing to change playbooks
as the terrain dictates.
— *Grier McAllister – Blog at Jane Austen Girl*

It was nearly ten, and Grier intended to head straight for
the inn. But the county road leading from Bobby Jack's
and Andy's house back into town was a familiar one, and
as she neared the road sign for 219, butterflies danced
through her stomach. Just as she was about to pass the
turn, she hit the brakes, flipped her turn signal and hung a
right.

The road was smaller than the one she'd just been on, and curvier, too.

The moon was a mere sliver tonight in the dark, enveloping the car, thick enough to prevent her recognizing anything along the way except for the fact that she still knew this road as if she had just driven it yesterday.

Three miles. Four miles. Five. And then six. The Potter farm sat on the right. And the sign for Marcie's hair salon – the one she ran out of her basement – still hung at the end of the Garmon's driveway. Another half-mile and the gravel driveway appeared. She slowed, eased the car into the turn and instantly saw there was very little gravel left. She hit the bright switch on her headlights and peered into the darkness at the spot where the house she had lived in with her mother once sat.

It was no longer there. Gone. Completely. As if it had been picked up and dropped elsewhere. Or had never been there to begin with.

Grier felt a smack of shame for the fact that she hadn't known. And right on its heels a little spurt of anger that no one had bothered to tell her. But then who would have? Her mother herself? Grier was the one who had returned all the letters she'd written during those early years. Grier was the one who had cut off all communication, chosen to act as if her life here had never even existed.

For so many years, anger had fired the furnace of resentment inside her to the point that it had been almost easy not to write, not to pick up the phone and call. She had never let herself question her decision. Her mother had made her own choices long ago, choices that overrode the ordinary protection a mother provided her own child.

At some point in her late twenties, and it had taken that long to get to this point, Grier made the decision to put it all behind her. To move forward in a future that did not include that past. It had taken many thousands of dollars and nearly that many hours for her to get to a place that did not include dwelling on her past.

It had been a choice to kill the store of memories that ate away at her self-esteem, nipped at her heels with constant reminders that something in her had been deserving of what had happened to her. How could anything else be true? This was the question she'd asked herself over and over again until the truth one day simply exploded to the surface of her consciousness, literally waking her up one morning with a bolt of pain that pierced straight through to the core of her.

It hadn't been her fault. She'd done nothing, nothing, to deserve what had happened. She had been a victim. A victim of another human being's evil.

It sounded so simple in retrospect, from this place of awareness in which she now lived. She had trudged through years of blaming herself for everything from wearing clothes that were too revealing to a smile that was too friendly, eye contact that said something other than what she'd intended. None, of which, of course had been true.

She had put it all behind her. Finally. And she did not want to open any of those old doors again.

In a few days, she would be leaving Timbell Creek and all its memories behind. What was the point in opening up old wounds that had finally healed to the point that she could live with them?

There was no point.

She pulled back onto the road and drove away.

20

---

*Love is not instant. Infatuation is instant. Love is
a thing that begins with the most shallow of roots
that reach the depths of our souls only after we've
given ourselves up to the helplessness of it. And
when it's true love, we are truly helpless.*
*— From a letter Bobby Jack wrote to Andy on her
sixteenth birthday*

Bobby Jack had breakfast ready for Andy when she came
downstairs.

She'd stuck her head in his door when she'd finally
gotten home sometime after eleven and told him she had
to be back at the inn at eight-thirty. He'd forced himself to
smile and say, "Don't forget to set your alarm."

Clearly, she hadn't. She came tripping into the kitchen,

fully dressed, fully made up with every piece of assistance available in that tackle-box of cosmetics her mother had given her for her last birthday. Bobby Jack bit his tongue, and said, "Pancakes?"

"Ah," Andy said. "That's awfully heavy. Maybe I'll just have some juice."

"Andy, you need to eat."

"I'll feel like a whale if I eat pancakes before going over there this morning."

Again, Bobby Jack forced himself not to say anything, reached for the orange juice, poured her a glass and silently set about slicing a pear.

"Andy, about what I said to your mama on the phone—"

She raised a hand to stop him. "Whatever, Daddy. You didn't need to tell me I was an accident. Clearly, you and mom never loved each other."

"Honey, that's not true either. Your mama and I—"

"Specialize in hurting each other?"

He started to deny it, but realized it was true. "Andy—"

But she cut him off with, "Where are you working today?"

Since it was more interest than she had shown in his schedule in weeks, he could only assume there would be a question to follow that he wasn't going to like.

"Out at the Bickman place," he said.

"How's that going?"

Now he was really suspicious. "Pretty good. We got the framing done."

"Daddy?"

Here it came.

"I was thinking we might could ask Grier—"

"Andy, no," Bobby Jack said firmly.

"No, what? I haven't even said it yet."

"I can tell by the look in your eye that what's coming isn't something I'm going to like."

"You could like her!"

"Andersen," Bobby Jack said, tossing the pancakes into the sink and flipping on the disposal with more aggravation than was logical.

It wasn't the first time Andy had tried matchmaking with him. But Grier McAllister was a far cry from the polar opposite of Priscilla, which was normally the type she steered his way.

"She's beautiful," Andy reasoned.

"She's Darryl Lee's ex-girlfriend. And aren't you going to be late?" Bobby Jack suddenly preferred Andy heading off for today's duke pursuit over talking about why he should ask out Grier McAllister.

"You're not very good at changing the subject, you know," Andy said, picking up her purse and slinging it over her shoulder. "And if I want to invite her over, I guess I can."

"I guess you can't."

"Daddy!"

"Are you sure your interest is in fixing me up with her, or angling with points for the date with a duke?"

Her face turned into a storm cloud, followed by a thunderous, "I cannot believe you would even think such a thing!"

"Well, she's not the type you usually pick for me."

"She's not the type who usually hangs around Timbell Creek. You couldn't keep a woman like her anyway," Andy threw in for a finale and then huffed out the front door. He heard her crank the truck and gun out of the driveway, asking himself why he had just thrown that match on the current fire that was their relationship.

He gathered up the dishes, loaded the dishwasher, all the while trying not to think about those last few moments before Grier had left last night or the nearly physical pain he'd felt in looking at her. She was beautiful. Nobody could deny that Darryl Lee knew how to pick them.

There had been other times, not that this was one of them, when Bobby Jack and his brother set their sights on the same girl, and Darryl Lee always won in the short run because he threw everything he had into the contest. As soon as Bobby Jack got wind of Darryl Lee's intention, he'd always backed off, for the most part because getting into a pissing contest with his brother was a no-win proposition. With a couple of those girls, it wasn't that Bobby Jack didn't think he had a chance. He just cared more about his relationship with his brother than Darryl Lee seemed to care about his relationship with him.

For the sake of everyone involved, Bobby Jack hoped that Darryl Lee hadn't decided to rekindle his old flame with Grier. He had a damn good marriage with Dreama, if he could only open his fool eyes and see it. They had three beautiful boys, and Dreama had made a good home for them.

There had been a time when Bobby Jack would have given anything if Priscilla could have been like her, determined to make a home for him and their daughter, stitched together a life that made sense for all of them and not just for herself. But she hadn't. And Darryl Lee didn't. And that was that. There wasn't anything he could do about it.

He wasn't going to do a single thing but mind his own business.

21

It is impossibly difficult to be a teenager in today's world. We are pitched fast food ads on one TV channel while the very next one lifts up stick figure women as the ideal to aspire to. It's hard to know what to do with that as an adult – how is a teenage girl supposed to reconcile the two?
— Grier – Blog at *Jane Austen Girl*

By eleven o'clock that morning, Grier had long begun to wonder what she'd been thinking to take on the crazy task of picking one single girl from this hopeful sea of teenagers on the basis of a few skimpy interviews, an essay, and their ability to throw a dinner party. What girl in this day and age, at sixteen, would know how to throw a dinner party?

Since arriving at the inn this morning, she'd reached for her cell phone no fewer than six times with the intent of calling her network contact and cancelling the whole thing. It was only the ensuing vision of her sure-to-be tattered career that had stopped her.

It had seemed like such a great opportunity in the beginning, a chance to get her business out in front of potentially millions of people via the reality TV show special. A chance to prove that she could come back home and no longer feel the wounds of her life here. But now it seemed like the proverbial apple in the Garden of Eden, and she wished she had never taken that first bite.

They had narrowed the selection to twelve, among which Andy Randall was one. The relief in her eyes when Grier called out the names was so palpable that Grier could not even begin to let herself think what would happen if it came to the point where she was cut. Grier would not have the final say among the last six. Two network executives would be flying in to take part in the last round of judging.

While she had initially not really cared to share that last part of the decision making, Grier was now exceptionally glad of it.

The session ended at one, and Grier felt a gigantic sense of relief for a reprieve from the pressure. The clutch of girls who remained in the room was as buoyant as a flock of goslings on choppy water. They had survived the most recent storm and lived to tell about it. Grier tried to be happy for them and not dwell on the other group of girls who had trooped dejectedly from the room just minutes earlier.

"Wow, that was intense."

Grier looked up from the front table where she was still sitting to find Andy smiling a sympathetic smile.

"Yeah," Grier said. "Really."

"I don't envy your job."

"Kinda wondering why I took it," Grier said. "I don't think I realized I would have to break so many hearts."

"Not everyone can win. Hope I can remember that in a couple of days."

Grier didn't really know what to say to that, so she just smiled back.

"What are you doing for the rest of the day?" Andy asked.

"I don't really know," Grier said. "Thought I might revisit a few old haunts."

"I'd be happy to take you around, show you some of the new stuff," Andy said hopefully.

"Oh, you don't have to do that, Andy," Grier said.

"No, really, I'd love to."

"Are you sure your dad would—"

"He wouldn't care any."

Grier wondered at the accuracy of that, but she wasn't looking forward to spending the rest of the day alone anyway. "If you're sure," she said.

"Absolutely."

"Do you have clothes to change into?"

"Yeah, in my backpack."

"Why don't I just run up and change into jeans, and I'll meet you back at the front desk?"

"Okay," Andy said.

It didn't occur to Grier until she started up the stairs to her room what others involved in the contest might wonder about her spending time with Andy. The more she thought about it, the less wise it seemed. Granted, when it came to the final decision, she would only be one vote. She thought her own professionalism would lead her to make what she truly considered to be the best choice based on the parameters she had been given. That didn't mean anyone else would agree with that.

By the time she'd changed and headed back to the front desk with Sebbie in tow, she'd decided to explain all of this to Andy in the hope that she would understand the potential conflict of interest. But when she saw Andy standing by the front desk with a look of anticipation and excitement so clearly etched on her face, Grier didn't have the heart to change the plan.

"Hey," Andy said.

"Hey," Grier said. "Andy, meet Sebbie. Sebbie meet Andy."

"Hey, Sebbie," Andy said, squatting and giving him a two-finger rub under the chin.

Grier liked her all the more for that, since most people patted him on the head, which he hated.

"Aren't you the cutest thing?" Andy said.

"Oh, no doubt he thinks so," Grier agreed.

Sebbie wagged his tail.

They walked out to Grier's BMW, newly replenished with oil and returned earlier by Marty from the tow shop. She clicked the remote, opened the door and pushed the button to roll back the convertible top.

She picked Sebbie up and set him in the front seat. "Okay if he rides on your lap?"

"Sure," Andy said, clearly thrilled. "You have the coolest car!"

"Thanks," Grier said, "You up for some lunch?"

"I'm starving."

"What's your recommendation?"

"Good local food?"

"Yep."

"Well, you can't beat Sullivan's out on Arrowhead Point."

"Is Sullivan's still there?" Grier asked, surprised.

"It is."

"Was it there when you were growing up?"

"Sure was."

They drove out of town and headed down one of the quieter county roads to Arrowhead Point. As far as the lake was concerned, it had been one of Grier's favorite places to go when she had been a girl, and an opportunity had arisen, like a church youth group trip. The place had a beach where anyone could come and hang out, and the restaurant sat right on the water with a clear view of passing skiers and fishing boats.

"There's music on the iPod," Grier said. "Pick something."

Andy scrolled through the song list and punched play. "I can't believe you like country," she said.

Grier smiled. "Oh, yeah. From way back."

The song was just right for a sunny day cruising for the lake with the top down. It was something Grier almost never did. City life didn't exactly allow for it often.

Sebbie sat on Andy's lap with his paws on the doorframe and his face pointed joyfully into the wind.

They were silent until they reached the entrance to Arrowhead Point. Grier lowered the volume as they rolled down the short gravel drive to the back of the restaurant where a line of pickups and cars sat parked in the nearly full lot.

Andy stared hard at one particular truck and then said, "Maybe we ought to go somewhere else."

Grier glanced at the truck's logo, realizing that it was Bobby Jack's. "Will he mind you being here with me?"

"No, it's not that. We just had kind of a little fight this morning."

"Ah," Grier said. "I was looking forward to one of those grilled cheese sandwiches—"

"We can still go," Andy said, getting out and helping Sebbie from the car. "It's not a problem."

"If you're sure."

"I'm sure."

They walked inside then, and Grier asked the hostess if it would be all right to bring Sebbie in if they ate outside.

The young girl smiled and said, "Sure thing," picking up two menus and leading the way through the restaurant.

Most of the tables were still full, the deck less so, maybe because of the warmth of the day. Grier saw him immediately from the corner of her eye, awareness shooting through her like sugar-tipped needles, sweet and ill-advised. She was just beginning to wish she'd gone along with Andy's suggestion that they go elsewhere when one of the men at Bobby Jack's table called out, "Hey, Andy! What are you doing out here?"

Forced then to look their way, Grier planted a smile on her face and followed Andy to the table where the men sat.

"Hey, Daddy," Andy said.

"Hey, punkin. Grier," Bobby Jack said. "Y'all finish up early?"

"We did," Grier said. "Andy offered to tour me around for a bit."

Bobby Jack nodded once, clearly uncomfortable.

"Well, she sure knows the county," one of the men said. "The lake at least. She's helped build enough houses out here."

Andy immediately looked embarrassed. "That's not true."

"You know it is," he disagreed. "I'm expectin' you to take over your daddy's business one day."

Andy shook her head and said, "Hardly."

Grier didn't miss the immediate hurt that flashed across Bobby Jack's face or the way he stood quickly, dropped some money on the table, and said, "Boys, we better get on back to work."

"Yeah, that house ain't gonna build itself, is it?" the man said, looking at Andy with disapproval.

Andy looked down, as if she might have regretted her harsh reply.

"Y'all enjoy your lunch," Bobby Jack said and walked off without another word.

Grier saw Andy look after him, start to call him back, and then just as quickly press her lips shut.

The other men followed Bobby Jack's path, a couple of them murmuring, "See ya, Andy," the others ignoring her.

Grier and Andy sat down at their own table then, leafing through the menu in silence.

"Sorry about that," Andy said. "He just makes me so mad sometimes."

"Well, if you were looking to hurt him, I think it worked," Grier said.

"That's not what I want to do. It's just—"

"Hey, I know. It's not easy being a teenager. Might want to think about the fact that it's probably not all that easy for him either. Your being one, I mean."

"I know." Silence and then, "Did you fight with your parents when you were a teenager?"

"I never knew my dad. And my mom and I didn't really

argue. She was kind of—" Grier hesitated and then said, "Caught up in other things."

"Her work and stuff?"

"No, not really."

"What then? I'm sorry. It's none of my business."

"It's okay. She drank. A lot."

"Oh," Andy said. "Is that why things seemed weird between you yesterday?"

"Yes."

"I talked to her for a few minutes. She seemed like a nice lady," Andy said and then pressed her lips together as if she thought that might not be what Grier wanted to hear.

"Except for when I was very young, I never really knew her like that. Without the alcohol, I mean."

"That's awful," Andy said.

"It is, isn't it?"

The waitress came then and asked for their order.

Grier went for the grilled cheese and fries, adding on impulse a Dr Pepper. It was what she'd always gotten here as a teenager. And it seemed like a day to relive a little bit of that.

"I'll have the exact same," Andy said, and they smiled at each other, partners in corruption.

"Do you ever miss her?" Andy asked, once the waitress had gone to get their drinks.

"I don't really know how to answer that," Grier said. "I guess I miss what might have been. But no, I've never missed the way our life was when I left."

"I'm sorry," Andy said.

"Don't be. I just did what I thought I had to do."

"She didn't look too well," Andy said. "Yesterday at the inn."

The words made Grier's heart flutter a little, and she realized she hadn't allowed herself to look at her mother long enough to notice much more than her obvious aging. How sad was it that this girl, whom Grier had just met, knew more about her mother than she did?

"I could find out more if you wanted me to," Andy said.

"No," Grier said, her voice sharper than she'd intended, and then, a softer, "That's okay."

The waitress arrived with their Dr Peppers. Grier thanked her, stuck a straw in her glass and took a long sip.

"How long has it been since you had a Dr Pepper?" Andy asked, as if she felt the need to lighten the atmosphere.

Grier couldn't even remember, but the sweet taste somehow mingled with memories of being here with other kids when she'd been Andy's age, laughing about silly things. It suddenly hit her then that she had allowed the bad things in her life to color the entire picture, so that she had not let herself remember the good.

Sitting across from a young girl who looked at her as if she had answers to important things, Grier wanted to tell her that she didn't have answers to anything. Anything she thought she might have figured out over the years now seemed questionable at best.

"I'm sorry for bringing all this up," Andy said, taking another sip of her drink.

"Don't be," Grier said. "It's not your fault. What happened, happened, and none of it is erasable."

"If you decide you want to see her, while you're here, I could—"

"I won't, Andy. I can't."

"Okay," Andy said. She changed the subject, and from then on, they didn't talk about anything personal at all. Andy told Grier about how much the lake had grown up in the past ten years, how many houses her daddy had built, to the point, really, where he worked way more than he even wanted to.

"I'd love to see some of the ones he's built," Grier said.

"Maybe when we leave here, we could drive by a few."

"That would be great."

They ate their grilled cheese and French fries with equal enthusiasm, and it wasn't until they'd finished that Grier said, "I don't even want to think about how many miles I'm going to have to run to make up for that."

"You look awesome. You don't have to make up for anything."

"Hah," Grier said. "I will if I eat like that very often."

"Guess you don't want to split a sundae then?" Andy said, teasing.

"I don't have an inch of room," Grier said.

"Me, either, actually," Andy agreed.

They left the restaurant and drove around for an hour

or so, Andy proudly pointing out house after house that her dad had built over the past several years. They were impressive, to say the least, styles varying from Cape Cod to English Tudor to Old World French. The one ingredient they had in common was size. They were enormous, ten thousand square feet plus. Grier marveled that such wealth had found its way to rural Timbell Creek.

"Your dad does incredible work," she said.

"He's pretty smart," Andy agreed. "He gets on my nerves a lot, but he always tries to be there for me."

"You can't ask for much more than that," Grier said.

"He could let up on my curfew."

They both laughed then, and Grier pointed the car back toward town.

They finished the drive mostly in silence, the music blaring, Sebbie snuggled up asleep now on Andy's lap. Grier wondered how the two of them had gotten so comfortable with each other so fast.

When they pulled up at the inn where Andy had left her truck, Grier turned the music off and said, "Thank you for that. I really enjoyed it."

"Me, too," Andy said, looking as if she wanted to say more, but bending down to give Sebbie a kiss on the head. "Later, sugar."

Sebbie sat on the seat and wagged his tail, clearly sad to see her go.

22

I don't want to be bitter. I just want to forget.
— Grier – at twenty-five to the first therapist she
allowed herself to be honest with

Grier remembered the Sunset Years Retirement Home as a place where old people sat on the front porch in rocking chairs, looking as if they had nothing left to do in this life but wait for the end. Growing up, she'd driven by with her mother nearly every morning on the way to school. She actually remembered asking once why people had to end up at a place like that, and her mother had said, "Well, I suppose it's when they don't have any place else to go."

The memory of that answer arrived with a stab of guilt sharp enough to bring an ache to Grier's midsection. If her mother really was living there now, and she supposed it was true, was that the point she had reached? No place else to go?

The straight county road gave way to curves and hills, the asphalt narrowing in this more rural section of Timbell Creek. Grier drove without letting herself think about what she would do when she arrived at the home, telling herself she just needed to see it.

But when the small sign – Sunset Years Retirement Home – appeared on the right-hand side of the road, she flicked the blinker, and turned into the parking lot, gravel crunching beneath her tires.

The front porch was empty now at four o'clock. She debated putting the car in reverse, backing out, and leaving as unnoticed as she had arrived. But something kept her hand from reaching for the gearshift. Sebbie whined and looked at the door as if to say, "Are we going in?"

"I don't know," Grier said. He whimpered again, and she turned off the ignition, rolling the key between both palms. Before she could decide against it, she reached for Sebbie and got out of the car. Her feet led her to the front porch as if they had a mind of their own, and then refused to go a step beyond the main entrance door.

A woman with very short, very bleached-blonde hair appeared at the screen door, her smile wide and welcoming. "Hello there, can I help you?"

"I'm not sure," Grier said.

"Are you here to see someone?" she asked patiently.

"Maxine McAllister."

"Maxine?" The woman lit up. "Why, she'll love having a visitor. Can I tell her who's here?"

Grier swallowed hard. "Her daughter."

The woman blinked once, as if surprised, and then said, "Well, sure, I'll be right back."

It was clear to Grier that the woman had no idea Maxine had a daughter. She felt like running, but her feet had turned to concrete blocks. She stood planted while two men ninety years old or better, and three humpback little women shuffled into the open room just inside the front door. One of the men looked up, smiled a gap-toothed smile, and winked at her. Grier smiled back at him, and felt the hard knot in her chest loosen just a bit.

Two or three more minutes passed before the woman reappeared and said, "Your mama's not feeling too great right now. Would you mind coming back to her room?"

It took every ounce of courage Grier possessed to force an answer from her mouth. "Yes, yes, sure."

The woman waved a hand for her to follow, and then led the way down a long white hall, rooms laid out on either side in hospital fashion. Through the doorways, Grier could see that each was a mini-home to its occupants. Crocheted throws in rainbow colors lay at the foot of several beds, homey reminders maybe of things each individual had made over the years. Just the sight of them made Grier swallow back a thick lump in her throat.

The nurse in the Hawaiian-pattern shirt looked back as

if to make sure Grier was still following, and said, "She's just down here." The woman turned into the last room to the left at the end of the hall, and Grier felt for a moment like she would be physically sick if she stepped over that threshold. But she tucked Sebbie up tighter under her arm, blinked, and stepped inside the doorway.

Her mother sat in a hospital style bed against three stacked pillows, an IV attached to her left arm. "Grier," she said, her voice an instant reminder of the unfiltered cigarettes she had smoked when Grier was a little girl. Grier could almost smell them now, remembering the early morning car rides. Her mother would drop her off at school on her way to the factory, windows rolled down, even in December to let out the heavy smoke.

"Hello, Mama," she said, hardly recognizing the two-word croak as her own voice.

Her mother stopped, and then said, "Oh. It's so good to see you, Grier."

"How are you?" Grier said, even though she heard the lameness of the question.

Her mother's smile appeared forced when she said, "I'm good. How are you?"

"Okay," she managed, beginning to feel that this was a very bad idea.

"Come in and sit down, please."

Grier walked over and took the chair by the window. The room smelled of lemon-scented cleaner. And even though the building had clearly seen better years, there wasn't a speck of dirt, dust, or grime anywhere to be seen.

"Who's your friend?" her mother asked.

"This is Sebbie."

Her mother reached out, and Sebbie licked her hand, wagging his tail. "Aren't you a cute young man?"

Sebbie wagged harder, as if he liked the sound of her voice.

"I'm sorry for just showing up like that the other day," she said then, looking up at Grier.

Grier shook her head and shrugged. "It caught me off guard, I guess."

"I should've known better."

"It's okay," Grier said.

"No, it really wasn't. But, I'm glad you came today."

Grier nodded, looked away, then glanced back and said, "What happened, Mama? Why are you here?"

Her mother glanced at the IV, shook her head, and said, "You know, the years just catch up with you eventually, honey."

The endearment struck Grier like a slap, reminding her of her anger. She sat straighter in her chair. "I'm sorry," she said.

"It's not your fault. I earned ending up here, I guess."

The admission surprised Grier to the point that she couldn't think of a single thing to say. Memories of her mother's drinking binges, the faces of men she had long ago forced herself to forget rose up like bannered reminders of the choices that surely had contributed to her mother's current state of health. But those reminders came with no sense of satisfaction in knowing that there had eventually been a price to pay.

They sat for a few moments, simply looking at each other, words eluding Grier altogether.

"Is there anything you need?" she finally asked.

Her mother shook her head. "No, they're … they're really good to me here."

A man appeared in the doorway just then. Tall, dark-skinned, slumped over at the shoulders. He looked at Grier and said, "Well, Maxine, it looks like you got a visitor."

"I do," her mother said. "Come on in, Hatcher, I'd like for you to meet my daughter, Grier."

Grier heard the note of pride in her mother's voice. She realized this was the first time she ever remembered hearing that. Tears rolled up, and she blinked them back, standing and extending a hand to the man.

"Hatcher Morris," he said.

"Grier McAllister."

"Awful nice to meet you ma'am," he said. "Heard a lot of good things about you."

Grier glanced at her mother, surprised by this.

"She's kept up with you over the years, you know," he said.

Grier had no idea what to say. She couldn't imagine how

her mother kept up with her. It wasn't like she was famous and in the newspaper every day or anything.

As if sensing her questions, her mother said, "Amazing what you can find out at the county library. I just wanted to know you were all right."

"Well, she sure is every bit as pretty as you said, Maxine," Hatcher said.

"Isn't she though?"

As if she had suddenly stepped into some kind of dream from which she would surely at any moment wake up, Grier felt dizzy and disoriented, her breathing short and shallow. "I think I have to go now," she said quickly, picking up Sebbie and turning for the door.

"Grier!" her mother called out.

But Grier simply said, "I can't. I can't."

She brushed past Hatcher and started running down the hall. And it wasn't until she was in her car, driving fast down the county road that she felt as if she could begin to breathe again.

But her heart still raced as if propelled by jet fuel.

In reality, Grier supposed the fuel was fury. Old. Buried. And still able to revive itself despite the deep hole she had spent so many years digging for it.

Grier could hardly reconcile the woman in that retirement home as the same woman who had brought home new man after new man, ever in search of the right one, the one who would at last, be the kind of daddy she'd wanted for Grier.

And they never were. Not for more than a couple of weeks. A month, at best. A breakup was always followed by a new hairdo, a new dress and a string of late nights making the rounds at local watering holes until the new Mr. Right had been lassoed and brought home to introduce to Grier.

By the time she was thirteen years old, Grier did her best to avoid those introductions. Eventually not bothering to get to know them in any capacity, since their shelf life barely outlasted the milk in their refrigerator.

Grier had just turned eighteen when one of those new catches came into her room one night after he and her mama had closed down The Tank, a bar with the watermark of serving its customers until they could no longer say, "Another round, please," in intelligible English.

Grier had woken up to find his liquored breath choking her lungs like the thick black smoke of burning tires. It was like having a whale on top of her, and for a moment, she could do nothing but panic, unable to breathe or even to get out a scream.

He'd yanked up her nightgown and unzipped his pants when a sound erupted from her throat that she didn't recognize at first as coming from her. Rage. Pure rage. She'd shoved him off her with the same kind of superhuman surge of strength that might allow a mother to save her child from the imminent jaws of death.

He'd rolled backward and hit the carpet of her bedroom

floor with a thud that brought her mama running down the short hallway between their rooms, her voice floating out ahead of her. "Walt, where are you, honey? I just went to the bathroom and you disappeared—"

Grier had never forgotten the way her mother stood swaying in the muted light of the doorway, the look on her face falling somewhere between disappointment and disbelief.

Her mouth hung slack, the red lipstick she'd left the house in earlier that night now smeared above and below in sickening evidence of what they'd been doing before the whale had decided to pay Grier a visit during their intermission.

Grier had pulled her knees up under her nightgown, turned her head and squeezed her eyes shut, praying as hard as she knew how that when she opened them, they would both be gone. And they were.

The next morning, she packed what she could fit inside her suitcase and walked out of town with it in one hand and a grocery bag full of books she loved in the other.

The mother she'd left behind bore little resemblance to the mother she'd just seen. And yet, they were one and the same, weren't they?

The question felt too big to answer.

And so she just drove.

23

"Find your own girlfriend, butt-face!"
— *Second-grader Darryl Lee to Third-grader*
Bobby Jack during lunch period when Cassidy
Frampton couldn't decide who she liked best

It was nearly eight o'clock when Bobby Jack left the spec house at the lake. He'd stayed late to make sure the last bit of roof got completed, before the rain they were calling for set in tomorrow.

He was fiddling with the radio as he passed by the log house structure of one of the county's most frequented beer joints. Bobby Jack nearly missed the BMW parked smack dab in front. Seeing it in the corner of his eye, he automatically hit the brake, even as common sense waved its caution flag.

He rolled on, but then just as quickly, swerved into the Babbett's Hair Salon parking lot, threw it in reverse, backed up, and wheeled into the Beer Boot.

He could hear the crowd from his lowered window, and already it was pretty rocking. What was Grier McAllister doing here? He sat for a moment under the immediate realization that it was none of his business what she was doing here.

Still, he threw a glance around the parking lot for Darryl Lee's truck. Relief washed through him when he didn't see it. He could hear the band kick into a new set. Drums crashing and banging before a Jason Aldean wanna-be slammed into a country rocker. As if his boots had a mind of their own, Bobby Jack found himself getting out of the truck and heading inside, not giving in to doubts about the wisdom of it.

The place was jam-packed, and he stood for a moment, taking in the crowd. He recognized a few faces, and then spotted Grier on a barstool bestowing a flirtatious smile at a grinning bartender. He was clearly under her spell, despite the fact that he looked barely legal enough to be serving liquor, much less entertaining the notion of being seduced by Grier McAllister.

Bobby Jack walked over and eased his way in between Grier and the soon to be too-drunk-to-sit-up-straight man next to her. "I'll take a Bud Light," Bobby Jack said to the bartender.

Grier swung an inebriated glance at him, her eyes going

wide in recognition. "Bobby Jack Randall! What are you doing here?" He heard the slur in the words and wondered exactly where she might've ended up tonight if he hadn't stopped by. Maybe it was a place she wanted to end up. Something in the thought bothered him for reasons he didn't really want to look at. He leaned one elbow on the bar, hung his gaze onto her, and said, "Just stopping in for a beer."

She made a sound of disbelief. "Are you checking up on me?"

The words hit a little too close to the truth for him to voice a denial, so he simply rolled his eyes and took his beer from the obviously disappointed bartender.

"Don't you have better things to do?" she asked, a little roll at the end of each of the words.

"The question is, what are *you* doing here?" he asked.

"You don't think I like places like this?"

"It's not the worst place I could picture you in," he said on a note of reason.

"Would you like to dance?" she said, alcohol no doubt letting the question slip out.

He shook his head. "You are going to regret this in the morning."

"It's not morning yet. It's still night, and I'm not done." She waved her hand to the bartender and called out, "Can I have another, please?"

The bartender said, "Sure thing," reached for a glass,

poured a splash of gin, added some tonic and lime, and slid it across the bar top.

"You sure you oughta do that?" Bobby Jack said.

"Who are you, my daddy?"

"So not your daddy," he said with immediate conviction.

She pulled back and gave him a long, assessing look. "You sure aren't."

This brought another smile to his lips, despite the realization that he was playing with fire. The question was, which one of them was going to get burned?

The band cranked up another beat thumper. Grier took his hand and said, "You never gave me an answer, but come on, anyway."

What made him slide off that stool and follow her had nothing to do with common sense or anything remotely related.

She led him out to the dance floor, her hips already finding the song's groove and simultaneously drawing his eyes to their center.

Grier slipped her arms around his neck, and he looked down at her, feeling suddenly more than a little drunk on the look in her eyes.

"Grier," he said, her name half protest, half plea.

"Anybody ever call you uptight?"

"A time or two."

"For now, let's go prove them wrong." She led the way then, and he was helpless but to follow. It had been a very long time since he'd felt this kind of pull to any woman. The song ended, and another started up.

The crowd immediately picked up the increased tempo, so that the floor felt like a living sea of rhythm-drunk bodies.

Bobby Jack realized then that he didn't need alcohol to get drunk on Grier McAllister. He could lose all hold on reason by the simple sway of her hips and the way her hair felt against his fingertips.

In fact, just then, he wanted to get hammered on the woman in his arms. Stone cold oblivious to anything else but the way she was staring at his mouth.

"What the hell is going on here?"

Bobby Jack heard his brother's voice and started to turn just as a fist slammed into his jaw. The impact sent stars whirling out in front of him.

He heard a scream, and then Grier screaming, "Darryl Lee! What are you doing?"

Darryl Lee gave Bobby Jack a two-palmed shove into a no-longer-dancing couple, knocking him to the floor and scattering folks left and right while the band kept playing. "Get the hell up and fight back!" Darryl Lee snapped. "You two-faced son of a—"

Bobby Jack was up now and went at his brother, not giving himself a second to think about the consequences. He line-backed Darryl Lee straight across the dance floor to the main entrance where somebody held the door open, and they both staggered into the parking lot, along with half of the bar patrons.

Darryl Lee started swinging like a kindergarten bully, and Bobby Jack put his right shoulder into his brother's chest, flipping him once so that he landed on his back with a loud "umph!"

Bobby Jack stood over him, breathing hard, "You had enough?"

"Hayyyle, no!" he yelled, getting to his feet and aiming a tackle at Bobby Jack's midsection.

"Have you two lost your minds?" Grier appeared in the parking lot, screaming for somebody to break them up. When there weren't any takers, she ran at them, pole-vaulting herself in between them.

"Stop! Stop it right now!" The action served to separate them long enough so that they stood there breathing like two fighting bulls.

"And you call yourself a brother!" Darryl Lee threw out.

"Darryl Lee! He didn't plan to meet me here! It was an accident."

Darryl Lee croaked a laugh of disbelief. "Oh, yeah, right. It was an accident that you two were cozied up out on that dance floor like he already had the key to the motel room in his pocket."

Grier reached out and slapped Darryl Lee, a ringing smack that made his eyes go wide. He stood there staring at her, clearly shocked.

"What right do you think you have to even comment on

who I might or might not be dancing with? Or anything else for that matter? You're a married man! Does that mean nothing to you?"

He had the decency then to look a little ashamed, hanging his head the way Bobby Jack had seen him do at age thirteen when their mama had caught him about to steal her car and take it to town one night after everyone had gone to bed.

Darryl Lee looked at them both for one long second and then pinned his gaze on Bobby Jack before saying, "It's sure true that I don't have any right, Grier, but it's also true that I deserve some respect from my brother."

Bobby Jack opened his mouth to throw something back at Darryl Lee. But something inside him snapped with softness for the little brother who'd followed him around, copying everything he did from the day he was born. On some level, Darryl Lee was right. He was a chicken-ass traitor. Hadn't he been the one telling Darryl Lee that Grier McAllister was a bad idea? And here he was dancing with her – Darryl Lee's words came back to him – like he already had the motel key in his pocket.

The itch to hit his brother leaked from his clenched fists like water through a flyswatter. He backed up, holding his palms in the air. "Darryl Lee, man, let's just take some time to cool off. We'll talk tomorrow."

"Shit!" Darryl Lee said, slapping his palms against his blue-jeaned thighs. "You'll be lucky if I ever talk to you again, brother." He stormed off, slammed his way into his pickup, threw it in reverse, and spit gravel all the way out of the parking lot.

Bobby Jack and Grier stood there, silent, for a long string of moments. He finally looked at her and said, "Well, this is awkward."

She shook her head and ran her hands through her hair, shaking it loose, and then lifting it off the back of her neck. "I don't even really have any idea what to say," she said.

He could hear that the former state of inebriation had all but evaporated. The crowd pretty much turned in unison and filed back inside, now that the show was over, a man in the front calling out, "Sure wouldn't wanna be you tomorrow, Bobby Jack."

"I'm sorry," Grier said, looking at him.

"It's not your fault," Bobby Jack said.

"Well, actually, it is."

He dusted off his jeans, knowing he was going to regret the question even as he asked it. "What are you doing out here anyway?"

Grier blew out a breath, didn't answer for a few moments, and then, "I went to see my mother out at the Sunset Retirement Home this afternoon."

Bobby Jack heard the thread of pain in her voice. "I knew she was out there."

Grier laughed a short laugh. "Yeah, well, I didn't."

He shook his head, confused. "What do you mean you didn't?"

"Before I came back to Timbell Creek, I had no idea she was in a nursing home."

He waited, unsure what to say.

She was quiet for a few moments, and then said, "Can we ride around for a bit? I don't think I should drive quite yet."

Bobby Jack knew this would be another bad idea. Still, he nodded and said, "Come on." He opened the passenger door of his truck, and she climbed in while he went around to the driver's side and got behind the wheel.

"Where's your dog?" he said.

"I took him back to the inn earlier. He was ready for a nap."

Bobby Jack nodded, silent then, as he drove away from the Beer Boot. "Anywhere in particular you wanna go?"

"No," she said.

He thought then that she sounded like someone lost. Maybe someone who'd been lost for a while.

He took one of the small roads that led out to the lake. It was quiet out here. Most of the land was still used for cow pastures, a few houses scattered here and there. He'd bought a piece of land before the prices rocketed up. He turned onto a gravel road and they bumped along until they came to the end where the lake began just a few yards away. They had the windows rolled down and Grier said, "Did somebody just cut hay?"

Bobby Jack said, "Yesterday."

"I love that smell."

"Me too," he said.

"Can we get out?" she asked.

"Sure." He opened the door, a little surprised when she scooted across the seat and slipped out behind him. His pulse drummed the base notes even as his brain reminded him of what had just happened with Darryl Lee. And the absolutely crazy fact that he was out here with this woman. He stepped away from her, thinking distance might be his only saving grace. He walked down to the edge of the water, and she followed.

The night air was cool now, stars decorating the ink black sky like white lights on a Christmas tree. The moon hung high, a beacon of light illuminating the water's surface.

Grier slipped off her sandals and sat down at the edge of the bank, dipping her feet into the water. "Ahh, that feels so good," she said.

He sat down as well, careful to keep space between them. She glanced at him, clearly aware of the effort he was making to avoid her.

"I'm really sorry about everything that happened tonight," Grier said.

"It wasn't your fault."

"Yeah, it kinda was. I all but bullied you into dancing."

He'd like to agree with her, certainly could if it would save face by doing so. But it would've been a lie. He'd wanted to be out there on that dance floor with her, wanted her close against him. He wanted it even now.

"How long will he be mad at you?" Grier asked.

"Ohh, maybe a little longer than usual, but he'll get over it."

Grier sighed. "You know he doesn't really still have a thing for me. It's just. . .a pride thing, I guess."

"I don't know."

"I do."

Bobby Jack let that hang for a moment. "So what happened with your mama today?"

She reached down and trailed her fingers through the water.

"That was the first time I've talked to her since I left over nineteen years ago."

"Whoa," he said.

"Yeah."

He waited, aware that poking his nose in where it wasn't wanted or needed would be another ill-advised move.

"We have a pretty complicated history," she said. "She used to drink."

Bobby Jack remembered seeing her out in public places after she'd clearly had a few. It hadn't been pretty.

"When I left at eighteen, I guess I was so full of anger, I never wanted to see her again. She . . . let some pretty awful things happen. But the woman I saw today wasn't that woman."

Bobby Jack could almost feel her pain. He wanted to reach out, pull her to him and absorb it. At least a piece of it, so it wasn't so heavy. But he forced himself not to. Waiting instead until she went on.

"I wanted her to be. . . I wanted to have a reason to still hate her." Tears choked her voice then and she dropped her head back, staring up at the sky, something in between a laugh and a sob breaking free from her throat. "Like you need to hear any of this."

"I'd like to hear," he said quietly.

"I don't know why I went. I shouldn't have. It's too late for anything to change. And now she's sick." Her voice broke on the word, and she started to cry now. Huge, gulping sobs that seemed to wash over her like angry ocean waves.

Bobby Jack reached for her then, unable to stop himself. He pulled her up tight into the curve of his arm, forming a barrier around her like sandbags against a flood. He would let her cry as long as she needed to.

And she did for a good long while. It felt as if she released an entire lifetime's worth of grief there in the circle of his arms. He didn't know what else to do except hold her until it loosened its grip.

When her sobs finally quieted, she leaned limp against him as if she didn't have the energy to move away.

An owl hooted from a nearby tree. A fishing boat started up a cove or so away and idled off into the distance. They sat there, silent, while he felt the shift of something inside him.

It left him with the certainty that this night would

change his life, and there wasn't a thing he could do to stop it.

24

A first kiss can be an utter disappointment.
Or a life-changing, forever-not-to-be-lived-up-to
revelation. Or so I've been told.
— *Grier McAllister – Blog at Jane Austen Girl*

Grier never wanted to move. It made absolutely no sense, but not once in her life had she ever found herself in a place that felt like it was the only place she'd ever been meant to be. Here in the circle of Bobby Jack Randall's arms.

Her hand lay pressed to the center of his chest, even though she had no memory of putting it there. She only knew she didn't want to move it. He rubbed his thumb across the top of her shoulder. Something about the simplicity of his gesture broke down the wall of need inside her, and she lifted her face to his. "Would you please kiss me, Bobby Jack?"

"Grier. We both know this isn't a good idea." His voice was rough at the edges, as if it wasn't easy to say what he'd just said.

"Would you do it anyway?"

He hesitated for a second during which she thought he would simply say no. But then he made a low sound of defeat and sank his mouth onto hers.

The kiss was unlike any she had ever known. Grier thought maybe this was what the princess in all those fairy tales felt like when the prince finally kissed her and brought her back to life.

Because that's what Bobby Jack's kiss did for her. Filled her with helium-like happiness so that she turned into him and looped her arms around the back of his neck, seeking any way at all to get closer to him.

He made another sound of defeat and slipped his hands under her arms, lifting her quickly, deliberately, onto his lap. They kissed like that for minutes on end. Two people who hadn't realized their thirst for each other until now. There simply wasn't enough for either's quenching.

He rolled her onto her back, flat onto the grass, following her, his body heavy and pleasantly hard, one leg in between hers. He slipped a hand under her thin T-shirt, anchoring his palm to her waist.

The kissing went on until Grier felt all but drugged by

it: her response to him was one that she had no desire to control.

"Grier," he said, "one of us has to stop this."

She wanted to ask him why, but, at the same time, knew she could recite at least a dozen immediate reasons for the fact that he was right.

He rolled off her, lay flat on his back looking up at the sky, dragging in deep, leveling breaths, and then clamoring to his feet as if someone had just taken a bullwhip to his back.

He walked straight to the truck where he opened the door and braced himself against the frame with two hands. Grier waited for her breathing to even, stood, picked up her sandals, and walked back to the truck, getting in on the passenger side and putting herself as close to the door as she could.

After a couple of minutes, Bobby Jack got inside, leaned both elbows on the steering wheel, still not letting himself look at her.

"I'm sorry," he said.

"You don't need to be sorry. I asked you to kiss me."

"I wanted to kiss you."

"Are you apologizing for giving in or for wanting to?"

"Both."

"It's okay, Bobby Jack."

They sat quiet for a stretch of minutes, during which reason got a foothold.

"Tell me about you," he said, his voice low and interested.

"What do you want to know?"

"Right now, everything."

A spark of surprise fluttered through her. "I doubt you'd really want to know everything."

"You'd be wrong."

"Ask me a question."

"Favorite way to spend a Saturday morning?"

"Getting in a long run. Yours?"

"A hike with Flo up on the Blue Ridge Parkway." He hesitated and then, "Best book you've ever read?"

"*Pride and Prejudice*. Yours?"

"*Swiss Family Robinson*. Taught me how to be enterprising."

Grier smiled and nodded.

"I read your blog," Bobby Jack said, turning his head to look at her.

Surprised, she said, "Oh?"

"Good stuff."

"Thanks."

"Why 'Jane Austen Girl'?"

She considered the question for a moment and then, "I think she tried to be truthful about life as she saw it. I guess as a reminder to myself to do the same."

"Even when the view's less than perfect?"

"Even when."

Outside the truck, cricket frogs chirped in unison. The

sound reminded Grier of summer nights as a child when she'd slept with her window open. And she felt something for this place where she had grown up, something deep and connected. The feeling surprised her, in light of everything that had happened that afternoon and her mixed emotions about her mother.

"I like you, Grier."

"I like you, too, Bobby Jack."

"But this probably isn't going to work, is it?"

"Probably not," she said, honesty forcing itself out.

"We'd be crazy to act on lust alone, right?"

"Right."

He reached across and twined his fingers with hers, stroking the back of her hand with his thumb. "Wanna be stupid?"

"I really do," she said, tracing his palm with one finger.

He leaned over and kissed her, hard and deep. Her response felt like she'd been ignited from inside. She kissed him back, just as hard and just as deep.

When they were both breathing as if they couldn't get in enough air, he ran both his hands through her hair and stared down into her face. "I'm taking you back. And tomorrow, I know I'm going to kick myself."

"I should feel lucky, right?"

"And I should feel respectful, right?"

She smiled and dropped her head back. "That's us. Lucky and respectful."

"Dang, woman, you're not making this easy," he said,

a half-laugh accompanying the words. He cranked the truck, swung it around in the grass field, and headed down the narrow gravel road.

Grier lowered her window and stuck her head out in the night air, letting the wind cement her resolve.

By the time they arrived back at the Beer Boot, she was as sober as she had ever been in her life.

Bobby Jack pulled in next to her BMW. "You sure you're okay?" he asked.

"Perfect," Grier said.

"Grier—"

"Don't," she said, raising a hand. "I know exactly how much I'm going to regret all this in the morning."

"I'll follow you back to the inn," he said.

"No, really, I'm good." She got out of the truck, found her keys and got in the car, all without looking at him again.

She pulled out of the lot and headed back toward town. It didn't surprise her in the least that Bobby Jack's headlights stayed in her rear view mirror until she made the turn into the inn's parking lot.

25

"I think inconsistency is the main weapon women use to keep us guessing. The only thing I don't guess about anymore is that whatever assumption I make where a woman is concerned will end up being wrong. That's consistent."
— Darryl Lee to Bobby Jack two beers short of a six-pack after a college girlfriend broke his heart

The downstairs lights were all on when Bobby Jack let himself in the front door to the house.

"Andy?" he called out, walking through the foyer to the kitchen. His daughter sat on a bar stool, her gaze on a book, a glass of milk in her right hand. "Hey."

"Hey," she said, without looking up. "Where've you been?"

Bobby Jack blinked at the sharpness of the question. "Out," he said, opening the refrigerator and pulling out a half-gallon jug of orange juice.

"Who with?"

Uncomfortable with the answer, he started to say no one, but he never lied to Andy. He wasn't going to start now. "Grier."

Andy looked up then, surprise widening her eyes. "I thought you didn't like her."

"I never said I didn't like her."

"Didn't want anything to do with her then."

"She was out at the Beer Boot. She went to see her mom this afternoon at the retirement home. She'd had a little too much to drink."

"Oh," Andy said. "So you took her home?"

"We drove around for a bit, and I followed her back to the Inn." He left out the part about Darryl Lee acting like an ass, figuring they didn't need to go there tonight.

"So you do like her?"

Bobby Jack took a long swig of his orange juice and avoided answering. "I just helped her out, Andy."

"Then why's your hair all messed up? And is that lipstick at the corner of your mouth?"

He ran one hand across the top of his head and scrubbed the other across his lips. "Long day," he said.

"Does that explain the hair or the lipstick?"

"Okay, smarty pants. Time for bed."

Andy got down from the bar stool and closed her book. "You like her."

Bobby Jack didn't think she sounded too happy about the conclusion. "You better head up to bed," he said. "What are you still doing up, anyway?"

"Waiting on you," she said and brushed past him, leaving the kitchen without saying goodnight.

Bobby Jack stood still, listening to her footsteps on the stairs. What the heck? Would the day ever come when he could even begin to understand women?

He started to go to her room and ask for an explanation, but it was late, and he wasn't sure he had the energy.

Instead, he went outside and sat on the patio, stretching his legs in front of him and staring up at the star-speckled sky.

Grier's face came taunting, and with it instant memory of what it felt like to kiss her beautiful mouth. Sweet, soft, insistent.

Bobby Jack was no stranger to kissing. He'd dated his share of girls before Priscilla. And Priscilla herself had taught him a thing or two.

But he didn't remember it once ever feeling the way it felt tonight with Grier. Like the lock had never really fully clicked into place until he kissed her. Felt her melt into him. Wrap her arms around him as if she never wanted him to let her go.

And Heaven help him. He hadn't wanted to.

Sitting here with nothing but darkness and common

sense surrounding him, he knew what a mistake it would have been to let that happen.

Ever since the split between Priscilla and him, Bobby Jack had focused his whole life on raising Andy. There had been a few casual relationships along the way, but nothing that had ever threatened to redefine his life. They'd been women he had no intention of marrying, and for the most part, they had known as much.

But Grier was different. Grier was a life changer. The kind of woman who made a man toss out every resolution he'd ever made about staying single and keeping life simple.

Nothing about Grier would be simple. As if her history with Darryl Lee wasn't enough, she lived in New York City, another planet as far as he was concerned. Their lifestyles couldn't be any more different had they designed them to be polar opposites.

And wasn't that what they were when it came right down to it?

He had a teenage daughter who clearly needed his focus. And Grier had a career that she put everything into.

By his own admission, taking things any further would have been a gigantic mistake. Some things were right. And some weren't.

Why, then, didn't he feel grateful for the save?

26

I believe it was Cicero who said we should not
consider every mistake a foolish one. I'm not so
sure he was right about that.
— *Grier McAllister – Blog at Jane Austen Girl*

Grier woke the next morning to the kind of headache that felt as if every ounce of moisture had been sucked from her body, leaving her brain to thump out its pitiful plea for water in regreter's Morse code.

The alarm beside the bed began its squawk of warning that she was about to miss the start of the day. She slapped the top of the clock with an open palm until she hit the right button, and the squawking ceased. She sat up on the edge of the bed, heard Sebbie thump his tail against the pillow behind her, and managed, "Good morning."

He thumped harder, and she felt a sympathetic lick at her elbow.

"I know, I know, I deserve it." She walked to the bathroom, downed a couple glasses of water, all the while refusing to look at herself in the mirror. She got in the shower and stood under the spray, letting the water slide across her face.

Would there really be anything so wrong with packing up the car and heading back? It had been a horrible, horrible, horrible idea to come here in the first place. What would happen if she simply tore up the contract and drove back to the city? The answers were obvious. She'd be facing enough lawsuits to choke the last few breaths of air from her business, for one. And her personal banking account couldn't afford those kinds of legal fees, either.

She got dressed, grabbed Sebbie's leash, and took him outside to go potty. She then took the sidewalk to the bakery just down the street, hoping they'd be open with some hot, fresh coffee.

They were open, but Priscilla Randall's banana-yellow Corvette sat parked out front. If the pull of caffeine hadn't been so strong, Grier would have turned around and left right then. Her pounding head prodded her on, and she scooped up Sebbie and went inside.

Priscilla turned at the sound of the door's tingling bell, her eyes going wide at the sight of Grier.

"Good morning," Grier said.

"Well, good morning to you," Priscilla replied with sauce in her voice.

Grier walked to the counter, determined to order her coffee and leave. But she could tell by the other woman's stance that it probably wasn't going to be that easy. "You don't waste any time, do you, honey?" Priscilla said.

Grier tried not to roll her eyes. "What do you mean?"

"Well, news around town is you got both the Randall boys wrapped around your pinkie finger. And my daughter, too."

"Whatever you're hearing," Grier said wearily, "isn't true."

"Well, there's always a speck of truth to every rumor. The question is, how big is the speck?"

The young boy working the cash register asked for Grier's order, and she requested a large black coffee. "Be right back," he said.

"No bagel?" Priscilla prompted. "Oh, but I guess carbs probably aren't part of the Jane Austen Girl plan, huh?"

By now Grier had had enough. She tucked Sebbie tighter under her right arm, angled her body at Priscilla, and said, "You have no idea exactly how much I want to leave this place right now and never look back. Whatever it is you think I'm here to get, you're wrong if it includes anything other than finishing up this show and going back where I belong."

"Well, that's just fine, as long as you don't plan on taking any of us with you. Or what belongs to any of us."

Grier told herself to bite her tongue, but the words were out before she could stop them. "I was under the impression that you and Bobby Jack are divorced."

"That may be, but you know there are still times when I lie awake at night, and think about the way he used to make love to me. Like one long passionate adventure. That I'd like to have back again."

The boy turned the corner of the counter just then with a brown bag that slipped from his hands, bagels hitting the floor and spinning off in four different directions. Priscilla looked at him, rolled her eyes and he scurried to the back for more.

"I'm not interested in your love life, Ms. Randall," Grier said, tucking Sebbie closer under her arm.

"But you are interested in Bobby Jack, though, aren't you?"

And with that, she cat-walked out of the store, the doorbell dinging behind her.

"You forgot your bagels!" the cashier called out behind her.

"Apparently, she no longer wants them," Grier said.

"Wow," the boy said. "She's usually so nice."

"May I just have my coffee, please?" Grier asked, not wanting to hear another word about Priscilla Randall.

"Sure thing." He grabbed the cup, snapped a lid on it, and handed it to her. "It's on the house," he said. "After that, you deserve it."

"Thanks," she said.

Two more days, she told herself, leaving the store. Surely anybody could handle anything for two days.

27

---

*"Sometimes I wish we never had to grow up. You
promise you'll still like me when we do?"*
— Kyle to Andy – age eight

Kyle was in line at McDonald's, waiting for his breakfast
order when he felt a hand on his shoulder and turned to
find Kari Bitner smiling at him.

"Hey," she said, the sparkle in her green eyes somehow
still surprising him. Kari had been making it clear for a
couple of weeks now that she was interested in him. Given
her family background, and the fact that her daddy owned
half the real estate in Timbell Creek, he didn't get it.

"Hey," he said.

"I waited for you after school yesterday."

"Yeah, I ended up having to leave right after class."

"Oh," she said. Kari flashed him a wider smile. "I thought you might be avoiding me."

He shook his head, keeping his gaze on her face, and trying not to notice the low scoop of her sleeveless tank top and the shadow of cleavage just above the neckline. "No," he said. "Why would I do that?"

"Well, I don't know," she said. And it was clear to him that she really didn't. But then with nearly every boy in the junior and senior classes hot after her, she probably really didn't know.

"Come over and join us?" she said, tipping her head at a table full of kids.

"Gotta get going. I have a makeup test this morning."

"Wanna try to meet up again after school today?"

He started to invent some excuse. Then he thought about Andy, and that stupid contest she'd entered, and he wondered what the heck he was waiting for. Andy was all but pushing him out the door of their friendship, relationship, whatever the heck a person was supposed to call it. And what was he going to do, stand around and wait for her to make up her mind?

"Sure," he said. "I'll be at your locker at three."

"Well, okay," she said, lifting her hair from her shoulder with two fingers. "I'll see you then."

KYLE PULLED INTO the high school parking lot, spotted Andy's truck in one corner, and parked beside her. She was sitting behind the steering wheel, and in the second before she saw him, he could see that she'd been crying.

"Crap," he said to himself. That was the thing about Andy. If he wasn't nursing a hurricane of anger at her, he was trying to figure out how to keep her from breaking his heart. He got out, went around her truck to the driver's door, and pecked on the window. She looked up with a start, her eyes wide and tear-filled.

"Go away, Kyle," she said through the closed window.

He sighed, turned and leaned his back against the truck bed, folding his arms across his chest. "I'm not going away, Andy. Might as well tell me what's wrong."

She opened the door and slid out.

"What are you doing here anyway?" he asked. "I thought you had your duke thing this morning."

"It's not until this afternoon," she said.

"So what's wrong?"

"Nothing."

"Andy, the bell's gonna ring in ten minutes. What's wrong?"

She let out a big sigh. "Everything?"

"We don't have time to go over everything, so maybe you can just start with the basics." This brought an actual smile to her face, and he remembered then how much he liked doing that, making her smile.

"Oh, it's just nothing is working out the way I thought it would."

"Nothing as in—"

"Daddy came home at one o'clock last night. He'd been out with Grier McAllister."

"Who's that?" he asked.

"She's the lady running the contest. She's also Darryl Lee's ex-girlfriend."

"Oh," Kyle said.

"Yeah, oh. He came in looking like they'd been rolling around in a hayloft somewhere."

Kyle couldn't help but laugh. "Well, all right, Mr. Randall."

Andy jabbed him with her elbow.

"Hey!" he said. His arm naturally found its way around her shoulders, and he pulled her to him, ruffling her hair. "So what's wrong with any of that?"

"At first I thought it would be cool if they liked each other. But then after I sat up waiting on him for two hours, I don't think I want him to fall in love."

"You probably won't have a whole lot to say about that."

"What if he ends up loving her more than he loves me?"

The question came out as if it had been issued by a three-year-old, and if Kyle hadn't known her the way he knew her, he might've been tempted to laugh again. But he didn't. He just pulled her up close to him and said, "Andy, your daddy's never gonna love anyone more than he loves you."

"You don't know that."

"Yes, I do. I've never known any father or mother so crazy about their kid."

"You think I'm being unreasonable?"

"Uhh, yeah, a little."

She pressed her cheek into the curve of his shoulder, breathed in, and tipped her head back to look up at him. "I miss you, Kyle."

The honesty hit him in the back of the knees. He wanted, more than he wanted his next breath, to lean in and kiss her. "Andy, I—"

"Kyle!"

He looked up to see three of his football player buddies making their way through the parking lot, throwing their fists in the air and saying, "Yeah, Kyle! Go, man!"

Andy instantly pulled away, straightened her shirt, then opened the truck and grabbed her backpack. "Looks like your friends are calling you, Kyle."

"Andy! Andy, wait!"

But she was running then for the door of the high school. And even as he called her name again, she didn't look back.

28

Prince, duke or regular guy – he's only worthy of
you if he treats you like royalty.
— *Grier McAllister – Blog at Jane Austen Girl*

Grier's phone vibrated on the table. She glanced at the number, saw KT network on the caller id, then excused herself from the table.

"Grier McAllister," she said.

"Hey, Grier, this is Elizabeth Arbon. I'm the executive producer for Dream Date. I'll be working with you on the Jane Austen Girl episode. I tried Gill's number, but he didn't pick up."

"I think he just went out for a short break," Grier said. "Would you like me to get him?"

"No, no, I can talk with you, that's fine. We've had an

interesting development, actually. George, the duke, has decided he would like to participate in the last round of judging. He'll be replacing the judge originally coming with me. So I'll be flying down with him tomorrow to take part in the final twelve elimination round. I know this changes things a bit, but I'm thrilled that he made the suggestion. Having him take part in the process will make it all the more interesting."

"I . . . of course," Grier said tentatively.

"Our flight is scheduled to get in at ten a.m."

"Will you need someone to pick you up?"

"The network hired a limousine to bring us in."

"Great," Grier said.

"Why don't you ask everyone to be ready to meet the duke at eleven?"

"I can only imagine what they're going to say," Grier said.

Elizabeth laughed. "I almost wish I was one of them. He's pretty cute."

Grier smiled. "I know they think so."

"See you in the morning then," Elizabeth said.

Grier hung up and stood for a moment, realizing that her trip had just been extended, at least for another day. Leaving Timbell Creek as soon as possible would no doubt be the best thing for her, but it wasn't like she had any choice. So she went back into the conference room and shared the news that George would be joining them tomorrow.

Twelve faces stared back at her in open-mouthed disbelief. And then the girls all exploded in a fit of squeals and giggles. Everyone, that was, except Andy.

When the furor settled a bit, it was Andy who spoke up. "So . . . will he actually be involved in choosing one of us?"

"Yes," Grier said. "That's the idea."

"But it wasn't set up that way," Andy began.

"Apparently he decided he wanted to be a part of it."

Andy slid back her chair and reached for her purse, the look on her face crestfallen. She left the room, the door clicking closed behind her while the other girls stared after her.

"What was that all about?" one of the girls asked.

"She's weird," another girl chimed in.

"All right, that's enough," Grier said, starting to feel like a schoolteacher. "We're done for the day anyhow. You girls be back here tomorrow and ready to meet the duke at eleven a.m."

They floated out of the room on a nearly visible cloud of euphoria.

Gil came back into the room, glancing over his shoulder at the departing group. "I'd say they're happy."

"Elizabeth got in touch with you?"

"Yeah. I wonder why he decided to come down," Gil asked.

"I don't know," Grier said.

"Maybe he got a little afraid he would end up going out with somebody he didn't want to go out with."

"Maybe," Grier said.

Gil set about packing up his equipment. Looking over at her, he said, "Hey, you wanna grab a drink or a bite to eat or something?"

Grier heard the interest in his voice and said carefully, "I have some personal stuff to take care of. But thanks, Gil."

"Sure, no problem. Kind of hard to believe you grew up here."

"Sometimes it's hard for me to believe, too," she said, hearing the irony in her own voice.

"You got family to visit with?"

"Not really," she said. And for the first time since she'd returned to Timbell Creek, the answer somehow felt wrong to her.

29

"I've heard it said that we are the sum total of every choice we've ever made. I don't think anyone could be a better example of that than I am."

— *Maxine McAllister at her first AA meeting*

Maxine had slept through the night. She'd finally conceded to the next level of pain medicine. But she wasn't sure if it was that or Grier's visit that had allowed her to sleep so deeply.

The visit could hardly be called successful, but for Maxine it had at least created an opening through which she could begin to see letting go. She had been sick for a while now, and she didn't need the doctors to tell her that her body was losing its battle. Maybe it was her mind alone that had held the line these past couple of years.

Aware as she was of things left unresolved with Grier, she wasn't delusional enough to think that the two of them had resolved anything at this point. It did feel, at least, as if a door had been opened. And while she wouldn't expect anything as complete as forgiveness from her daughter, it would be nice to die knowing that Grier no longer saw her as the woman she had once been.

Hatcher appeared in the doorway, the county newspaper in his hand. "Share it with you?"

Maxine nodded and said, "Come on in."

Hatcher sat down in the chair next to the bed. "That medicine work last night?" he asked.

"Must have," Maxine said. "I slept like a baby."

Hatcher nodded, looking pleased. "Glad to hear it. You deserve a good night's rest. Seeing Grier have anything to do with it?"

"Maybe," she said, quiet for a few moments. "You ever find yourself hoping your children might one day forgive you for the things you did?"

Hatcher folded the paper on his lap, glanced off out the window, and then looked back at Maxine. "I'd be lying if I said I didn't. But I also know that it ain't too likely. I guess I decided some time ago that the first thing we have to do is forgive ourselves. If we don't do that, how can we expect anyone else to?"

Maxine thought about Hatcher's words when he left

her alone again to go back to his room for his midday medication. She wondered then if she had ever actually done that, forgiven herself. And she knew that the answer was no, she hadn't. How could she? She'd messed up beyond redemption as far as she was concerned. Made choices that pretty much ruined Grier's childhood. And yet she knew she couldn't go back and change any of that. Was there a point at which forgiveness wasn't even a possibility? It occurred to her then that she had never asked Grier for forgiveness. She wondered what forgiveness would even feel like. If it might finally free the burden of guilt lodged inside her. What if she could leave this world without the awful weight of regret?

Did she deserve to ask for such a thing?

No.

But did she want to?

Yes.

30

"What's the difference between beauty you're
born with and the kind you get in a beauty parlor,
Mama?"
— *Andy, age five, to Priscilla*

Andy parked her truck in front of her mama's salon. Sitting with her arms draped across the steering wheel, she tried to decide whether to go in or not.

Ever since Grier had announced that George was actually coming to Timbell Creek tomorrow, Andy felt as if her heart might explode right out of her chest with anxious anticipation.

Why had she entered this contest in the first place? She regretted it more than she could put into words. But to drop out now would be to concede that her daddy was right, that Kyle was right, that she had no business even trying to win such a thing. And so, here she was, on the verge of asking for her mama's help, something she had never even once in her life done.

Telling herself that it was her only hope, Andy slid out of the truck, slammed the door, and marched into the salon.

Priscilla, working at one of the stations near the front door, looked up when Andy stopped at the front counter, staring at her mother with as little expression as she could muster.

"Well, hey, Andy," she said, clearly trying hard to hide her surprise.

But Andy saw the little crack in her mama's composure and some of the hardness inside her softened a bit.

"I was wondering if you might have time to give me a—" She stopped there, unable to say the words, pride, fear and too many other emotions to identify choking them off.

Priscilla waited a few seconds, then said, "A makeover?"

"Yeah," Andy said, suddenly feeling ridiculous.

"Well, you know I'd love to, honey," her mama said, delight overriding her surprise. "Let me just finish up with Ellen here. I'll be with you in about five or ten minutes, okay? Why don't you sit down over there and read a magazine?"

Andy did as she suggested, flipping through the pages of Vogue and then Vanity Fair, the pictures of current supermodels and other glamorous people reinforcing her awareness that this guy she was trying to win a date with could probably get a date with any of them.

She felt her cell phone buzz in her pocket and reached for it. The text was from Kyle. Where are you?

Like she was going to answer that. She turned her phone off, and put it back into her pocket. She'd nearly talked herself out of going through with getting in her mama's salon chair when Priscilla finished up with Ellen and waved Andy over.

Reluctant, Andy sat down, avoiding her image in the mirror. She focused on her mama's face instead.

"Are you going to tell me what you want, or just let me have my way with you?" she said, her voice teasing in a way Andy rarely heard.

"Just to look pretty."

Priscilla leaned back and gave her a long, leveling look. "Andy. You're already pretty. Surely, you know that."

Andy looked down, shook her head. "You're a little prejudiced, don't you think?"

"I may be, but I know beauty when I see it, too." She turned the chair and forced Andy to look at her. "It's time you let yourself see what the rest of the world sees when they look at you."

The words surprised Andy, and she couldn't deny that they felt nice to hear. The root of self-doubt that normally dissed such comments stayed quiet for once.

Priscilla trailed her fingers through Andy's hair. "A sprinkling of highlights, maybe. Just a sprinkle, mind you."

She stepped in front of the chair and ran her thumb over Andy's eyebrows. "And we could clean these up a bit. We're doing this wonderful new facial that ought to make your already peachy skin just glow. And then of course, there's a mani-pedi."

"How long will all this take?" Andy asked.

"As long as it needs to," she said with a smile. "You got somewhere else to be?"

"No."

"Wanna get started then?"

"Yes," Andy said, suddenly confident that if anybody could make her beautiful, her mother could. "Let's do it."

31

---

*"We give each other crap most of the time, but
you know I'd give you the shirt off my back."*
— *Darryl Lee on his wedding day to best man
Bobby Jack*

It was nearly five o'clock when Bobby Jack heard Darryl
Lee's truck pull up to the construction site. He didn't need
to look to know who it was. He knew the sound. And
anyway, he'd been expecting him.

From his spot on the ladder, just off the front porch,
Bobby Jack hammered another nail into a lantern wall
mount, refusing to look back.

"Hey," Darryl Lee said.

"Hey," Bobby Jack said, still not looking around.

Silence hung for several seconds before Darryl Lee threw out, "You think maybe we ought to talk?"

Bobby Jack hammered in another nail. "Talk about what?"

"Last night," Darryl Lee said.

"I don't guess there's a whole lot to talk about."

"I got a little crazy," Darryl Lee conceded.

Bobby Jack turned around and looked at his brother. "Not the first time though, is it?"

Darryl Lee scuffed a booted toe against the porch floor. "What were you doing with her?"

"Is that any of your business?"

"Man, you're my brother."

"And you're married."

"So you're really after her then?"

"I am not after anybody, Darryl Lee," Bobby Jack said, climbing down off the ladder, suddenly weary of the subject.

The two of them looked at each other long and hard. And then finally Bobby Jack began to feel the air seep from his anger, and he saw his brother as he always had. A little bit of a loose cannon, foolish at times. All that, and yet, he still loved him.

"You're a jackass," Darryl Lee said. "And you hit like a girl."

"Yeah, where'd you get that black eye then?"

"Good point."

"Where are the boys?" Bobby Jack asked.

"With Dreama."

"You two talking now?"

"Barely."

"You got any plans to change that?"

"Does it ever occur to you to cut me a break?"

"Not on this, no." Bobby Jack picked up his toolbox, sat down on a porch step and started cleaning it out.

Darryl Lee sat next to him, looking as if he wanted to say something but couldn't find the courage.

"What is it, Darryl Lee?"

"There's something I haven't told you."

"What?"

A good stretch of silence followed the question. When Darryl Lee answered, his voice was low and lacking its usual note of confidence. "I wasn't the one who cheated, Bobby Jack."

"Come again."

"You heard me."

"No way."

"Way."

Bobby Jack stared at his brother, not sure what to say that would in any way help. "Man, I'm sorry. I had no idea."

"I didn't want you to."

"Why?"

"Because I knew you would look at me exactly the way you're looking at me now."

"And you were willing to let me think you were the bad guy?"

"Yeah."

"Who is it?"

"Does it matter?"

"If I'm gonna kick his ass, I need to know his name."

This actually made Darryl Lee smile. "Nice to have you in my corner anyway."

"I've always been in your corner."

"I don't want your pity."

"It's not pity."

"Yeah, it is."

"No, it isn't."

"What is it then?"

"Regret, maybe, that I've been giving you such a hard time."

"I'd rather have you giving me a hard time than have you feeling sorry for me."

"You should have told me."

"Like it would change anything?"

"I could have been a little more supportive."

"Maybe," Darryl Lee said, aiming for a smile and falling short. He got up from the porch, dusted off his jeans, and walked to his truck, opening the door and then turning back to look at Bobby Jack. "I walked by Priscilla's this afternoon on my way to the hardware store. I saw Andy in there getting all fixed up. She looked amazing."

The news hit Bobby Jack with a thwack in the chest. "I didn't know she was going."

"Seemed like they were getting along real well. Actually talking to each other, you know?"

For minutes after Darryl Lee had backed out of the driveway and drove off, Bobby Jack thought about what his brother had said. In all fairness, he should be happy to hear that Andy was showing her mother a little grace. But all he could manage to feel was resentment and yeah, even a little jealousy. He'd had Andy to himself for a long time, and the wall that Andy had chosen to erect between her and her mother had, if he could admit it, served Bobby Jack well. As long as Andy was punishing Priscilla, he didn't have to.

32

"Even a caterpillar gets to turn into a butterfly.
Am I ever gonna be pretty, Daddy?"
— *Age twelve, Andy to Bobby Jack*

Andy closed her eyes and held her breath. "Okay, don't look yet," her mama said, slowly turning the salon chair to face the mirror. She fussed with the ends of Andy's hair. She fluffed a little here, fluffed some more there, as if she were nervous about whether Andy would like it. And then finally she said, "Okay, you can look."

Andy slowly opened her eyes, and then sat staring wide-eyed at the girl looking back at her from the mirror. Was that really her?

"Well," Priscilla said, her voice wavering a note. "What do you think?"

"I. . .I can't believe that's me."

"Well of course it's you," she said with a nervous laugh. "Don't you like it?"

"I. . .I love it." Andy looked at her reflection, hardly able to believe what she saw. True to her word, her mother had streaked in some highlights to her medium-blonde hair. The resulting effect was something like dapples of sunlight. Andy's previously one-length hair now looked stylishly tossed. Her eyebrows were arched and neat, and one of Priscilla's assistants had darkened them just a shade so that all of a sudden Andy's light blue eyes looked lighter and bluer. She had even waxed her legs and performed the manicure and pedicure while the foils in her hair developed.

"Thank you," she said, finally letting herself meet her mother's gaze. And what Andy saw there surprised her. It was relief. Her mother actually felt relief that Andy liked what she had done. They watched each other for a few moments while something new settled in around them. Something Andy didn't remember feeling before. The seeds of friendship.

"I'm really glad you liked it, Andy."

Just then the front door swung in, and Andy glanced up to see her daddy standing at the entrance, looking like a Texas thundercloud.

"Bobby Jack," Priscilla said. "We're just finishing up."

He stared at Andy for several unnerving moments, his gaze clearly taking in the new changes in her. She waited for him to say something, willing herself not to speak first, not to seek his favor the way she always ended up doing. But he didn't say anything at all. He just turned around and left.

33

Virginia Tech Expected to Make Play for
Quarterback Kyle Summers
— Timbell Creek Gazette Headline Sports Page

Kyle was sitting at the stoplight on Amherst and Main when a big, black limousine drove by. Not something regularly seen around Timbell Creek, the car immediately caught his eye. Just as he wondered who might be inside, he saw the magnetic sign on the back door that read, Jane Austen Girl – *Dream Date*, Coming to the KT Network. Check Your Local Listings.

The light turned green, and he pulled into the intersection behind the limo.

Five different emotions hit him at once.

One of the girls from the contest had been at the Dairy

Queen last night, talking about the fact that George would be arriving the next day to help judge the end of the contest. The very thought of that namby-pamby, very likely royal jerk talking to Andy set his nerve endings on fire.

He'd stopped himself from calling Andy last night, not trusting the jealousy inside him to keep itself contained. How much more ammunition was he going to give Andy to shoot him in the heart? Whether she knew it or not, she already had.

On both sides of Main Street, people started coming out of stores and offices to stare and wave at the limousine. Kyle rolled his eyes, and got close enough to the long car's bumper to see the back of a tall, young guy's head through the rear window. A woman sat on his left, laughing at something he had just said. The guy lowered the back window and waved back at the people waving at him from that side of the street.

Kyle resisted the urge to blow the horn, tailgating instead to show his irritation with the car's speed. He was already late because he'd helped his dad get his old car running. But even though he should've taken the next left to get to school, Kyle followed the limo to the Inn, where it hung a right and slid to a stop at the front entrance.

Kyle pulled into a parking spot near the back of the lot, and slid down in the seat, hopefully low enough not to be seen, but still get a glimpse of the duke Andy was so high on.

The driver got out and opened the door on the woman's side first, and then walked around to open the duke's door. Kyle's heart pounded like a freight train, ridiculous as it was. He found himself holding his breath as the guy slid out of the car. For some reason, he had expected him to be tall. But when he realized the duke was well under six feet, Kyle felt a spike of gladness that surely ought to be beneath him.

He took a second to revel in the fact that Andy had always said she liked tall guys. Since he was six-three, that suited him. But then he noticed the way the duke held himself. Straight, shoulders back in the regal posture that only those born knowing they're important manage to carry off. His hair was thick and blond and cut stylishly long at the front, shorter at the back in a way that seemed to say Aristocrat.

A pretty woman came out of the inn, shook hands with the lady from the car, and then with the duke, smiling and saying something that looked like it was gracious and appreciative. The duke inclined his head and smiled a wide, white smile that drew out an instant response from both women.

The woman who had just come out beckoned for the two of them to follow her, and they disappeared inside. Andy's truck sat parked at the front of the lot, and Kyle knew she was in there somewhere waiting in anticipation with all the other girls to meet him.

Kyle let himself picture Andy's smile, and he knew it wasn't a smile many guys could resist. Not even a duke.

He cranked the truck, put it in gear, and eased back out onto Main Street, headed for school under the dead heavy certainty that any chance he'd ever had with Andy, he could now call gone.

34

"I'll always pick you first."
— *Kyle to Andy – Recess – Second Grade Red Rover*

Andy felt like she'd been holding her breath since seven-thirty that morning when she'd come downstairs to find her breakfast waiting and a note from her dad that said he had to meet the county building inspector on a site at seven.

She made some coffee, forced herself to drink it black instead of with the cream and sugar she liked, and dumped the breakfast in the trashcan. Eating seemed like way too much effort when all she could think about was the morning ahead and how much she wanted to make a good impression on George.

She changed outfits three times before finally settling on a fitted, sleeveless, pink dress that hit just above the knee, hoping it said appealing and not cheap.

She arrived at the inn way too early, and then not wanting to look like she was overly anxious hid out in one of the side rooms until she heard other girls coming in. Now that they were all sitting in their chairs, looking sick with nerves, Andy knew she was no exception.

It was eleven on the nose when the door at the back of the room opened, and Grier stepped inside. Another woman dressed in an expensive-looking business suit and the guy who could only be George was walking beside her.

Andy felt the air leave her chest, even as she couldn't tear her eyes off his face, which was actually really beautiful. He had high, well-defined cheekbones, and blue eyes framed in thick, dark lashes. He looked like an athlete, muscles clearly defined beneath the light blue polo shirt. The only scratch on the entire record was the fact that they would be nearly the same height. Andy was five ten, and she guessed him a dead ringer for that.

But then, if he had been taller than she was, he'd have to fall under the category of perfection, and she was almost relieved to see that he didn't have quite everything. She had a better shot with less than perfect.

Grier walked to the front of the room. The other woman and the duke stood at her side as she said, "Good morning, everyone. As you can see, George Fitzgerald, Duke of Iberlorn has joined us this morning."

A nervous upsurge of laughter followed Grier's words. When it settled back, she said, "So, please, let me introduce the executive producer for the *Dream Date* show at the KT Network, Elizabeth Arbon." The girls all clapped politely, and then Grier said, "And with her today is the Duke of Iberlorn."

The applause rose high and loud, and the duke smiled a very engaging smile that somehow showed both confidence and a hint of shyness. The combination surprised Andy, and she glanced around to see its effect on every other girl in the room. They were all but swooning.

Andy forced herself into polite composure, determined to appear a little less impressed.

Grier explained that they would be having a very informal chat session over the next hour, during which George would tell them a little bit about his life and take any questions they might have. After lunch, he would meet with each of them for a one-on-one session.

This brought forth nervous giggles of anticipation.

And again, Andy refused to join the fray. She sat straight in the chair with a composed smile on her face.

George took the podium. Grier and the producer walked over to sit in the front row.

"Good morning, everyone." Andy didn't have to look around to know that the greeting alone with its Irish inflection would win every girl in the room, including herself.

"Good morning," they all said back in unison, like a dozen pretty robots.

"I love those southern accents," he said, and there was nothing condescending in the assertion. That seemed to lower a sense of ease into the tense atmosphere, and Andy found herself leaning forward a little in her chair.

"Well," he said, glancing at the producer. "I don't suppose I could have twelve dates for the ball, could I?"

The producer laughed, and so did all the girls, Andy included. George certainly hadn't been shorted on charm.

"I'm afraid not," the producer said, smiling.

"Ahh, well, can't blame a guy for trying."

He went on then to talk about his life in Ireland and the small town where he had grown up, similar, he said, in many ways to this one. Andy found it hard to believe, but the way he described it, she could almost imagine that it was. He'd gone to a private school that was even more out in the country than his own home. They had not been allowed to have computers, telephones or TVs in their room, and so he had spent his time playing rugby and tennis. "Not," he said, "that I had any special gift for either one. I just didn't have much else to do, and if you do something for enough hours, you're likely to get good at it."

The modesty that threaded his words together surprised Andy. She kept expecting something more in line with what she would have imagined in a guy who had clearly known a life of privilege. But during his twenty-minute talk and his answers to the questions that followed, she never saw it.

By the time the last question had been answered, and everyone had asked him something except for Andy, the hour was nearly up.

"Is there anyone else?" George asked.

When no one spoke, he looked directly at Andy and said, "Is there something you would like to ask about me?"

Anything resembling a reply seemed to be stuck in her throat, and she could feel the eyes of the other girls resting on her, assessing, questioning why he had singled her out.

"I . . . uhh . . . well, what's your favorite song of all time?"

The other girls laughed, echoing Andy's own realization of how completely lame the question was.

"Ahh," George said. "I think a person's taste in music says a lot about them. All-time favorite. Can't Always Get What You Want."

Forgetting her discomfort, Andy smiled at the answer and said, "Stones. Good one."

"And yours?" he said, smiling that full, charm-infused smile directly at her.

"'Go Your Own Way.'"

"Fleetwood Mac," he said.

Andy smiled and felt a blush creep into her cheeks.

"Did somebody tell you he liked old rock or something, Andy?" one of the girls piped up from the audience. "That's hardly fair."

Grier stood then without acknowledging the question,

and walked back to the podium. "All right, why don't we head in to the other room for lunch, and, afterwards, we'll start the individual sessions. I have each of your names in a basket, and the duke will draw one at a time. That will be the order you go in."

The girls stood then and, to Andy's surprise, George, Duke of Iberlorn, looked at her and smiled again.

THE HOUR-LONG LUNCH turned out to be an exercise in misery for Andy. The duke sat in the middle of one side of the rectangular table, every girl there vying for his individual attention. Every girl, that is, except for Andy.

Andy sat at the far end of the table on the opposite side. And even Casey, the usually shy girl sitting next to her, managed to lob a couple of conversational points at the duke, to which he responded with what seemed like genuine smiles and interest. Andy wasn't normally one to give up so easily, or to knock herself out of the running without a good effort. But there was something about his actually being here that made the whole thing seem even more far-fetched than it had when he was really nothing more than a mental image.

He was real, all right, and while it would've been a little easier to write him off had he been a jerk, he seemed anything but. His interest in Timbell Creek sounded entirely genuine. He wanted to know about their high school, how many kids went there, what they did for fun on the weekends, who their favorite bands were, what movies they liked, and whether any of them still preferred hardbacks to digital books. It was on this question that he looked straight at Andy and actually said her name.

"What's your take on that, Andy?" She jumped in her seat at the sound of his voice on her name. "Do you like to read?" he added.

"Uhh, yes," she said. "I do, actually, a lot."

"I would have guessed that," he said. She wondered then if she should regret that statement, whether it made her sound boring. But then he said, "Me, too. So which is it? Hardcover? Paperback? Digital?"

"It depends on the situation," she said. "If I'm trying out a new author, I like digital. One, they cost less. And two, if I love their book, I can immediately download the rest of what the author has written. But if I'm on a vacation or something, I like sitting on the beach with a hardcover."

"Exactly," he said.

All the other girls looked at Andy, and not one of them was smiling. It was like Wimbledon or something, where she hadn't been the designated favorite, but had somehow managed to slam home a winning shot.

He held her gaze for a moment or two longer than she would've expected, and when he smiled, it was like the ceiling above them opened up and in shot a big beam of sunlight.

Andy felt beads of sweat pop out on her upper lip, and she forced herself not to reach up and wipe them away.

Charlene Myers took the reins of the conversation then, and Andy found herself only too willing to let her, half listening as Charlene babbled on about some show she was watching on MTV, and how she couldn't stand waiting a whole week for the next episode because it was just so good.

For the remainder of the lunch, George did not look at Andy again.

But then that didn't really surprise her.

ONCE THE INDIVIDUAL interviews started, Andy pulled her Kindle from her backpack, anxious for some means of escape other than the most obvious one of leaving the competition all together.

As it turned out, she had plenty of time to read because she was the last girl to be called. And while that might have bothered her on some level, she was so engrossed in her book that at the sound of her name, she looked up with a start.

"You mind if we just talk in here?" George asked.

Andy glanced around to see there was no one else in the room. She started to stand and dropped her Kindle. When she reached for it, she all but stumbled on her backpack.

He walked over, clearly trying not to smile.

"Uhh, sure," she said.

"Can I help you with that?"

"I'm good," she said, her cheeks blazing hot.

"Why don't we go for a walk?" he suggested.

"A walk?"

"Maybe just down the street or something?"

"Oh. Okay."

"Do you want to leave your stuff here?"

"Sure," she said. The interviews were supposed to be no more than fifteen minutes, so she didn't think it would be at risk that long.

She led the way out of the room, too aware of how close he was behind her. They walked through the lobby and out the main door. Andy spotted Grier near the reception desk and raised her hand in a little wave when Grier gave her a questioning smile. Andy had no idea what Grier was thinking, but since she didn't know what to think herself, she forced her attention back to putting one foot in front of the other. That seemed like something she could actually manage at the moment.

"Where would you like to go?" she asked when they'd reached the sidewalk outside the inn.

"Wherever you'd like to take me. What's interesting?"

Andy couldn't imagine what he would find interesting in Timbell Creek, but they did have that cute coffee shop three or four blocks away, so she set off in that direction, and he followed. Only now he walked beside her, and the mere inches separating their shoulders felt like it contained electricity instead of air space.

"I'm sorry you had to wait so long," he said.

"That's all right, I was reading."

"What was it?" he asked.

"A mystery," she said. "I like trying to figure out who did it before I get to the end of the book."

"Me, too," he said. "Who's your favorite writer?"

She started to say the Nancy Drew Files were her all-time favorite, but it sounded like something that would make him laugh. So she said, "Harlan Coben is good."

"I like his books."

They had walked at least half a block before either of them spoke again.

"So what made you enter this contest?" he asked.

The question was so unexpected that Andy's mind went completely blank, and she couldn't think of a single thing to say. Finally, she shrugged and said, "I don't know. Just to do something different, I guess. Why did you decide to do this contest?"

"That, I'd rather not go into."

"Sorry."

"No, don't be. It's—"

"You don't have to explain anything. It just doesn't seem like something you'd need to do."

"How's that?"

"Well, you're royalty. You look like a movie star. You could clearly have a date with pretty much anyone you wanted."

He laughed again. "I'm not as good as I look on paper. I'm moody in the mornings. I don't like to share popcorn at movies. And I'm really not a very good driver."

Andy considered this and said, "Those are real deal

breakers, for sure." She met his gaze then, and they sized each other up for a few moments before she said, "Why did you ask me to come out here?"

"Because I think you're interesting."

This wasn't at all what Andy expected to hear.

"I kind of sat there like a bump on a pickle when you were talking to everyone," she said. "I don't think I looked all that interesting."

He laughed. "I wasn't really thinking of pickles when I saw you at the end of the table."

Andy's face went instantly warm, and she felt a little curl of happiness at the words. "Do you like coffee or tea?"

"A cup of hot tea would be great. I'm still feeling a bit of jetlag."

"There's a coffee shop another block down."

"Let's do it," he said.

They walked the rest of the way without talking. He opened the door for her and then followed her inside.

A few kids sat in oversize leather chairs with laptops, their focus lasered on the screens in front of them. But it only took a few seconds for the buzz to begin, and Andy tried to ignore it as they stepped up to the counter.

"Hey, Andy," Jennie McPherson stood at the register. She owned the place and went to Andy's church.

"Hey, Jennie," Andy said. "This is George. Duke—"

He cut her off there and stuck out his hand to Jennie. "Just George," he said. "What kind of hot tea do you have?"

"What kind do you like, Just George?" Jennie said with a smile.

"Earl Grey?"

"Earl Grey, it is," Jennie said. "How 'bout you Andy? What can I get you?"

Realizing she hadn't brought her purse with her, Andy shook her head and said, "Nothing, I'm good, thank you."

"I've got it," George said. Andy started to refuse again, but then said, "Just an iced tea, please. That would be great."

They waited while Jennie got their drinks together, and then found a couple of chairs situated by the window. Andy could feel the stares of pretty much everyone in the shop, but she kept herself from meeting eyes with anyone, and took the seat that put her back to their audience.

"I guess you're kind of used to that," she said, sitting down.

He took a sip of his hot tea. "What's that?"

"People looking at you."

He shook his head and said, "It's not real."

"What do you mean?"

"Well, they're looking at their interpretation of who they think I am. It isn't usually very accurate. So I never think of it as real. If I really were all the things they think I am, maybe I would be a little intimidated by the stares. You know, thinking I had to live up to that. But I'm not, so it almost feels like they're looking at somebody else."

Andy didn't really know what to make of that. "Doesn't it get old?" she said. "People looking at you all the time?"

"It's only when I'm out in public and someone actually knows who I am. But that's not as often as you would imagine."

"So you're saying that you're just a normal guy then?"

"Pretty much," he said.

"A normal guy who gets a reality show made about him. A chance to pick a date from a dozen girls who are all gaga over him."

He smiled. "All?"

"You know what I mean."

He looked pleased by the admission, even if it wasn't a complete one.

"So tell me who you are, Andy. What's your life like?"

"Is this the interview part?"

"If you want to call it that. Actually, I just really want to know."

"There's not a lot to tell," she said. "Kinda just an average girl living in a small town. Mom and dad are divorced. No brothers, no sisters."

"Boyfriend?" he threw out.

She hesitated. Then, realizing it was an honest answer, she said, "No."

"Are you free tonight?"

"Ah, yes," she said. "I am."

"Good."

35

"Isn't it better to just leave some doors in our lives closed?"
"Not if you're always going to wonder what might have been behind them."
　　—Grier with therapist – ten years ago

Grier was sitting on the bed, sharing her room service tray with Sebbie when the phone rang at just after six. She reached for the receiver, picked it up, and said, "Hello?"

"Grier?"

She absorbed her mother's voice for a moment before saying, "Yes?"

"I hope I'm not disturbing you or interrupting anything."

"No," she said. "You're not."

"I was wondering if you might come out for another visit before you go. I wasn't sure when you would be leaving. But—" Her words dropped off there, as if she weren't sure where to go next.

The question surprised Grier and set off another flutter of panic in her chest. "I'm really not sure I'll have time to."

"I know you must have a full schedule, but it would mean a lot to me if you could."

She considered sparing her mother's feelings, and then let truth change her mind. "I don't think it's a good idea," she said.

"I understand how you feel," her mother said. "I wouldn't expect you to feel anything else."

Resentment swirled through Grier and then settled like bile in her throat. Guilt was not a card her mother had any right to play. "I really have to go," she said, and hung up.

Grier sat on the side of the bed, willing her hands to stop shaking. She couldn't decide whether the cause was anger or sadness, but she had no desire to indulge either one. Grier had spent years getting herself to a place of indifference. A place that gave her the ability to live a life unencumbered with the weight of her past. The last thing in the world she intended to do was give her mother the chance to ignite any of those old feelings. And especially not if she was doing it for her own peace of mind. Wasn't it true there were some things people just had to live with? Some things that couldn't ever be forgiven or pushed aside like they'd never happened?

Grier had to believe it was true. She couldn't say that she had actually healed in the past nineteen years. But she could say that she had finally reached a place of acceptance for the things she would never be able to go back and change. For the things that had happened to her that had never been her fault. She didn't want to open any of it back up again. Because despite everything, she knew the wounds were still there, raw and painful beneath the surface. And she just couldn't let herself feel any of it again, not even to give her mother peace.

36

Does real love appear as a choice? Or does it
arrive, inevitable, irresistible?
— Grier McAllister – Blog at _Jane Austen Girl_

Restless and completely wide awake, Grier left the room
around nine o'clock to take Sebbie for a walk. She'd
reached the middle of town when her cell phone rang.
She pulled it from her pocket, glanced at the number, and
recognizing it as local, answered "Hello?"

"Hey." It was Bobby Jack's voice, and just the sound of it
sent a jolt from her midsection straight to her heart.

"I. . .how did you get my number?"

"Beaner," Bobby Jack admitted.

"They really should fire him," Grier said.

"Yeah, they really should," Bobby Jack agreed. "Where are you?"

"Walking," she said. "Actually, near the bakery on Main Street."

"Can I pick you up?"

She hesitated. "I'm not sure that's such a good idea, Bobby Jack."

"But can I pick you up?"

Totally devoid of any energy to fight her own doubts, she said, "Yes."

"Be there in less than five minutes," he said and hung up.

Grier sat down on the bench outside the bakery, which was now closed. Sebbie hopped up beside her and rested his head on her lap. She rubbed his back and said, "I should've said no, shouldn't I?"

He whined his agreement.

Bobby Jack pulled up in less than five minutes, lowered the window on the passenger side, and just looked at her, silent. Grier scooped up Sebbie and got in the truck, as if the whole thing was inevitable. Which, she supposed, based on what had happened last night, it was. "Where are we going?" she said.

"Where do you want to go?"

"I don't know. Where do you want to go?"

"We could go to my house. Andy's staying at her mama's tonight."

Grier considered this and then said, "I'm thinking that's probably not such a good idea."

"I'm thinking you're probably right," he said. "Want to come anyway?"

"Yes," she said, and he drove.

37

---

*People are almost never what you think. Don't
even try to figure them out.*
*— Something Andy once read in a
magazine. Turns out it's true.*

So the plan was that Andy would pick George up at the
inn at seven o'clock.

Andy felt a little funny at the thought of picking a duke
up in a truck, but when she'd told him that's what she
would be driving, all he'd said was, "Cool."

He definitely got points for that.

She spent a good two hours getting dressed, fixing her
hair with hot curlers, changing outfits half a dozen times
until she finally closed her eyes and just picked one.

She had left a note for her dad on the refrigerator,

telling him she was going out and then spending the night with her mom. She'd felt a little ping of guilt for the hurt she knew this would cause him. But then he hadn't been exactly sensitive to her feelings lately, so why should she be to his?

All the way to the inn, she drove with the radio cranked and the windows rolled down, partly to drown out her conscience and partly to subdue her nervousness over seeing George again. Of all the girls he had met today, she still couldn't figure out why he'd picked her to hang with.

He was standing in the parking lot, waiting for her. She'd barely rolled to a stop when he popped the door latch and slid in.

"Hey," he said with his megawatt smile.

"Hey," she said back. "Don't you have a bodyguard or something?"

"Do I need one?"

"From me? Maybe." She heard herself flirting with him and wondered at her sudden confidence.

"I think I'll take my chances," he said.

"You may not like your odds."

"Oh, I think I will."

Andy pulled out of the parking lot and took a right, her hands shaking on the steering wheel. She felt as if a whole flock of butterflies had taken flight in her stomach. "Where to?"

"Wherever there's action."

"Not a lot of that around here."

"Then we can make our own."

She glanced over at him, and his smile made her feel like she had everything in the world going for her. "There's a place I'd like to show you."

"Drive on, then," he said, reaching over to crank the radio.

They drove through town, blasting Nickelback, their windows down, hands stretched out into the night air. The county road that led to the lake had little traffic, and Andy kept the speedometer at the edge of the speed limit.

Fifteen minutes outside town, she slowed the truck and turned onto a narrow paved road, drove a few minutes more until they reached the gravel turnoff that led up the mountain overlooking Clearwater Lake.

"You game?" she asked him, pointing out the windshield at the rutted path ahead of them.

"Definitely," he said.

Andy hit the accelerator, and off they went up the curving mountain road, bouncing and laughing most of the way. Some of the curves were near right angles, and she glanced at George to see if he'd lost his nerve yet.

"I take it you've done this before," George shouted over the roar of the engine.

"Four-wheeling is part of driver's ed here," Andy teased.

"Good to know."

She laughed, negotiating the last turn before the road straightened to flow out along the ridge of the mountain. She pulled the truck over, cut the engine and locked the emergency brake. "Come on," she said, opening the door and sliding out.

He followed her, moonlight guiding their way. Large rocks dotted the edge of the woods, and Andy used them as stepping stones until they were far enough in for the view to open up before them. Stretched out below the base of the mountain, Clearwater Lake lay like a jeweled carpet, boat lights winking in the distance, house lights dotting the shoreline.

"Wow," George said, standing close behind her, close enough that she could feel his chest against her back. "That's beautiful."

"It's my favorite view in the county."

"I can see why."

She pointed out a blinking light in the distance. "That's Arrowhead Point. Great place to eat there. And see that boat? That's the Lennox Lee. It's like a Mississippi riverboat. They do dinner cruises."

George slipped his arm around her waist and eased her back against him. His mouth close to her ear, he said, "Do go on."

"If you . . . if I—"

"If you turn your face a little more to the right, then I am going to kiss you."

Andy went completely still, the instant kick of her heart proof of her inability to do anything other than exactly that. She lifted her face to his, her lips parting automatically.

He slipped both arms around her waist and turned her fully to him. Andy dropped her head back to look into his face. "I really want you to kiss me."

"I really want to kiss you."

And he did. A soft test of a kiss, at first. His lips wonderfully coaxing and insistent against hers.

Clearly, this wasn't his first kiss. Except for the few experimental sessions she and Kyle had undertaken when they were fourteen, Andy would call this her first real kiss. By someone who knew what he was doing. How to whisk her up and make her want to follow him along a path on which he held the only light. She didn't have to try and see what was ahead. All she had to do was hold onto him, let him take her wherever it led.

And that was exactly what she did, while an owl whooed somewhere down the mountain, and a boat engine hummed on the distant lake.

This kind of kissing was like dancing, dip and sway, give and take, seek and find.

Andy could hear the rasp of her own breathing and with it a ping of reason that made her pull back slightly, look up at him through somewhat dazed eyes. "Wow," she said.

"Yeah, wow," he said back.

"That was really nice."

George laughed. "Should I be pleased with that assessment?"

"You should," she said.

He pushed her hair back from her face and added, "You're incredibly pretty, you know."

She shook her head, starting to voice a denial, then pressed her lips together and said, "Thank you."

"You're welcome." He studied her for a moment, and then added, "I get the feeling you don't think you are."

She shrugged. "Life in the shadow of a drop-dead gorgeous mother."

"She couldn't be any more gorgeous than you."

Andy couldn't deny the words were nice to hear, but he hadn't met her mother. "She's pretty gorgeous."

"Do you like her?"

Andy smiled. "Does anyone like their mother when they're sixteen?"

"I like mine," he said, smiling back.

"Yeah, but you're a boy."

"True enough."

"I just mean, I don't know, my situation's kind of different, I guess."

"How so?"

"She left my dad and me when I was three. She was out of my life completely until a few years ago."

"That sucks."

"Yeah. It did. I'm not exactly sure how I'm supposed to feel about her. My dad tries to act like he's okay with me having a relationship with her, but I can tell it bothers him."

"That puts you in an awkward position, huh?"

"A bit. She kind of pushes me to do things he doesn't agree with."

"Like this contest?"

She shrugged, looking off at the lake. "I wanted to enter."

"Mind if I ask why?"

"Have you looked in the mirror lately?"

"I already know you well enough to guess that's not why you would enter."

"Why do you think I did?"

"To prove something, I suspect. But you know what, you don't need to prove anything. I don't need to have someone else tell me that you're a winner."

The words flowed over Andy like warm honey, easing into the cracks of uncertainty deep inside her. "That's really nice," she said.

"That's really true," he said.

"And I don't need anyone to tell me what a catch you are. Aside from the royalty and all."

He turned away from her then, facing the lake that lay at the foot of the mountain. "I'm not being honest with you, Andy."

Andy heard the now-serious note in his voice and wondered what he could mean. "How so?"

He was quiet for several moments, as if he were having difficulty figuring out how to answer her. "I really have no right to be kissing you."

"But I wanted you to."

"And I wanted to. Believe me."

"So what's wrong with that?"

"There is someone I am expected to marry when I turn twenty-one."

The answer stunned Andy into silence. She struggled to find a response. "You mean. . .like an arranged marriage?"

He lifted his shoulders in a shrug. "For lack of a more modern term."

"But why?" She heard the crack in her own voice.

"For lack of a better explanation, I believe it might be the only thing that will allow my family's estate to continue its existence."

"Because she has a lot of money?"

"I'm afraid so."

Andy didn't know what to say. "That sounds so—"

"Medieval?"

"Sort of."

"Practical is the term my parents use."

"That's a lot of expectation for you to shoulder at your age."

"I guess it's better than bankruptcy," he said, a note of bitterness at the edges of the assertion.

"Is she nice?"

"Actually, yes, she is. And probably no more thrilled about the match than I am."

"What's in it for her?"

"Her family's estate borders ours. When we both inherit, the two will be joined."

"And that's important, why?"

"It would be hard for me to explain exactly. Ancestral pride, maybe? I don't know. But her family wants the marriage as much as my own."

"Mind if I ask why you've been kissing me then?"

He turned back to her, and even in the shadowed light, she saw the apology on his face. "Sometimes, I just want to be someone totally different from who I am. I'm sorry for pulling you into that."

She tried to summon up offense or even anger, but neither one would come. "I wanted you to kiss me. I don't regret it."

"You don't?"

She shook her head. "It's nice to be wanted."

"Who wouldn't want you, Andy?"

"Oh, you'd be surprised."

He took her hand, led her over to a very large rock. They climbed to the top and sat looking out at the moon-sparkled water below. "Who is he?"

She shrugged. "No one important."

"Clearly, he is."

"Someone I used to be really close to."

"What happened?"

"We grew up?"

"But you still care about him?"

She shook her head and then, "I wish I didn't."

"Does he know how you feel?"

"Kyle's too busy dating the cheerleading squad."

George looked at her, a small smile at his mouth. "Slight exaggeration?"

"Maybe just slight."

"Is he a good guy?"

"Except for the cheerleader thing."

He laughed. "You should tell him how you feel."

"I'm not sure it matters anymore."

"Love always matters."

"I didn't say it was love."

"You didn't have to."

She considered this, started to deny it, but realized she wouldn't be convincing. He'd been honest with her. She would give him the same. "I'm really glad I met you, George, Duke of Iberlorn."

"And I'm really glad I met you, beautiful Andy of Timbell Creek."

38

"It is never easy to tell someone what they don't want to hear."
— *Grier McAllister – Blog at Jane Austen Girl*

All the lights were out when they got there. Bobby Jack flicked on a couple of lamps as they stepped into the foyer. "Want a drink?" he asked, turning to look at her.

"I think I'll pass on that tonight. Okay if I put Sebbie down?"

"Sure," he said, calling out, "Flo?"

From the back of the house, Bobby Jack's elegant hound came trotting up to them. She wagged her tail at Grier, and then she and Sebbie sniffed each other for approval. Flo turned around and trotted off again with Sebbie right behind her.

"She's probably going to show him the best napping spots," Bobby Jack said.

Grier smiled. "His favorite activity."

"Why don't we go outside?" Bobby Jack said.

Grier followed him through the kitchen to the rock terrace where they'd eaten a couple of nights ago. It seemed as if several lifetimes had happened since then.

"Too cool out here?" he asked.

"I'm good," Grier said, rubbing her arms against the chilly spring evening air. Bobby Jack walked over to the stone pit at the edge of the terrace and fixed a small fire from a nearby woodpile. Once it was blazing, he pulled two chairs over, and they both sat down.

"Why did you call tonight?" she asked.

He looked at her then, and didn't answer right away. "I kind of needed somebody to talk to. And I wanted it to be you."

She tried to look surprised, but she wasn't. She felt this thing between them as clearly as he did. To deny it to him would be an insult to both of them. "So what is it?" she asked.

He was quiet for a moment before saying, "I think I've handled this thing with Andy all wrong."

"Parenting's not the easiest job in the world, and besides, Andy's lucky to have a daddy who cares about her choices and what happens to her."

"I don't really think she's seeing it that way right now."

She could hear his hurt and wanted suddenly to ease it

for him. She got up from her chair and walked over to him. She took the spot on the wooden bench next to him. "It might feel like she's pushing you away, but I can tell how much she needs you."

"Thanks," he said.

"It's true."

They didn't say anything for a good long while. Night sounds played out around them. A whippoorwill repeating itself again and again. A cow mooing somewhere nearby.

"Darryl Lee came by to see me earlier," Bobby Jack said, breaking the silence.

"You two didn't get in another—"

He shook his head with a look of chagrin. "He actually came by to apologize."

"Oh," Grier said, surprised.

"He asked me if I was interested in you, and I said no."

Grier met his gaze then, unable to deny the crashing sense of disappointment the words brought down on her. "Oh," she said.

"But I lied."

"You lied?"

"Yeah, I did."

"What does that mean?" she asked, shaking her head.

"What do you want it to mean?"

Dancing around the question might have been the wisest choice. Grier couldn't deny that. But wisdom didn't win out. "I want it to mean that you're feeling everything

I'm feeling. That every time you see me you want to eliminate every speck of distance between us."

He stood, reached for her hand and pulled her up in front of him.

"I do feel that," he said, his voice dropping so low that she could barely hear him. Still husky, but louder, he added, "In fact, it's all I think about."

He slipped his hand to the back of her neck, pulled her to him and kissed her.

There was kissing.

And then there was the art of kissing.

Bobby Jack Randall had definitely elevated it to an art. Grier didn't care to dwell on how he'd come to be so good at it, but even so, Priscilla Randall's voice came taunting. *There are still times when I lie awake at night, and think about the way he used to make love to me. Like one long passionate adventure—*

Grier pulled back and looked up at him, running her thumb across his lower lip. "You know your ex-wife wants you back, right?"

Bobby Jack made a low moaning sound, kissing the side of her neck and teasing her earlobe with his tongue. "Do you have any idea how much I do not want to talk about Priscilla right now?"

"Nonetheless, it's true."

Bobby Jack smoothed a hand across her hair and said, "Hey. If there's one thing you need to know about

Priscilla, it's that she only wants something when she thinks she can't have it or somebody else might want it."

"Ah."

"The truth is she didn't want me when she had me. It took me a long time to figure that out, but once I did, it wasn't a place I wanted to revisit."

"Okay."

"You don't sound one hundred percent certain of that."

"She seems to think she has reason to believe she has a chance with you."

"There's only one woman right now I want a chance with."

"Is that so?"

"That's so."

"Does that woman know about this?"

"I'm working really hard to make sure she does," he said, kissing her mouth lightly and then again more deeply.

Grier closed her eyes and drank in the kiss, one hand absorbing the warmth of his chest. "Are you sure you're working hard enough?" she whispered at the corner of his mouth.

"Oh, I can work harder," he said.

"I would suggest you give it your all."

He dropped an arm to the back of her knees and swept her up in a single, fluid motion. She laughed and let her head fall back to study the star-dotted night sky. "Now what?"

He kissed the hollow of her throat and said, "Now we go upstairs and figure out the rest as we go."

Grier knew there had to be a thousand reasons why this was a really bad idea. But honestly, at the moment, she couldn't think of a single one.

When they reached his bedroom, he kicked the door shut behind them, dropping her onto the king-size bed and staring down at her as if he couldn't drink in enough of her. He reached for the top button of his shirt, undid it, and then one-by-one, the remaining buttons, shrugging out of the shirt and tossing it on the floor.

He looked like a man who used his body in everyday life, his shoulders wide and carved with muscle. His arms were equally rippled and fit, not in the way of some of the New York City guys she had known, whose fitness came from daily gym workouts. Bobby Jack was the real thing.

She held out her hand to him, and he took it, twining his fingers with hers and sliding onto the bed beside her. He held their joined hands against his chest. Her skin tingled with the feel of him.

The room was nearly dark, but light enough that she could see the fierce want in his eyes, something inside her shifting beneath the realization that it was for her, about her. Not once in her entire life had she ever been drawn to anyone the way she was to this man.

She could feel the empty spots in her heart and her soul begin to fill with something so overwhelmingly real and alive that tears burned her eyes and spilled out.

"Hey," he said, leaning in to kiss first one eye and then the other, absorbing her tears with his lips.

She closed her eyes then and kissed his mouth as if she had been thinking about it all her life and could not wait another single moment to act on it.

And Bobby Jack kissed her back, a full-on assault to mind, body, and heart. He anchored his hands to her waist, fitting her to him, as if they were two parts of a whole, which finally, after a lifetime of searching, had clicked into place.

They kissed each other with all-consuming need, and Grier really couldn't tell whose was greater, hers or his.

He rolled her across the bed, fitting himself on top of her. He was so much taller, so much broader, and she felt everything that she'd ever imagined she would feel in the arms of a man she knew was right for her.

The phone on the nightstand rang.

Bobby Jack glanced at it, then back at Grier, the look in his eyes telling her how much he wanted to ignore it.

"You better see who it is," she said.

He grabbed it as if it were a snake he wanted to fling out the window, looked at the caller id and then answered in an even voice. "Hey, what's up?"

He listened for a moment, and Grier saw the seriousness enter his face. "Yeah, okay, I'm leaving now."

He clicked off the phone and put it back on the nightstand.

"What is it?" Grier asked.

"The fire department. I'm a backup volunteer when extra men are needed."

"Something bad?"

He slid off the bed and reached quickly for his shirt. "There's a fire out at the retirement home."

"Which. . .which home?"

"The Sunset Years Retirement Home," he said and she could tell he was trying hard not to sound alarmed.

She swung to her feet even as a sickening wave of anxiety swept through her. "I'm going with you," she said.

"Grier, I don't think that's a good idea. Why don't you wait here? I'll call you as soon as I know something."

"No!" she said. "I'm coming with you."

39

"A prince rarely arrives on a white horse. You'll recognize him all the same."
— *Grier McAllister – Blog at Jane Austen Girl*

Bobby Jack put the flashing red light on top of his truck and drove according to the urgency he had heard in Billy Mire's voice a few minutes earlier. Apparently, it was bad. The only time he got called was when it was bad. He didn't have a good feeling about Grier coming with him, but he couldn't exactly stop her.

They'd left Flo and Sebbie at the house, sleeping beside each other on the living room couch. Bobby Jack assured Grier that Flo would show him the doggie door to the fenced back yard if either of them needed to go.

They said nothing else during the ten-minute drive.

Bobby Jack concentrated on taking the curvy roads as fast as he could. And Grier sat straight and silent, looking out the passenger door window.

He saw the flames licking at the skyline before the actual building came into sight. Bobby Jack heard Grier's sharply indrawn breath and reached over to put his hand on hers. "You wait in the truck," he said. "I'll be back as soon as I know something." But one look at her face told him his words were a waste. When he pulled up alongside one of the county fire trucks, they both got out.

The scene was one that barely made sense to him. The entire front of the retirement home was engulfed in flames, six men hosing different sections of the fire. People were strewn across the yard in wheelchairs, on cots, and on the ground as well, as if they had been rescued from the burning building and left there while others were helped.

Bobby Jack spotted the fire department captain and ran to him, asking, "What can I do?"

"They need help on the back side."

"I'll go," Bobby Jack said, and then called out to Grier where she stood, staring at the people around her, "Grier, stay here. I'll be back as soon as I can."

Bobby Jack circled the building, recalling the jut-out of rooms at the far end.

Marty Crawford, another volunteer, waved him over and said, "The flames haven't gotten back here yet, but the smoke has engulfed the whole place. Some of the guys are inside, bringing people out. Why don't you grab a hose from the truck in case the fire comes this way?"

"How many people are still in there?" Bobby Jack asked.

"We don't know for sure," Marty said.

"I'll go in and help," Bobby Jack said.

"Hey man, that's not a good idea!"

But just then a fire fighter in uniform struggled out with a barely conscious woman in his arms. Bobby Jack ran into the building, aware that every second counted. The smoke was thick and black, and he put a hand over his nose and mouth, feeling along the walls for the doors to the rooms.

The first one was empty. He ran his hand along the bed and called out, "Is anyone in here?"

The second and third rooms were also empty. But in the fourth, he heard soft moans coming from the bed at the room's center. The man lying there was thin and frail. When Bobby Jack reached down to lift him up, the man felt like a bird in his arms.

"Hold on," Bobby Jack said, "we're getting you out of here." He made his way to the door, then reminded himself to turn left for the entrance to the building. He tried to hold his breath while he walked, and by the time he burst through the doors with the fragile man in his arms, he was gasping for air. He sucked it in, then carried the barely conscious man to the far end of the yard and set him down beside the woman who'd been brought out a few minutes earlier. "You stay right here, everything's gonna be all right. Someone will be here to help soon."

He gulped in as much air as he possibly could, and then bolted back into the building. At the sound of cries for help, Bobby Jack felt as if he had just run back into a nightmare. He followed the sounds, counting down the number of rooms from the entrance and checking the fifth room on either side of the hall. Both were empty, and so was the sixth.

But in the seventh, he found another man crumpled to the floor. "I'm not sure I can get up," he said.

"It's okay," Bobby Jack said. "I've got you."

"Have they gotten Maxine out?" the man asked.

Recognizing Grier's mama's name, Bobby Jack told the man, "I'm not sure. We'll check when we get outside."

This man was far heavier than the last, but Bobby Jack somehow managed to lift him from the floor and fight his way back through the smoke to the entrance.

Again, Bobby Jack carried him to the far end of the yard and lay him down on the grass, next to the other people there. He could hear the rescue squad blaring toward them, and assured the man that someone would see to him soon.

"That's all right," he said. "I'm fine. What's your name, young man?"

"Bobby Jack Randall. What's yours?"

"Hatcher. Please. Can you find out if anyone's gotten Maxine?"

Marty ran over and said, "Bobby Jack, it's not safe for you to go back in. The fire's broken through the wall between the two buildings. And it's started in on this one."

Just then Grier appeared at the corner of the building, calling out his name. "Bobby Jack, have you seen my mama?"

"Did you not see her out front?" he said.

"No," she said, fear in her voice.

Bobby Jack glanced around, not recognizing any of the faces. "I'll go back in." He looked at Hatcher and said, "Which room was she in?"

"The eighth one on the right."

"Okay."

"I'm coming with you," Grier said.

"No, you're not," Bobby Jack said. "Stay here, Grier. I'll be back as soon as I can."

She was going to defy him. He could see it. "Grier, if you come with me, I may not be able to save your mother because I'll be watching out for you instead."

Eyes pleading, she folded her arms across her chest and said, "Please, go."

Marty called out for Bobby Jack to stop. "Wait until the others get here!"

But he ran back in, covering his nose and mouth again, reaching out with one hand and counting the room doors, hot to the touch. The building now felt like an inferno, and he tried not to think about anything other than the next step in front of him.

When he got to the eighth room, he found Maxine in

bed, struggling to breathe. She tried to speak, but Bobby Jack told her not to and leaned in and picked her up.

They were halfway down the hall when he saw the blaze spit through the roof and drop tiles onto the floor in front of them. He fumbled his way around the flames, clutching the tiny woman in his arms, close to his chest.

Bobby Jack stumbled onto the lawn with Maxine in his arms, dragging air into his lungs.

Grier ran to them, crying, "Are you okay? Mama, are you okay?"

But Maxine had gone limp. Bobby Jack placed her on the ground while Grier frantically called for one of the paramedics who had just arrived. The paramedic immediately began CPR.

Grier knelt on the ground beside her, looking frozen with disbelief. Bobby Jack touched her shoulder and said, "I'm going back in to make sure there aren't any others."

"Are you sure it's safe?"

"I'll be right back," he said.

She stopped him with a hand on his arm, her gaze holding his. "Thank you," she said.

He followed two other volunteers into the building, and together, the three of them searched each room. The sound of crying drew them to the end of the hall where they opened door after door until Bobby Jack found an older woman huddled inside a cleaning closet.

Compassion coursed through him when he leaned

down and picked her up. "Come on, sweetheart," he said. "Let's get you out of here."

He lifted her up. The flames were licking at the roof now, as if announcing that they meant business. Water from the fire truck hoses rained down through the newly created holes. It was impossible to see through the black smoke billowing up around them, but Bobby Jack knew they had to be close to the door.

He heard the crack in the roof above, and lunged forward, trying to get out of the way. But the section of ceiling came crashing down.

Someone screamed, and that was the last thing Bobby Jack remembered hearing.

40

"It's what we take for granted that is actually most important to us."
— Andy's favorite quote from last week's sermon at Timbell Creek Baptist

Andy woke up to a phone ringing somewhere in her mother's house. At first she thought she was dreaming, or that it was her cell phone, and she groped a hand through the dark for the spot on the nightstand where she'd left it, only to find that it wasn't her phone.

From down the hall, she heard her mother's voice. Even at first, then rising like something was wrong.

"Where is he? Darryl Lee, where is he? In the hospital? Is he okay? I'll meet you there."

Andy swung out of bed and ran to her mother's room. "What's wrong?" she said. "Is Daddy okay?"

Priscilla glanced up with something that looked like shock widening her eyes. "There's been a fire out at the retirement home. Your daddy was in one of the buildings when part of the roof collapsed."

Andy started to cry then, with no ability whatsoever to control herself. Tears just turned on inside her, and she cried like a little girl. "Daddy," she said. "Daddy."

She repeated the word over and over again until her mother quickly slipped on her clothes, and then helped Andy into hers. They ran for the car, leaving all the lights on in the house and not bothering to lock the front door. They drove to the hospital, holding hands the entire way.

41

"*Most important quality in the man of your dreams? No, my dears, it isn't great hair. Or even killer abs. In my book, it's selflessness. Give me a man who puts others before himself, and that's a man I'll keep.*"
— *Grier McAllister – Blog at Jane Austen Girl*

Grier sat in the small hospital waiting room, numb with shock.

The doctors had just wheeled both her mother and Hatcher back to separate areas of the ER. Grier had ridden with them in the rescue squad, alternating between praying and blanking her mind altogether of what might lie ahead for either of them.

A second ambulance had brought Bobby Jack and one

of the other injured firefighters in behind them. When Grier had all but pleaded for information on how Bobby Jack was doing, the nurse told her in a firm but gentle voice, "We'll get back to you as soon as we know something, dear."

Grier leaned forward now with her head between her knees, breathing in several long gulps of air and willing herself to calm.

"Grier!"

At the sound of her name, she raised her head to find Andy staring at her, eyes wide and terrified. Priscilla stood behind her, looking nearly as distraught. "Where's Daddy?" Andy said. "Is he okay?"

Grier stood, her legs shaky with the effort. "The doctors are with him."

"Is he all right?" Andy cried, the question shrill now. Grier started to pull the girl to her, but glanced at Priscilla, and kept her arms by her side.

"Can we see him?" Priscilla said.

"The nurse said to wait here," Grier said.

"How can we just wait here?" Priscilla said then, pressing a hand to her mouth. And Grier could see in that moment the woman's clear feelings for Bobby Jack. Whatever had passed between them over the years had not extinguished the basic root of love.

Grier eased her way back into the chair, a wave of dizziness forcing her to sit.

"What happened?" Andy said.

"Bobby Jack was getting people out from the back side of the building. When he started, there was just smoke. But by the time he came out with the last woman, the flames had gotten through to that area, and part of the roof fell in."

"On him?" Andy cried again.

"I'm not sure," Grier said carefully. "The firefighters were hosing that area, and got the blaze out quickly."

"Is he burned?" Priscilla said.

"I don't know," Grier said. "They wouldn't let me see him."

"Oh, Daddy!" Andy said, sinking down into the chair beside Grier.

Andy started to sob then. Priscilla sat down next to her, putting an arm around her shoulders and pulling her to her chest, rubbing her hair, and telling her that everything would be all right. But Andy continued to cry, her shoulders shaking, and Grier could feel the girl's pain vibrating against her own.

Andy sat up abruptly, tears still streaming down her face. "Your mama," she said, as if just remembering. "Was your mama in there?"

"Yes," Grier said. "Your daddy saved her and her friend Hatcher, and several other people as well. So many of the firefighters were working on the front side of the building that they were shorthanded in the wing where Mama and the others were. Most likely, he saved their lives."

This brought a fresh wave of tears to Andy's eyes, and

they rolled down her cheeks, dropping on her hands, which were clasped in her lap.

A nurse appeared in the doorway just then. "Is there family here for Bobby Jack Randall?"

"Yes," Andy said, popping out of her chair. "I'm his daughter."

Priscilla stood too, saying nothing. The nurse waved for them to follow her. Andy glanced back at Grier, and said quickly, "I hope your mama's okay," and then followed the nurse from the room.

42

"You ever heard the word restoration?"
"Can't say that I have."
"It means figuring out how to make right our wrongs."
"I guess that would be a fine place to be. If a person knew how to get there."
— Maxine and Hatcher – a summer night conversation on the front porch of the Sunset Retirement Home

Maxine opened her eyes to a blinding white light. Its glare hurt intensely, and she squeezed her eyes shut, trying to figure out where exactly she was. Sounds echoed in her ears, voices urgent somewhere nearby. A sudden awareness of pain in her chest made her gasp. She tried to sit up, but weakness hit her so hard that she slumped back to the pillow.

A nurse stepped inside the curtained area and said, "Mrs. McAllister, nice to have you back with us."

Maxine tried to speak, but the effort was too great, and she simply shook her head.

"No, no, don't try to talk now. Everything is all right," the nurse said in a soothing voice. "Does anything hurt?"

Maxine started to answer, but she didn't have the breath to recite the list, so again she simply shook her head.

"I believe there's someone outside to see you," the young nurse said. "All right if I tell her to come in?"

The word no tried to form itself on Maxine's lips. She didn't want anyone to see her like this, and least of all Grier, if it was Grier waiting to see her.

But the nurse took her silence as acquiescence and slipped behind the curtain, her shoes squeaking on the tile floor. Maxine closed her eyes, and when she opened them again, Grier stood by the bedside, looking down at her with naked concern. Maxine tried to speak, but her throat was so dry that no sound came out.

Grier put her finger to her lips and said, "Shh."

She reached for the chair next to the bed, and pulled it closer, sitting down. They watched each other for a few moments until Grier said, "You rest, I'll be right here."

It was on those comforting words that Maxine let the wave of exhaustion slide over her, and she slept.

43

---

*"The brain may rationalize with why should I
care? But the heart takes a different route with
how can I not?"*
— Grier McAllister – Blog at Jane Austen Girl

For the next two hours, Grier sat in the chair, unmoving.

On some level, she was afraid to, glancing every few
seconds at her mother's chest to make sure she was still
breathing. She looked so pale and fragile against the white
hospital sheets that it was easy to see how frail she was.
The emotions assaulting Grier at regular intervals were
so tangled, that she had no idea how to separate them,
much less identify them. She wanted so badly not to care,
to stand up and walk out of the hospital without looking

back, yet she knew, with utter certainty that was no longer a choice.

Watching Bobby Jack carry her mother out of that smoking building had snapped something inside Grier. The walls of the dam she had erected around her heart so long ago, collapsing and flooding her with the most painful kind of regret. Not regret for the bad things that had happened between her mother and her, but regret for the fact that she had never allowed herself to seek some kind of peace between them. Tonight had shown her how quickly an end can come, and how deeply the realization that all chances are gone can cut.

She took in the lines of her mother's wrinkled face now, and knew somehow that at least part of their origin was self-incrimination. The woman lying here wasn't the same woman Grier had grown up with. All the anger that her mother had nurtured during Grier's childhood had evaporated somewhere along the way. It no longer possessed or controlled her.

Grier had never known the why of it; she had just known it was there. And for her mother's own peace, she felt suddenly grateful that it was gone.

She bowed her head then, and said a prayer of gratitude for the mercies granted tonight. To her mother, to her friend Hatcher, to the others from the nursing home who were helped to safety. She prayed, too, that the mercy would be extended to Bobby Jack, for all that he had done tonight.

She opened her eyes, suddenly needing to know if he was all right. Assured that her mother was still sleeping, Grier slipped through the curtain.

44

Clarity comes with the light.
— *Today's truism from Bobby Jack's desk calendar*

If Bobby Jack had ever wondered how it would feel to have a hammer taken to the back of his head, he now knew.

Awareness hit him with a blow, and his eyes flew open, panic clutching at his chest.

"It's okay, Daddy."

He heard the words, tried to focus, and then settled his gaze on Andy standing at the side of his bed. He realized then that he was in a hospital bed, the antiseptic smell confirming the realization.

Andy took his hand and twined her fingers with his. "How do you feel?"

Bobby Jack tried to raise his head, and then let out a soft moan. Priscilla stepped into his line of vision and said, "Don't, Bobby Jack, just stay where you are."

Something in her voice nagged at him. Panic, concern, worry? He let his eyes settle on hers then, and saw conformation of all three. "You're going to be all right," she said.

He could hear that she believed it, but his body was telling him something entirely different. His lungs felt as if they had been scorched with a blowtorch, and the back of his skull throbbed like a freight train. Memory slammed back then, and he rose up on his elbows, forcing out the question, "Are they okay?"

"Who, Daddy?"

"The people. . .at the nursing home."

"I think so," Andy said. "You saved a lot of lives tonight, Daddy."

He heard the near accusation in her voice, and then understood when the tears started to slide down her cheeks. She leaned her head on to his chest and cried as he hadn't heard her cry since she was a young child. He put his hands on the back of her hair and rubbed gently. "It's okay, baby. Everything is all right."

"You could've died tonight, Daddy!"

"But I didn't," he said gently. Priscilla reached for his hand, and patted softly.

He met her gaze, and saw then what had once been between them.

"It's amazing what you did tonight, Bobby Jack," she said. He shook his head, not trusting himself to speak. And when he opened his eyes again, he saw Grier standing next to Priscilla. Her eyes were red, her cheeks flushed, and he could see that she had been crying.

"Your mama," he said. "Is she?—"

"Yes," Grier nodded, "Thanks to you."

"And the others?"

"I think so."

He focused on that thought, the fatigue deep in his bones pulling him towards sleep. He wanted to resist it, but couldn't find the strength. He closed his eyes and let it in.

45

Compassion is the predecessor to understanding.
— Grier McAllister – Blog at *Jane Austen Girl*

It seemed like days passed before a doctor finally came into the room where Grier sat with her mother. At some point, during the hours while Grier sat at the side of the bed, her mother's breathing had grown more peaceful, steadier, with the assistance of the oxygen mask. Her face retained its pallor, and Grier pressed the back of her hand to her cheek a number of times, reassured by the warmth there.

She felt an overwhelming urge to take her mother's hand between her own and squeeze it tight, but resisted the impulse for fear of waking her. She looked so tired, as if she had been on some incredibly long journey and only just now found a place to rest.

Emotion squeezed Grier's heart like a vice in her chest, the pressure making tears sprout in her eyes and trickle down her cheeks.

How was it possible to feel such an overwhelming mix of pity and pain? A rope of regret suddenly lowered into her own well of pain. And she wondered if that rope could pull them both back to a place called forgiveness.

46

"My Daddy can do anything."
— *Andy to her first grade teacher*

Andy sat at her father's bedside for the entire night while he slept. She'd asked the nurses who came in the room every twenty minutes or so if he was actually sleeping. Somehow, she didn't quite trust their reassurances. She'd never seen him sleep this deeply.

A couple of the nurses had offered her coffee to help her stay awake, but she refused. She didn't need coffee. Her nerve endings felt as if someone had lit a match to them, the flame of fear leaping up every few minutes like the flames that had destroyed the old nursing home.

Her mother had offered to stay as well, but Andy told her to go. Somehow, it didn't feel right, her being here.

Tonight for the first time in Andy's memory, she'd seen the love her mom must have once felt for her dad. It had been there in the naked worry in her eyes when she looked at him. Andy wondered why people didn't protect that kind of love, why they did things to abuse it, to pound away at it until it finally dissolved into nothingness.

She didn't know the answer to that question, only that the love they had once felt for each other was gone. Divorce sucked that way, when you were the kid in the middle of it.

She loved them both for different reasons, because they were such different people. But pieces of them were what made her what she was. In seeing each of them a little more clearly tonight, she saw herself a little more clearly as well.

For a long time, she'd been banging on all the things she considered wrong with her. She wasn't as pretty as her mom. Not as responsible as her dad. But then again, she was only sixteen. Where had she read that it was so mandatory that she already have everything figured out at her age?

"Andy?"

Andy jerked her gaze to her dad's face, her heart beating at a sudden gallop in her chest. "Daddy?"

"What time is it?"

"Five-thirty?"

"In the morning?"

"Yeah. You've been sleeping."

He tried to sit up on his elbows, frowning. "Why am I still here? And what about everybody else? Are they?—"

"Daddy, everything is fine. You're here because the doctors wanted you to stay overnight and make sure everything is okay."

"Grier? Grier's mom? Is she?—"

"She's resting, too. Here, sit back, okay?"

He fell against the pillow, as if his muscles had suddenly remembered their fatigue.

"Hard work being a hero, isn't it?"

He looked at her, clearly a little surprised by the comment.

"I forgot, you know," she said.

"What's that?"

"When I was a little girl, that's what I thought about you. That you were this big superhero kind of guy. And if I ever needed saving, you're the one I hoped would be around."

"That all went away, didn't it?" he said, a sudden note of sadness in his voice.

Tears welled in her eyes. "It's not you, Daddy. It's me. I've been a jerk to you for a good long while. I don't know why, except that I've been kind of mad and disgusted with myself and I guess I took that out on you."

"Why would you be mad at yourself?"

She took her time answering this one. When she spoke, her words came out as a question. "If it weren't for me, would you and Mama still be together?"

"Ah, Andy. Your mama and me. We were so young and stupid when we got together. We didn't know anything about the real work it takes to make a relationship last. We tried for a long time to be what the other one wanted. But when it comes down to it, that doesn't get it. People are who they are. And I don't know why we end up sometimes with someone who's looking for something different. They think they see some of it in us, and maybe we'll change enough to be the whole picture of what they want. But that's not how it usually goes. We're just born with certain things that make us who we are. Maybe our challenge in life is to grow from that. And be the best of that we can be. When we ask someone to be something they're not, maybe that's the worst kind of rejection. When we refuse to see the good that's already there in a person because it's not our good. Their good ought to be enough, don't you think?"

Andy glanced out the window at the sun creeping up behind the park that lay to the side of the hospital. She knew her daddy was right. And she knew, too, that was exactly what she'd been trying to do as well. Be something other than what she was.

She wasn't a girl who liked to get up in front of other people and walk down a runway in an evening gown. She liked jeans and T-shirts that let people know what she thought about something. She didn't like to wear makeup all the time. It was okay when she went out at night or did something a little special. And if she had to actually roll her hair on those hot curlers every single morning of her life, she would never get anywhere on time. A ponytail with a rubber band was her stand-by, and it worked just fine.

So why was she turning herself inside out trying to be something she wasn't, attract the attention of a duke with a life on the other side of the world, a guy who would be nothing more for her than a memory at some point in the not-so-distant future?

She looked at her dad, stood and leaned forward to loop her arms around his neck. "I'm sorry, Daddy."

"Hey," he said, pressing the back of his hand to her cheek and tucking her hair behind one ear. "I'm proud of you, you know."

"Yeah," she said, "but I'm not a superhero."

"You are to me," he said.

And that was all it took. Those four words, filtering through to her heart, seeping outward to the farthest parts of her until she felt as if she glowed with their warmth.

47

---

*Give two boys who think they're enemies a
football.*
And then see what happens.
— *Kyle's Sandlot league football coach*

It was just about six-thirty a.m. when Kyle rolled through
the green light at Main and Yardley. He recognized the guy
immediately. It was the posture. Straight shoulders, the
blue blood walk that royals must start teaching their kids
right after they take their first steps.

If it hadn't been for that, he could have been mistaken
for any other guy. He wore blue jeans and a hoodie
sweatshirt, BEAT IT, emblazoned across the back.

He should have kept on driving. Common sense told
him as much. Which in no way explained why he hit the

brakes and lowered the passenger side window. "Hey, duke" he said, "you need a ride?"

George, Duke of Iberlorn swung him a glance of dismissal.

"They teach you that in royalty school?" Kyle asked.

George kept walking without looking at him. "Fuck you," he said in his high-brow accent.

"Bet they don't teach you that. Hey, man, I was just kidding. I'm Kyle. You need a ride somewhere?"

George slowed, looked at him and said, "Andy's Kyle?"

Too surprised to respond, Kyle stared at him for a moment before saying, "Why would you say that?"

"Because she told me about you."

"Told you what?"

"About the cheerleading squad for one thing."

"What?" He looked off and then said, "That's crap."

"Not to her."

"What do you know about it?"

"Enough."

"Not as much as you think you do."

"Maybe."

Kyle had a feeling he would be wise to drive on, but common sense wasn't winning out. "You need a ride?" he repeated.

"I was headed for the McDonald's."

"Me, too. Get in."

Reservation clear on his face, George opened the door and slid inside. "Just so you know, I left a note at the inn where I was going. In case you decide to do away with me or something."

Kyle smiled. "Why would I want to do that?"

George cut him a look. "Maybe because you think I'm stealing your girl?"

"She's not my girl."

"So in addition to being a jerk, you're also delusional."

"What's that supposed to mean?"

"Well, maybe neither one of you has figured it out yet, but she is your girl."

Kyle swung a left into the McDonald's parking lot. "Wanna go in or drive-thru?"

George shrugged. "Drive-thru's fine with me."

They pulled up to the speaker, gave their orders, pooled their change for the cashier at the first window and then waited at the second window for their food.

"What's the real rift between you two?" George asked.

"No rift," Kyle said.

George rolled his eyes. "Okay, no rift."

"Actually," Kyle said, "you're the rift."

"You might think I am."

"You and what you represent," Kyle said. "Andy doesn't want to be here. She wants some other place, some other life, some other guy."

"Has she said that to you?"

"She didn't have to say it."

"Oh, so you're a mind reader?"

"I could punch you, you know."

"I expect you could. But you won't. Because you know what I just said is true. You haven't asked her."

"Why would I ask her when I already know what she'll say?"

"That just seems plain stupid to me."

The cashier opened the window, handed their two bags of food and cups of coffee to Kyle.

George gave her a smile that visibly weakened her facial muscles into an audible sigh.

Kyle rolled his eyes and jerked the truck into drive, gunning it forward. "You practice that in front of a mirror?"

"It was just a smile. You ought to try it some time."

"I smile plenty."

"Bet you don't smile at Andy very much."

"'Cause she's always making me so damn mad."

"Arguing's better than not talking at all."

"What's that supposed to mean?" Kyle asked. He drove without thinking, waiting for George's answer. When it finally came, it had an acceptance of sorts etched at its edges.

"You're lucky to have a girl like Andy, Kyle."

"Well, that's where you're wrong. I don't have her."

"You could if you wanted to."

"So what are you doing? Just stringing her along or something?"

"When I agreed to do this ridiculous show, I never imagined I would meet a girl I liked," George said.

The words cut Kyle like a knife. "But you did."

"Yeah, I did."

Kyle rolled the truck into the high school parking lot, coming to a stop at the edge of the football field. He turned off the ignition, reached for his coffee and took a sip. "What would make a guy like you do a show like that?"

George laughed. "You mean a guy like you think I am?"

"Whatever," Kyle said.

"What else? The money."

"Ah. You're working on restocking the royal bank vault?"

George stared out at the far end of the football field. "Something like that."

The way he said it made Kyle feel like he'd said something he shouldn't have. "So, what, like it wasn't your idea?"

"Not exactly."

"Whose was it then?"

"Our family agent," George said.

"You mean like movie agent, TV agent?"

"Media agent," George said.

"Media agent." Kyle took a bite of his biscuit, then said, "You don't want any part of all that?"

"It doesn't matter whether I want it or not," George said. "It's just the way it is."

"Your family really needs this to keep the silver polishers coming regularly?"

"Will you cut it out?" George said.

They ate the rest of their food in silence. When they were done, Kyle got out of the truck, grabbed a football from the back. "Throw a few?"

George finished off his coffee. "Why not?"

They walked across the field, the dew dampening their shoes.

Kyle stopped, and George kept walking until he was far enough away for Kyle to pass him one.

Kyle put his best arm on it, rivalry impossible to deny.

George caught it with a solid whump, and then just as quickly, passed it back with an arm that made Kyle raise his eyebrows.

"Whoa. Where'd you get that?"

"Boarding school. Out in the country. Nothing else to do."

"Play rugby?" Kyle asked.

"Yeah."

"You any good?"

"Yeah."

Kyle missled him another one, which George caught and fired off just as quickly.

"Crap, man," Kyle said, taking it in the stomach with a doubled-over groan.

George grinned. "You're the big football star, aren't you?"

"Yeah."

"Modest, too."

Kyle rolled his eyes. "Not like you got that market cornered."

Both boys grinned then, throwing the football back and forth, each determined with every pass to show the other one up.

"So what's your plan?" Kyle threw out, as he whizzed the ball at George. "Have some fun with Andy, and then you're jet-setting back off to the royal palace?"

George gave him a good long glare before saying, "You're the one she's crazy about. Beats me why you're the only one who can't see it."

"Yeah," Kyle said, "that's why she's been hanging out with you and ignoring me."

"Maybe she's been hanging out with me because I'm nice to her. This thing I'm doing with the TV show, it's not a real date."

"What is it then?"

"Entertainment," George said.

"Oh, yeah, for the masses," Kyle said.

George launched the ball at him. "It's all funny to you, isn't it?"

"What do you mean it isn't real?"

"I'm engaged," George said.

"Engaged? Aren't you like seventeen or something?"

"Yeah, I'm seventeen."

"Then how, why—"

"Our families arranged it."

"And you're cool with this?"

George dropped the ball on the ground, sank down beside it, wiping his forehead on the sleeve of his sweatshirt. "It's just the way it is."

"Are you serious about all that money stuff?" Kyle said, walking over and dropping down next to him.

"Yeah, it takes a lot to maintain the royal coffers as you say. Her family still has it, mine not so much these days."

"That kind of sucks," Kyle said. "What's she like?"

"She's nice," George said.

"Are you like in love with her?"

When George didn't answer, Kyle said, "Man, do you think it's right to lead all these girls on? Letting them think you're some available bachelor duke when you're not?"

"I told her," George said.

Kyle looked at him for a long moment, shook his head and said, "Told who?"

"Andy. Everything. I told her everything."

"So she knows you're not really available?"

"She does."

"Why'd you tell her, man?"

"Because she's great, and I like her. And if I weren't already engaged, I'd be giving you a run for your money."

"And she was cool with that?"

"Maybe you don't know Andy quite as well as you think you do," George said, getting to his feet and sticking out his hand. "I look forward to watching you on the big screen one day soon."

The words surprised Kyle, and he guessed it showed

on his face because George said, "Yeah, you're that good, man. Stay with it, okay?"

Then he turned and headed off across the parking lot, the blue blood posture clearly back in place.

48

We may think we have forever. . .no one does.
— Grier McAllister – Blog at Jane Austen Girl

It was just after nine o'clock when Grier left her mother in the care of two nursing assistants intent on sponging away the soot marks still on her arms and chest.

Grier sought out an information desk and asked for Bobby Jack's room number. She found him sitting up in bed, drinking an enormous glass of orange juice while Andy fussed around his hair with a comb.

"That's enough, Andy," he said. "I don't comb my hair that many times in a week."

"You've got this cow lick thing going on," Andy said.

"There is the cow lick thing," Grier said.

Both Bobby Jack and Andy looked up at the same time.

"Would you please find her somebody else to fuss over?" Bobby Jack said playfully, smacking away Andy's hands.

"You sure don't look like you saved a bunch of people's lives last night," Grier said, walking closer to the bed.

"How's your mama?" Bobby Jack asked, his face suddenly serious.

"She's here," Grier said. "Thanks to you."

"And a lot of other people," he said.

Andy rolled her eyes. "Modesty's just one of his things, you know." She glanced back and forth between Bobby Jack and Grier and said, "I'm starving. I think I'll run down to the cafeteria and get something. Would you like anything, Grier?"

"No, I'm good, thank you."

"Daddy?"

"All full," he said, "with that delicious hospital breakfast."

"Back in a few," Andy said.

"Hey, Andy," he called out.

She turned to look at him, "Yeah, Daddy?"

"Could you run home and feed Flo and Grier's Sebbie? We left them there last night. I'm sure they're wondering where breakfast is."

"Will do," Andy said, and she was out the door.

"Thank you," Grier said in the silence that followed her departure. "I can't believe I hadn't thought about them yet."

"I'm sure they're fine. Just a little hungry."

"And no doubt mad at us both."

He smiled. "No doubt."

Grier sat on the chair next to his bed. "How are you? Really?"

"I'm fine," he said. "Breathed in a little smoke, took a beam to the back of the head, but the docs say there should be no lasting damage."

Grier glanced down at her hands and then forced herself to meet his eyes. "Thank you," she said, "for what you did last night."

"You don't have to thank me. I'm just glad I was there to help."

"Have you heard anything about the damage to the place? How much?"

"One of the other volunteer firefighters came in earlier and said it was pretty much a loss," Bobby Jack said.

They were quiet for several seconds, before he added, "You worried about where your mama's gonna go?"

Grier shrugged. "If you had asked me a week ago if my mother and I would ever speak again in this lifetime, I would have said no. And now, here I am, worrying about what's going to happen to her."

Bobby Jack reached out and covered her hand with his. "I don't think even your mama would deny how badly she messed up when you were young. But people change, you know, and get to points where they realize they could have done so much better. I kind of suspect your mama's already reached that point."

Grier started to deny it, but she knew it was true. She'd seen the look of regret in her mother's eyes. And she knew, deep in her heart, she would take it all back if she could, redo it all if she could. But she couldn't. "I don't know if I can," Grier said. "Forgive her."

"I've got a feeling, it's something you need to do not just for her, Grier, but for yourself, too. Speaking from experience, it's a lot easier to walk around this world without the weight of anger and resentment sitting on your shoulders. I've been doing that myself for a long time, and you know what? I just don't want to do it anymore. There was actually a moment last night when I was running in and out of that fire that it occurred to me I could actually die in there, along with those other people. I'm not sure that reality has ever hit me quite as square between the eyes as it did then. But it was kind of like someone flashed this big light in front of me, and I could see what really matters in my life."

Grier felt herself holding her breath, her chest tight and full with something she couldn't even name.

"I thought about Andy," he said, "and how I've been so royally screwing up things with her lately. Worrying and fussing over things that, I don't know, probably in ten years, we won't even remember. What I do know is she's everything to me. I can't imagine my life without her. I thought about my mom and my brother. How they know me better than anybody. How all I have to do is call, and they'll come running."

They sat, silent for a string of heartbeats. Grier could hear her own pulse pounding in her ears, and wondered if he could hear it as well.

A sudden sense of urgency swept over her, a feeling so strong and overpowering that she stood suddenly, the chair sliding out behind her and making a harsh scraping noise on the floor. She pulled her hand from his and stuck it behind her back, as if it had just been burned. "I should go check on Mama," she said.

She had reached the door when he called out, "Grier?"

But she didn't turn around. She walked faster and faster, propelled by something she couldn't even name until by the time she reached the end of the hall, she was running.

49

Friends come and go in life.
But brothers will always be brothers.
— Grandma Randall to Bobby Jack and Darryl
Lee after breaking up a swinging match in her
backyard

Darryl Lee stomped into Bobby Jack's room and took the chair next to his bed, looking about as mad as he had the day somebody stole the hubcaps off his truck.

"I let you out of my sight for less than twenty-four hours, and you turn into Clark Kent?"

"I'm fine," Bobby Jack said. "Sit down."

"What were you trying to do? Kill yourself?" Darryl Lee pulled the chair up close to the bed, then leaned back and glared at him.

"Actually, I was just trying to save some lives."

"You scared the heck out of me, brother."

"I'm fine," Bobby Jack said.

"Well, you might have been—"

"I wasn't."

"Coulda been."

"Wasn't. Where were you anyway? Nobody could find you."

Darryl Lee glanced out the window, then back at Bobby Jack with a look he didn't recognize on him. "Trying to work things out with Dreama."

"Did you?"

Darryl Lee shook his head. "I don't think so."

"What happened with you two? You had a good thing once."

"We got lazy, I guess. Maybe I got lazy. Taking things for granted, you know."

"You still love each other?"

"I still love her."

Bobby Jack heard the note of vulnerability in his brother's voice and felt a pang of actual pain for him. He wasn't used to seeing Darryl Lee in a state of anything remotely resembling second chair.

"I guess what I know now," Darryl Lee said, "is that you can't look away and think things will still be there when you decide to look back."

"What can I do?"

Darryl Lee shoved his hands in the pockets of his jeans,

lifted his shoulders in a shrug. "Make your own happiness. And then don't look away."

"If you're talking about—"

"Grier. Pissed me off at first, but clearly you've got it bad for each other." He stopped there, looking as if he wanted to say more but wasn't sure he should. And then, "Something real bad almost happened to Grier before she left here after high school."

Bobby Jack's heart jumped in his chest and he could see, just from the look on his brother's face, he wasn't sure he wanted to hear the rest of this.

Darryl Lee glanced out the window, his voice lower when he said, "You remember Sherry Apperson?"

"She was in your class, wasn't she?" Bobby Jack said.

"She and Grier were good friends in school. Several years ago when she came home to visit family, we ran into each other out at the Beer Boot. She started talking about why Grier had left town and how she didn't blame her. She said one night when her mama was loaded, she had a boyfriend over. I guess her mama must have passed out in the living room, and the creep tried to rape Grier. Apparently, it wasn't the first time that kind of thing had happened."

Bobby Jack felt the blood drain from his face, and a slow rage start to build inside him. He suddenly understood exactly how difficult what he'd just suggested Grier do would be for her. "Hell," he said. "I'm such an idiot."

Darryl Lee looked at him. "What'd you do?"

"I told her she ought to forgive her mother."

Darryl Lee considered this for a few moments. "That's probably the very best thing she could do for herself."

"And the hardest."

"That's usually the stuff that gets us where we need to go." Darryl Lee said, and then, "So are you gonna tell her how you feel about her?"

"I'm not sure it would do any good."

"As much as it galls me to say it, I saw the way she looked at you. She never looked at me like that."

"You were both kids then," Bobby Jack said.

"Love is love. Since when did it ever make any difference how old you are?"

Bobby Jack knew his brother and what it cost him to throw out this seal of approval. The strongest kind of love for Darryl Lee welled up in him.

They might not always agree on everything, but when it came to the real stuff in life, the things that mattered, he guessed they actually did.

50

---

*"The moment will come, as surely as we breathe,
when opportunity will disappear. Then, and only
then, will we realize what we have lost."*
— Grier McAllister – Blog at Jane Austen Girl

Grier stepped off the elevator and took the hallway to her
mother's room, her steps quickening until she was all but
running past the nurse's desk.

"Room 316!" she heard a nurse say. "Code Blue!"

Panic flared in Grier's chest and spread through her in a
wave of disbelief. She started to run outright then, a nurse
right behind her with a cart carrying a large machine.

Grier came to a jarring stop at the room's door. Two
other nurses were already there, giving her mother CPR.

She lay flat on the bed, her face as white as the sheet beneath her.

The nurses worked with capable, well-rehearsed movements, their voices steady and calm.

The nurse who had been behind her pushed by with the cart, murmuring a brisk, "Excuse me." And then glancing over her shoulder, said, "I'm sorry. You can't be in here. You'll have to wait outside."

"But what's happening?"

"Please," the nurse said firmly, but not unkindly. "Wait outside."

51

"I would rather take her pain a thousand times over than to watch her try to bear it."
— Bobby Jack to Darryl Lee after Priscilla left and Andy cried, broken-hearted, for her at bedtime

Bobby Jack spotted her as soon as the elevator doors opened.

Darryl Lee had brought him a pair of jeans and a shirt. After changing out of that ridiculous hospital gown, he'd slipped down the hall and into the open elevator before one of the nurses could spot him.

He walked as fast as his aching left leg would let him.

She sat huddled against the wall, her knees to her chest, her head hidden beneath her arms. He sank down beside her and put his arm around her, without giving himself time to consider that she might push him away.

"What is it?" he asked. "What happened?"

Grier looked up at him then, her face streaked with multiple tracks of tears. "They've been in there over twenty minutes. When I got here, they were . . . her heart must have stopped."

She began to cry then, deep, wracking sobs that came from a place of hurt so far down inside her that he could hardly bear to hear them.

"Grier." He folded her into the crook of his arm, holding her as tightly as he dared. She collapsed into him, as if she needed to absorb his strength, needed it to go on breathing.

He kissed the top of her head and held her while she cried. He had no idea what to say, if there was anything he could say, to lessen the pain.

People walked by. Stared at them. Shrunk away from the sound of Grier's grief.

He just pulled her closer. Held her tighter. Wanting to take the grief into himself. Feel the pain for her so that she didn't have to.

He wasn't sure how long they sat there. It seemed like forever because he couldn't stand knowing the agony she was in. And no time at all because having her here against him was something he never wanted to end.

"I wanted to tell her I—" Her voice broke then, sobs swallowing the words.

"Shh. It's okay," Bobby Jack said, rubbing her hair and sensing the recriminations she wanted to throw at herself. At the same time, he could feel her acceptance that it might be too late, that she might have waited too long.

Another nurse came running down the hall, opened the door and stepped in, her voice carrying into the hall. "She has a DNR. We were just now able to get it from the nursing home. There was a digital file of it on backup."

A man's voice, low and resigned, said, "Stop."

Bobby Jack felt Grier stiffen. She jumped to her feet, ran to the door and pushed it open. "No. Don't stop. She's my mother! Keep going!"

Bobby Jack stepped in behind her, saw the look of sympathy on the doctor's face. "I'm sorry," the doctor said. "But those were her wishes."

Grier sank onto the side of the bed, dropping her head onto her mother's chest, sobs now pouring from her. "I'm sorry, Mama. I'm so sorry. Please. Come back. Just come back."

The doctor laid a hand on Grier's shoulder and said, "She's gone, dear."

Bobby Jack looked at the doctor and the two nurses standing by the bed with downcast eyes. "Could she have a few minutes, please?"

"Of course." The doctor turned and left the room. The nurses followed quietly behind him.

"Do you want me to stay?" Bobby Jack asked, his voice breaking on the last word.

"No," Grier said, her voice barely audible.

"I'll be right outside," he said. "I'm not going anywhere."

And as he turned and walked from the room, he thought her pain would surely break his heart in half.

52

"When I grow up, Mama, I want to be as pretty
and good as you."
— *Grier, age four, on a picnic at the lake*

Grier pressed her face into the pillow beside her mother's
still head, trying to muffle the grief rolling from her like a
tsunami from the ocean floor. But it wouldn't be silenced,
and the tears wouldn't stop. She cried like she had never
cried before in her life, a child stricken by the realization
that her mother was gone and was never coming back.

She laced her fingers with hers, squeezing tight as if she
could infuse her with her own life force, will her back into
this world, into this room, into her life.

The words rose up and refused to remain within her,
silent. "I'm sorry, Mama. I'm so sorry." She said the words

over and over again, until they were nothing more than a weak whisper, slipping past her lips.

Ironic that she had come to this room to give her mother forgiveness, and now, it felt as if she were the one seeking it. Only now it was too late for any words that might heal either of them.

Grier sat up on her elbows, pushed her hair back from her face and ran a hand across her tear-stained cheeks. The lines in her mother's face had all but disappeared. She looked so much more like the younger woman that Grier remembered. She looked at peace.

"I know you never meant for anything bad to happen to me, Mama." She smoothed the back of her fingers across her mother's face, let them linger against the softness of her cheek. "Will you forgive me?"

But there was no answer in the silent room. She had waited too long, too late. She would have to live with that the rest of her life.

53

---

*"Sometimes, all you can do for a person is be
there. Just don't let them convince you that they
don't need you. They do. And they will."*
*— Bobby Jack's Grandma Randall after the
death of his father*

Bobby Jack stood outside until he could no longer hear
Grier crying.

He opened the door and walked quietly across the
room, putting his hand on her shoulder, and then rubbing
her back, compassion a weight on his chest. "Grier, honey.
Why don't we go now?"

She looked up at him then, her eyes and face a picture of
heartbreak. "You don't have to be here with me," she said.

"I want to be here with you."

He could see her resistance and then watched it ebb away beneath a need to hold onto someone, to anything, to keep from drowning in the current of emotion she was trying to navigate.

He held her hand tighter, pulled her to her feet and then encircled her waist with his arms, melding her into him with an all-consuming desire to absorb it all, take the pain from her and carry it as his own.

She pressed her face to his shirt. He felt her breathe in and anchored her more securely within the circle of his arms. "It'll be okay," he said. "You'll be okay."

"I'm not sure I want to be," she said, the words broken and full of self-blame.

"I want you to be," he said. "I want you to be."

AFTER WRANGLING A couple of doctors into hastening his release, Bobby Jack called Darryl Lee and asked him to drop his truck off at the hospital.

All the while, he kept Grier with him, mostly tucked inside the curve of his arm because he feared what might happen if he let her go.

He felt her fragility and how easy it would be for her to break right now. He wasn't going to let that happen.

By the time he had completed the paperwork to check himself out and Grier had answered the hospital's questions about funeral preparations, Darryl Lee already had the truck waiting in the parking lot.

He stood by the open door, his face compassionate and concerned. "Grier," he said. "I'm so sorry."

She looked at him, her eyes brimming again with tears. "Thank you, Darryl Lee."

"If there's anything I can do. . . anything at all."

She shook her head and said, "I appreciate that."

"Bobby Jack, are you sure you should be driving?" Darryl Lee asked.

"I'm fine. Really, I'm fine."

Under any other circumstances, Bobby Jack knew his brother would have argued. But he let him go, walked back to his own truck and waved a solemn wave.

Bobby Jack helped Grier inside and shut the door, walking around to the driver's side and climbing in. He drove slowly all the way to the inn.

When they pulled up in front, he said, "We could go back to my house."

"I think I'd rather stay here."

"Then I'm staying, too."

He expected her to argue, but she didn't. They walked inside and up the stairs to her room. She handed him the key and he opened the door.

Bobby Jack sat down in the chair next to the bed. "I'm here, Grier," he said, "and I'm not going anywhere."

54

"When the hurt is so big and so seemingly endless, the only thing that will ever get us through is love."
— *Grier McAllister – Blog at Jane Austen Girl*

Grier heard the cell phone ringing in her purse.

Bobby Jack said, "Do you want me to get that?"

She rose up on an elbow, wanting to say no, to turn it off, close out the world, but then she remembered all the responsibilities she had waiting and the fact that she hadn't shown up for the meeting this morning at the inn. She knew she couldn't put it off. "Yes," she said.

He reached in her purse and handed the phone to her.

Caller id flashed Elizabeth Arbon. Grier tapped the answer button and said, "Hello."

"I just heard what happened last night, Grier. And about your mother. I'm so very sorry."

Grier wondered who had told her but then realized Timbell Creek wasn't the kind of place where anything stayed unknown for long. Even when you were an outsider.

"Thank you, Elizabeth. I just need a little time to get myself together."

"Of course. We can go on this morning without you. That's not a problem."

"I appreciate it," Grier said.

"I'll check in with you later, okay?"

"Yes," Grier said and turned off the phone. She dropped back against the pillow then and stared at the ceiling. "I think I need to be alone for a little while," she said, looking at Bobby Jack.

"Are you sure?" he asked, sounding uncertain.

She nodded, biting her lip to keep the sob in her throat from slipping out.

"Is there anything I can do?"

"No. But thank you. For everything."

"You don't need to thank me. I'm a phone call away," he said and left the room.

It felt quiet and empty after Bobby Jack had gone. Grier felt drained of any recognizable emotion at all. It didn't seem possible that this could really have happened. She wanted to wake up and discover that the whole thing had been a dream. That she had come to her senses far sooner than she had. That she'd taken the chance to say the things to her mother that she needed to say.

But that wasn't to be.

Self-accusation after self-accusation circled through her mind until she felt limp with remorse.

How many times had she heard about other people who left important things unresolved in their lives until it was too late? Over the years, she'd had numerous friends tell her of regrets, things they wished they'd done sooner, not put off. But somehow, she'd never applied it to herself. Never thought, even for a moment, that she would regret not making peace with her mother. Logically, she knew that her anger had been justified. Somehow, right now, knowing that her mother was gone forever, none of it seemed to matter.

The only thing that mattered was the huge gaping hole in her heart, and the absolute knowledge that she would never again have the chance to fill it.

She thought about the days that lay ahead, of her mother's funeral and burial and she honestly didn't know if she could go through with it.

But then what choice did she have? She had failed her mother in the one thing that she could have given her. And she wouldn't fail her in this.

GRIER HIT REDIAL on her phone and made the call before she could give herself time to reconsider.

Elizabeth answered on the first ring.

"I'm so sorry to ask this," Grier said, "but can you find someone to replace me for the final judging?"

She heard the other woman let out a long breath. A couple of seconds passed before she said, "It won't be easy, Grier, but I can't say I wouldn't do the same thing in your place."

"I never dreamed I would be in this position," Grier began.

"I know," Elizabeth interrupted.

"If you could give me a few days—"

"I wish I could. But with the schedule, I really can't."

"I understand."

"Just take care of yourself, okay?"

"You, too," Grier said, before ending the call.

THE ROOM FELT too small.

She changed clothes and then walked to the parking lot where she got in her car with no destination in mind.

She cranked the music on the radio and just drove, aiming for some mindless zone where pain could not be felt. But no matter how fast she drove or how loud she played the music, there was no such place.

She felt raw to her very soul, every nerve ending blaring in protest.

She drove for two hours or more, finding herself at the entrance to Bobby Jack's driveway, turning the car onto the gravel road as if she had no ability to deny where she needed to be. It was late, dark now, and she pulled up in front of the house, Bobby Jack's truck the only vehicle in sight. She sat in the car and stared at the front door, telling herself if he didn't come out in the next sixty seconds, she would leave.

But just then, the door opened, and he stood there, looking to her the way a lighthouse might have looked to a lost ship. He walked out, opened the door of her car and all but lifted her from the driver's seat into his arms.

He held her tight against him, her feet not touching the ground. She wrapped her arms around his neck and buried her face in the curve of his shoulder. She wanted to sob there against him, but the tears would no longer come. She felt empty and wanted nothing more than to be filled with the presence of him.

He bent and looped an arm at the back of her knees, swinging her up fully into his arms and walking into the house, kicking the not fully closed door open with a booted foot and then just as quickly shoving it closed behind them.

He stopped at the foot of the stairs and looked down at her, his eyes saying the question he didn't need to ask with words. She nodded once, and that was all he needed. He carried her up the stairs as if she weighed nothing more than a bag of cotton.

Grier felt as if she had been standing on the other side of a glass window where nothing but sadness existed. The thought of ever seeing through to the other side again seemed impossible, until now, until this moment when

Bobby Jack's hard, fit body absorbed some of the pain from her, his embrace telling her how willing he was to carry as much of it as she would let him carry.

He took her to his bedroom, again closing the door behind them and deftly reaching out to turn the lock. He walked to the bed then and lay her down near the center. He sat on the side and smoothed the back of his hand across her cheek.

"I think I willed you to come here."

"What do you mean?" she asked softly.

"I wanted to come back. But I wanted it to be your choice. Coming here. Being here."

She wanted to say the words logic prodded her to say. But she couldn't force them past her lips. Truth, instead, won out, and she said, "I need you."

His green eyes darkened with a look so pure and powerful that Grier felt the force of it to the core of her very being.

"Grier," he said, her name ragged on his lips.

"Will you hold me?"

He folded her against him and leaned back against the headboard. "Forever if you want me to."

Lying there with her cheek against his chest, she wondered if even that might not be long enough.

55

*"We think we know a person. But we only know
what we see. We can't know what is hidden."*
— *Grier McAllister – Blog at Jane Austen Girl*

The funeral was simple. No service. Just a graveside
memorial with exactly four people in attendance. Grier,
her mother's friend Hatcher, Bobby Jack and Andy.

The pastor spoke what were supposed to be words of
comfort, only to Grier, they weren't. They felt empty and
hollow.

Among the few things recovered from her mother's
room at the retirement home had been a note requesting
that this service be exactly what it was. Plain and to the
point.

She didn't cry. She listened to the verses the pastor read,

absorbing each word. She stood by the grave, dry-eyed while his words fell like a rain too late to save the harvest.

Grier wanted to absorb them, take comfort in them, but the truth was she knew she didn't deserve the comfort.

When the service ended, the pastor walked over. "If there's anything I can do for you," he said, "please, just call."

"I appreciate that," Grier said.

Bobby Jack and Andy each hugged her, neither saying anything. She suspected they had no idea what to say.

"Thank you for coming," she managed. "I think I'll stay a bit."

"We'll wait for you," Bobby Jack said.

"No. Please. I'm fine. I'll call you in a while."

"Are you sure?"

She nodded, but she could see in his eyes that he was worried about her.

Bobby Jack reached out then to where Hatcher stood just to the side of Grier and shook his hand. "Can we give you a ride back to town, sir?"

Hatcher shook his head and said, "Thank you, Bobby Jack. But that yellow taxi over there's for me."

They left the graveside then, heading for the truck, Bobby Jack reluctant, Andy slipping her arm through his as if to lead him on.

Grier folded her arms across her chest and turned to Hatcher. "Thank you for coming today."

"Your mama and I got to be pretty close friends over the past couple of years."

"I'm glad she had you," she said.

Hatcher looked off across the graveyard and then with a troubled expression, said, "I might be overstepping my bounds here, but I can see you two didn't get things tied up before she passed."

Grier looked away, feeling the instant sting of hot tears. "No. I guess we didn't."

"We had a lot of long talks," Hatcher said. "I think you should know your mama would have given anything to be able to go back and change some of her choices. But you know we don't get to do that in this world."

"No, we don't," Grier said.

"She loved you. And there wasn't a day that passed that I didn't hear her say something about you. Something you used to like to do. Or something you were good at."

This surprised Grier. It would have been easier to think that her mother had closed her out of her thoughts in the years since she left Timbell Creek.

Hatcher drew in a deep breath and leaned hard on his cane as if it weren't easy for him.

"Are you all right?" she asked.

"I'm fine," he said. "Just old."

"Would you like to sit for a minute?" Grier sensed that Hatcher wanted to talk, and she knew somehow that he was the last lifeline she would ever have to her mother.

They sat on two folding chairs next to the casket, Grier

holding Hatcher's elbow as he cautiously lowered himself onto the seat.

The sun felt warm on her face, and the sky was a beautiful clear robin's egg blue. From somewhere, Grier had a flash of memory, a day very similar to this one when she and her mother had gone to the public beach on Clearwater Lake. Grier must have been five. Maybe six. This memory of her mother was one in which she had been so young with a beauty unmarked by the ravages of alcohol.

"She told me a few things she never actually told you," Hatcher said in his raspy voice.

"What things?" she asked.

"Did you know that she was accepted to the Atlanta School of Design?"

Grier frowned and tilted her head. "No. What do you mean?"

"Her senior year in high school. That was her dream, I guess. To be a designer. And she had planned to go there on scholarship, actually."

"Why didn't she?"

He hesitated a few moments before saying, "Because she became pregnant with you. Your father, the boy she was dating, wanted her to. . .not have you, I guess. That wasn't something she would ever do, she said. And at first she still planned to go to school. But right after she had you, your grandparents were killed in that car wreck, and your mama all of a sudden didn't have anybody to help her.

She let the scholarship go. I think maybe she thought in a couple of years she could go back to that dream. But it just didn't work out that way. Your mama never touched a drop of alcohol until she was twenty-three or so. She went out on a date with some guy who basically got her drunk and took advantage of her. She said she hated what the alcohol did to her, but it was kind of like once that button was turned on, it would always get the best of her, even when she had every intention of resisting it. I don't guess anyone can understand that better than I do. I had a good wife. Great kids. And I threw all of it away. I can't even explain my own addiction to the stuff. Much less your mama's. I just know what kind of hold it had on me. And from what she told me, the same is true of her. Being an alcoholic doesn't excuse wrongdoing, and your mama did some serious suffering after you left home."

"That was two of us then," Grier said softly.

"I don't doubt it. But she was a different woman from the one you knew who drank. I tried a bunch of times to get her to go up and see you. But then when she became sick, it really wasn't an option anymore. I think she was too ashamed to face you."

Tears welled up in Grier's eyes and tipped over to slide down her cheeks. "I wish I could—"

Hatcher reached over and took her hand. "I know, honey," he said. "But you can't torture yourself with that for the rest of your life. Your mama understood why you left home. And why you never came back. She knew she was to blame for that. Sometimes, we don't get to tie it all up with a pretty bow. But we need to make our peace with it. And I think Maxine did that. She forgave herself. Maybe there will be some comfort in that for you."

The sobs came up out of her before she realized they were even there. Once they started, Grier had no power to stop them. She leaned forward, elbows on her knees and cried like a broken-hearted child.

Hatcher reached his arm around her shoulders and tucked her up against him, smoothing his arthritic hand across her hair. "There now. It's gonna be okay," he said. "Everything's gonna be okay."

56

"Wouldn't it be nice if people never had to feel sadness?"
— *Andy – age eight*

Bobby Jack and Andy rode the first ten minutes back to town in complete silence.

"That was really sad," Andy said, staring out the window.

"Yeah," Bobby Jack agreed. "It was."

"Why do you think Grier didn't come home for so long?"

"Some really hard stuff happened to her that shouldn't have, things that didn't have to happen."

"You mean something Ms. McAllister did?"

"Yeah," Bobby Jack said.

Andy was quiet for a couple of minutes. "I guess people shouldn't stay mad at each other about stuff. Even when it seems big at the time."

Bobby Jack glanced over at her, saw the serious expression on her face and said, "No, honey, I don't guess we should."

"I'm sorry, Daddy. For being so mean to you."

"Andy. About what you heard me say to your mama on the phone that night. . .you're the best thing that ever happened to either one of us. Nothing else matters except that."

She glanced out the window, bit her lip. "You mean that?"

"With all my heart. And I'm sorry for saying anything that might make you think otherwise."

She leaned over then and put her head on his shoulder. "I forgive you."

He put his arm around her shoulder, smoothed his hand across her silky hair. "And about that contest. I might have been a little unreasonable."

"No. Actually, I think you were right. That contest isn't something I would ever have wanted to do except for—" she broke off and then added, "I kind of wanted to show Mama I could do something like that."

"I know," he said.

"I'm going to drop out," she said.

"You don't have to do that, Andy."

"I want to." She looked at him and smiled a soft smile. "Besides, I've already had a date with the duke."

"Oh, you have, have you?"

"Yeah," she said, smiling bigger. "I have."

"What does Kyle think about that?"

"I doubt that he would know without asking one of his cheerleader girlfriends."

"Is that jealousy I hear?"

"No," she said. "It's not."

"You forget I've known you both since you were as high as my knee. And I've seen the way you look at each other."

"Yeah, but he's not the same Kyle anymore."

"Maybe he thinks you're not the same Andy."

She was quiet for a couple of miles, and he could see she was thinking about what he'd said.

"You and mom really ought to mend your fences."

Bobby Jack's response was nearly automatic. But Andy was right. Life was short. Whatever had happened between him and Priscilla, Andy was smack dab in the middle of it. He'd never thought about it until now, but it could not be an easy position to be in. Being the tug rope between the two people she loved most.

"I'm sorry, Andy," he said. "I think your mama and I both need to grow up a little."

"Where each other is concerned, maybe just a little."

57

---

*"When the night is dark and seems as if it will
never end, just remember the morning is never far
ahead. Light will triumph."*
*— From a book Grier once read on hope and
healing*

When Grier let herself into her room at the inn later that
afternoon, she found a vase of white roses on the dresser.
She scooped Sebbie off the bed, gave him a longer than
normal hug and then went over to pull the card from its
perch among the stems.

> *I want to be here for you. Whatever it is you need. Just call
> me and I'll come.*
> *Bobby Jack*

Grier wanted to. She really wanted to. So much so that she had to force herself not to pick up her phone and call him right then.

But what would be the point, really? Bobby Jack lived here. She no longer did. And she didn't know how she could ever belong here again. The sooner she left and got back to the place where she did belong, the better for everyone.

Grier felt as if everything she had come to believe about herself was completely wrong. She had run away all those years ago for reasons that anyone would understand. She knew that. And yet she also knew that she would live the rest of her life knowing that her mother had asked for forgiveness and she had not given it to her. For that, Grier didn't think she would ever forgive herself.

IT WAS NEARLY nine o'clock when the knock at the door woke her. She sat up on the bed, still wearing the clothes she'd worn to the funeral that afternoon.

Sebbie barked once. She rubbed his head and got up to see who it was.

Gil stood in the hallway, a box of chocolate in one hand, a bottle of red wine in the other. "I figured one or the other might help a little."

She tried to smile, but felt her failure. "Thank you, Gil. That's really nice."

"How are you doing?"

"Um, I'm okay, I guess. How is everything going with

the selection process? I'm really sorry for dropping the ball."

"Everyone understands. And it's going fine. One of our favorites dropped out though."

"Who?"

"Andy."

The news surprised her at first, but then, maybe it wasn't so surprising after all. It had never seemed like something Andy wanted to do for herself. And maybe it was best that she'd figured that out. "I think she might have won it," Grier said.

"Yeah, I think you're right."

"So what else is left?"

"They'll announce the winner in the morning, and then it'll be back to New York to film the rest of the show. I don't think we'll need you again here, but we'll need you back in the city to tie it all up."

"No problem," Grier said. "I'm heading back tomorrow." The words felt final. And sad somehow.

"You'll be all right to drive?"

"I'm good."

"If you change your mind, I can cancel my seat on the plane. I'll be happy to drive you."

"I really appreciate that, Gill. But I think it will do me good to have the drive to sort a few things out."

"Okay. Well, you have my number if you need me."

"Thanks. Goodnight."

58

"We need each other. Nothing more
important to admit than that."
— *A line from Bobby Jack's favorite song*

Bobby Jack had been calling her for three hours.
Apparently, she had her phone turned off because voice
mail picked up immediately.

By the time he pulled up in front of the inn, he'd
convinced himself that something was wrong. He knew
how hard Grier was being on herself, and he'd conjured
up at least six different scenarios by the time he got to her
door.

He knocked once, hard. "Grier? Are you there?"

Two full minutes passed before she finally came to the
door. Her hair had come down from the clip she'd had in

it earlier in the day. Her eyes were red and puffy, as if she'd been crying.

"I've been worried," he said.

"I'm sorry," she said. "I didn't really want to talk to anyone."

"And I just needed to know you were okay."

She nodded, pressing her lips together, and then tears welled up, and she was suddenly crying and shaking her head. "Bobby Jack, please. I'm kind of a mess."

"All the more reason for me to stay," he said, stepping inside and closing the door behind him. He turned the lock, then led her over to the bed where they sat on the edge. "Let me take care of you," he said. "Okay?"

She turned her face into his shoulder as if she didn't want him to see her pain. "Don't be kind to me," she said. "I think I might actually break if you are."

"Then let me be here to pick up the pieces."

"I don't deserve—"

"Yes, you do. So let me."

And with a small sob, she did.

59

"Do you think we might kiss each other sometime
and if neither one of us likes it, just go back to
being best friends?"
— *Kyle to Andy – Fifth grade*

Andy walked into the kitchen to find a note from her
daddy taped to the refrigerator.

Have gone to check on Grier.

I have my phone on if you need me.

Andy heard the rattle of Kyle's truck in the driveway.
She started not to answer the door, but her own truck
was parked outside, and she suspected he would just keep
knocking until she answered.

She yelled, "Come in," from the kitchen, and he did,

walking through the foyer to stop in the arched entrance with a look she'd never seen on his face before.

"Is your daddy here?"

"No, he isn't. Why do you want to see him?"

"I don't want to see him," he said. He walked straight to her, slipped his hands under her arms and lifted her up, setting her firmly on the kitchen counter.

"Kyle, what in the world are. . . have you lost your mind?" She tried for outrage and heard her own failure.

"No," he said. "I haven't. And be quiet." He leaned in then and kissed her. Every thought of protest in her head shut down like the lights at the high school football stadium after a game. She put her hands on his chest, his very wide, very well-muscled chest. Slid them around his neck, snagging her fingers into his dark hair.

They kissed until they both had to stop for air, pulling back to look at each other, breathing fast and heavy.

"Do you know how many years I've wanted to do that?" he asked, looking straight into her eyes.

She shook her head. "How many?"

"Too many," he said. He ducked in, renewed the kiss, and Andy felt the heat of it all the way down to her toes.

"Why'd you wait so long?" she said in a voice that was little more than a whisper.

"Heck if I know. I guess I was intimidated."

"Intimidated?"

"Yeah," he said. "You can be intimidating."

She laughed then. "That is like the very last reason on earth I would have expected you to give."

"Andy. You're smart. And beautiful. And you've got a mind of your own."

"That Jane Austen girl thing then," she said.

"My Jane Austen girl," he said. "Not his."

"Is that so?"

"You belong with me, Andy."

She heard the vulnerability in his voice. And it surprised her. More like shocked her. "Is this Kyle of the star quarterback Kyle Summers?"

"Will you stop with that?"

"Well, it's true. "

"Andy, you've always been my girl. And I'm sorry it took some duke coming to town to knock some sense into my head and make me realize that it was about time I told you so."

"George is a nice guy," she said.

"Yeah, I know he is," Kyle threw out. "We kind of hung out. Threw some football."

"How did that happen?" she asked, surprised.

"He was walking down the street, and I picked him up."

"I figured you'd try to beat him up."

"I wanted to. At first."

"Until you realized he's pretty cool?"

"Yeah. Until that," Kyle conceded.

"I dropped out of the contest."

"You what?"

"It was no big deal."

"It seemed like a big deal to you."

"Yeah, but probably not for the right reasons."

"So, are you telling me you're not going to run off to New York City with the duke?"

Andy laughed. "I don't know. I guess that depends on whether he asks me or not," she said in a teasing voice.

"Andy," he said in a low growl.

He kissed the side of her neck, then it was back to her mouth again. When he pulled away to stare down at her with those dreamy eyes of his, he said, "Seems like I've figured out how to get certain notions out of your head."

"Seems like you have," she said, kissing the corner of his mouth.

"Seems like I could keep them out if I'm really, really good at diverting your attention."

"Seems like you could."

"Seems like I will," he said and pulled her to him.

60

_____

"To love someone who doesn't love you back – is
there anything emptier than that?"
— A question Darryl Lee had once asked of
Bobby Jack

It was after eight o'clock when Grier woke to find the other
side of the bed empty and no sign of Bobby Jack.

He had left a note on the pillow.

Running by a job site. Will grab breakfast and be back before
you know it.
Bobby Jack

Grier rubbed a finger across the paper and thought of

the tenderness Bobby Jack had shown her last night. She had needed it. Wanted it. Taken it.

Selfishly, she thought now. And what did she have to give him in return?

She slipped on her clothes and took Sebbie out for a quick potty break.

Back in the room, she started throwing her things in the suitcase before she had fully let herself admit that she really was leaving. It was cowardly and unfair. She knew it. But she didn't think she could look him in the eyes and then leave. She wouldn't have the will power.

She didn't bother with order. She just reached for clothing, blow dryer, makeup bag and threw it all in together, zipping up the suitcase and pulling it off the luggage stand.

Sebbie sat on the bed and watched her, a look of confusion in his sweet eyes. "I know. You don't have to tell me. There's nothing admirable about what I'm doing. But I don't know how to do anything else right now."

The door opened, and there stood Bobby Jack. He had two white bags in one hand, a cup carrier with two coffees in the other. He looked at her, at the suitcase and her purse on the floor. The hurt that crossed his face nearly buckled her knees.

"Bobby Jack."

"You're leaving," he said. He stepped inside and kicked the door closed, still holding the coffee and two bags. "You were really going to leave without—"

"It seemed like the best thing," she said softly.

"The best thing for who?" he asked.

"For both of us," she said.

He set the coffee and bags on the desk in the corner of the room and then turned to look at her. "Did I imagine?—"

"No, you didn't."

"Then why would you go without saying anything?"

"Because I knew if I saw you, I couldn't leave."

Unconcealed hurt crossed his face. "I don't want you to leave."

"My life is in New York," she said, and even to her ears, her explanation sounded pitifully inadequate.

"Life doesn't happen in a place. It happens when you're with people who love you. What exactly is there for you other than your business? Is there someone in your life you haven't told me about?"

"No."

"Then what?"

"A life I created for myself."

"When you ran away from here the first time," he said.

The words struck their intended mark. She glanced away, closing her eyes. "I didn't really have a choice," she said.

"I know you didn't. This time you do have a choice. But the truth is until you've made peace with things, really made peace with them, it won't matter if I love you. Or if anyone loves you. First, you've got to love yourself."

"You don't understand," she began.

"I think I do," he disagreed. "I've been left before. And I don't want to be left again. If you want me in your life, you come find me. Okay?"

He walked out then and closed the door behind him.

"Bobby Jack," she called out. She wanted to go after him, but her feet wouldn't move. She stood cemented to the spot, knowing in her heart that he was right.

She didn't love herself very much right now. And if she were honest, she didn't know when or if she ever would again.

61

"It's only through the passing of time that we gain perspective, insight. What once seemed impossible becomes infinitely possible."
— Grier McAllister – Blog at Jane Austen Girl

Two months and the city still didn't fit right.

Like a once-perfect outfit that had been tossed in the dryer by mistake, the size was no longer hers. Grier's infatuation with it seemed to have lost its shine.

Even Amy saw that she wasn't the same. She had long ago become more friend than assistant and she sat for hours at a time just listening to Grier talk about her mother, Bobby Jack and how unexpected the homesickness she now felt was to her.

Grier still loved her business. Loved working with

clients who appreciated the boost of confidence her suggestions often fostered. That was still rewarding in much the same way. But the difference now was that it no longer made her feel complete.

Before going back to Timbell Creek, there hadn't been this hole of awareness inside her. Awareness of a piece of life she had given up thinking would ever be hers.

She missed Timbell Creek.

She missed Bobby Jack. Missed what had been between them. The laughing and hand holding. The kissing and the way he had looked at her as if there were no possibility of any other woman making him feel what she made him feel.

And what she'd begun to realize in the couple of dates she'd ventured out on since coming back to the city was that she didn't want to see that in anyone else's face. Only his.

She'd come to realize a few other things, too. Things that didn't require sessions with her therapist to figure out. For the rest of her life, there would never be a day when she did not regret leaving things unresolved with her mother. She would have to live with that. She had finally accepted it. With resignation if not peace.

She wanted love in her life. Real love. Pure love. The kind she had seen in Bobby Jack's eyes when he had told her that last morning that he'd been left before and he never wanted to be left again. That if she wanted him, she would have to be the one to reach out.

And so, late one evening as she stood on the balcony of her apartment, holding Sebbie in her arms and looking out at the lights of a city that no longer felt like home to her, she made the decision to take the risk. Go out on a limb, fully aware that it might very well break beneath her.

62

"There's no limit to how much I can love. That
means I have more than enough room in my heart
for you both. Love isn't a competition."
— Andy to Priscilla and Bobby Jack during a
dinner she fixed for the three of them.

New York City was everything Andy had imagined it
would be and more.

She and her dad and Kyle had landed at LaGuardia at
ten that morning. They'd taken a taxi to the Plaza Hotel,
her dad deciding the splurge would be worth it since the
Jane Austen Girl Ball was being held there.

It felt like something out of a dream. That she and Kyle
were actually here in this city, a place she had always
imagined being larger than life. And it was. They spent the

afternoon walking street after street where shops held the most incredible clothes she'd ever seen.

Her dad was less than enamored with her darting in and out of store after store, but he didn't protest and followed along patiently.

They had just passed a Starbucks when he said he was going in for a coffee.

Standing in the middle of the sidewalk, Andy dropped her head back and stared up at the multiple skyscrapers within her view. "Can you believe this place?" she said, bringing her focus back to Kyle.

He had moved in close to her, standing right in front of her now, so close that her chin nearly bumped his chest. She put a hand out to steady herself. He slipped his arms around her waist and pulled her a little closer.

"I can't believe you," he said, looking down at her with an incredibly appealing smile.

"What?" she said, her voice coming out a little raspy.

"How beautiful you are."

She started to disagree, but her response dissolved beneath Kyle's lips.

He kissed her like she was the only girl he ever thought about, ever wanted to hold this way. And she kissed him back. In the very same way. Because it was exactly what she felt.

No one else knew her the way Kyle knew her. No one else looked at her as if she were the answer to every question he'd ever asked.

And that was what she wanted to be. Here in the middle of a busy Manhattan sidewalk, Andy realized that whatever she decided to pursue in life she wanted it to include Kyle. Knew in her heart that none of it would be the same without him.

She looped her arms around his neck and deepened the kiss, telling him all of that without words.

"All right, you two."

Andy and Kyle pulled apart to find her dad looking at them with not very convincing disapproval. "I can't leave you alone for a minute."

"It was just a kiss, Daddy," Andy said, reaching up to give him one on the cheek as well.

"Sorry, Mr. Randall," Kyle said, trying to look properly chastised.

Andy slipped one arm through her daddy's arm and the other through Kyle's. "Come on, we've got more shopping to do."

They both groaned as she led them down the street, one on either side of her.

63

"When something really, really good finds you,
welcome it, embrace it."
— *Grier McAllister – Blog at Jane Austen Girl*

One of the grandest ballrooms of the Plaza Hotel provided the setting for the Jane Austen Girl Ball.

Grier arrived on her own, a car service dropping her off at the front.

Butterflies had taken her stomach hostage, and she couldn't remember the last time she'd felt this kind of nervousness. All day long and while she'd been getting dressed, she could think of nothing but what it would be like to see Bobby Jack again. If he would even want to see her.

She honestly didn't know.

Her dress was a long, full, flowy thing, fitted at the top and strapless. A light silvery blue, it made a nice contrast to her hair and eyes. She'd searched the city for the past week, not once finding the right thing, until yesterday afternoon, when she'd pretty much given up before spotting it in a boutique window display.

She instantly knew it was the one, a dress to rival any she'd dreamed of as a girl.

Now, walking through the lobby of the Plaza Hotel in four-inch heels that cost nearly as much as the dress, she felt like a newbie going to her first freshman dance. What if Bobby Jack ignored her, didn't want to see her or talk to her?

It was a very real possibility, and one she wouldn't exactly blame him for. But if there was a chance. . .even the smallest chance that he might feel differently, she had to try.

At the entrance to the ballroom, Grier stopped, a little awed by the room full of beautifully dressed people. The music was hip and loud, instantly defining the ball as anything but stale and boring. Tables to either side of the room were filled with incredible displays of food that might have rivaled a Roman feast.

She forced herself to go in, glancing around for a familiar face. She felt a tap on her shoulder and turned to find George looking down at her with a charming grin.

"Wow," he said. "It's too bad you weren't one of the girls I got to choose from."

Grier laughed and felt some of her tension ebb away. "You're very kind."

"I'm very honest."

"I want to thank you again for inviting Andy and her dad tonight."

"I was happy to." He looked at her for a moment, a teasing expression on his face. "Am I to assume you have a crush on Mr. Randall?"

Blushing, she said, "Maybe a little one."

"Cool." He took her hand and started pulling her through the crowd. "They're right over here."

"Ah, wait. George, I'm not ready to—"

Either he didn't hear her, or deliberately wasn't listening. Holding onto her hand, he merged her right through the center of the room, and when they came out on the other side, there stood Bobby Jack.

Her heart rate dipped and then set off like gunfire.

Bobby Jack. In a black tux. Stark white shirt. His dark hair tamed into stylish appeal with some kind of gel that made it gleam. Oh. Dear. Heavens.

Then he looked up. Met her no doubt wide-eyed gaze. And he couldn't hide his reaction to her. She saw it on his face. An instant of absolute longing, so intense that she felt the heat of it ignite through her.

Just as quickly, he dropped shutters over all of it and pasted a polite smile on his incredibly good-looking face.

George walked her right up to him and said, "I believe you two have been waiting for each other."

"I wasn't—" Bobby Jack began.

"I didn't—" Grier started in at the same time.

"You two should really work this out," George said. "And I'd better go find my date."

With that, he left them alone.

Never in her life had Grier felt so incapable of putting a sentence together. Her mind seemed to have blanked itself of all verbal capability.

Bobby Jack stared at her, equally silent. She didn't look away, but let her eyes say what her mouth could not. All around them, people talked and laughed and danced and ate. And they just watched each other, as if they were the only two in the room.

"You look incredible," he said, his voice low and not quite steady.

"So do you," she said.

"How have you been?"

"I've been all right. And you?"

"Okay," he said, and it was clear that his answer was closer to the truth than hers.

And just like that, she decided she could no longer hide it from him. Her eyes brimmed with tears, and he made a sound of something almost like pain, reaching out to brush his thumb across her cheek and smooth them away.

He cupped his hand to the side of her face, and the connection between them melted all the doubts and yearning of these past months.

"I've missed you," he said.

"I've missed you," she said on a broken little sob.

He reached for her hand then and tow-boated her around the edges of the crowd and through a glass door to a terrace that looked out across Central Park. He led her to the far wall, not letting go, not even once looking at her until they had reached the shadowed edge outside the lights from the ball.

He slid his arm around her waist and reeled her in quickly, deliberately so that there wasn't an inch of space between them when he finally lowered his head and kissed her.

No slow reintroduction, either. But an open-mouth, full out I-want-you-now kiss that threatened to melt her silver blue dress to liquid.

And she kissed him right back. As if she had been thinking of nothing else in the two months since they'd last seen each other. As if she needed him to breathe. To think. To exist.

She couldn't deny that she did. Because now, only now that she was in his arms, did she feel complete again. Bobby Jack was the piece missing in her life, a vital piece that she not only wanted, but no longer wanted to live without.

His mouth found the side of her neck and then the soft spot just beneath her ear. She exhaled a sigh of sheer pleasure. "I . . . love . . . the way . . . you . . . kiss me."

The words came out as if she had no control over them, and really, she didn't.

He pulled back to run his thumb along the curve of her jaw. He looked down at her dress then, lowered his head and kissed the indention at the bottom of her throat. "Grier. If you don't mean this. . .I'm asking you. Don't give me hope. Letting you go the last time. . . I don't want. . . I can't do that again."

"I mean it," she said, placing her hand to the side of his face and drawing his sincere gaze to hers. "I so, so mean it."

He lifted her off the ground, one arm under her bottom, the other at her waist. And this time when he kissed her, she could feel the difference in him. A relaxed relief that freed him to show her everything he felt for her. And he did, setting her onto a rock wall well inside the shadows, shimmying her long dress up her legs until it was high enough that he could step in between, his hands at the base of her back.

They kissed themselves into a state of not caring where they were as long as they didn't have to stop. Or let each other go.

Bobby Jack came to his senses first. Stepping back just far enough that he could look at her through passion-hazed eyes. "Do you have any idea what you do to me?"

"The same thing you do to me?"

"How did I live so long without you?"

She put a hand to his face, leaned up and kissed him softly on the mouth. "I don't want to live another day without you in my life."

"You don't have to." He paused, and then, "I want to marry you, Grier. I don't want—"

She pressed a finger to his lips and stopped him. "Yes."

"Yes?" he said, the question carrying enough uncertainty that she realized he hadn't expected her to say yes.

"Absolutely, yes."

He smiled then, that smile that transformed his face from good-looking to downright beautiful. "The logistics we'll figure out as we go?"

"Yeah," she said, leaning in to kiss him with all the love she felt for him.

A sudden noise made her pull back and peer into the shadowed corner of the terrace. "What is that?" she asked.

Bobby Jack looked over his shoulder. "Unless my eyes are fooling me, a very large bird."

Grier could just make out the hooked beak, and then it lifted off the wall, wings widespread, soaring off into the night. "That was an eagle," she said, a little shocked, but somehow knowing she was right, even as she found it hard to believe.

"In the city?" Bobby Jack sounded doubtful.

Grier thought of her mother then, of the eagle they had once seen together so long ago. Had she sent it here tonight? Somehow, there was a warm comfort in the thought.

"I'm learning not to question the unexpected," she said.

"I'm just going to take it as a sign that I'm finally on the right track."

"I'll go with that," Bobby Jack said.

"And I'll go with this," she said, pulling him back to her with a promise of never letting him go.

Epilogue

Somewhere in the south of France

The enormous white hotel sat like the premier jewel at the cusp of a Mediterranean crown of royal blue.

Morning number three, and Grier and Bobby Jack had yet to venture out of the luxurious room on an upper floor that looked across a white silky-sand beach.

The sun had just tiptoed in between the sheer curtains. Grier always woke to the light, and despite some lingering jet lag, today was no exception. In that moment before complete awareness took hold, she panicked a little at the unfamiliar surroundings. But then she slipped an arm to the other side of the bed, and there was Bobby Jack.

She turned onto her side and explored the lean muscle of his nicely rippled abs. She loved his body, and now, one year into their marriage, she knew every delicious inch of him.

Just the thought of all the explorations that had led to such familiarity sent a little twist of heat through her.

"I'm not even fully awake and I'm wanting you again, woman." His voice was deep and still edged with sleep.

She smiled. "Excellent."

He flipped over, snagged her waist with one arm and sealed her to him, providing her with immediate proof of the accuracy of his statement.

"Are you aware, ma'am," he said, "that you aren't wearing any clothes?"

"I am, sir. Is there something you would like to do about it?"

"I might have to write you a citation. A French citation."

"Ooh, that sounds interesting. Is there a fine with my citation?"

"There is," he said, leaning in to kiss her neck and then the dip of her throat. He kissed upward and nipped her chin with his teeth. "Another day in bed, I'm afraid."

"Oh, no, not that," she said in mock distress. "But what if I can't think of any way to please you for all that time?"

He raised up enough to slip her under him, his beautiful body fully covering hers. "Just do what comes naturally," he said.

"And if I fail?"

He moved against her, and every part of her came awake to him. "Oh, you won't fail. Not if you practice some more."

"Ah," she said. "Want to practice then?"

"I thought you'd never ask."

A GOOD BIT LATER, when they lay staring up at the ceiling, their breathing still quick and uneven, he lifted up on one elbow to look down at her with love-hazed eyes. "Happy One Year anniversary, Mrs. Randall."

"Happy One Year anniversary, Mr. Randall," she said, running the backs of her fingers across his cheek. "You give nice presents."

"Are you trying to make me blush?"

"Is that possible?"

He nuzzled her neck and said, "Speaking of presents. I'm supposed to deliver a few."

"From?"

He got up from the bed and walked, fully naked, to the closet where he pulled a large shopping bag from the top shelf. He walked back and set it in the center of the bed, slipping under the sheet beside her. "Well, let's see."

She sat up and leaned against the headboard. "Where did you get this?" she asked, peering into the bag.

"I snuck it along in my suitcase."

"Oh, you did, did you?"

"I did." He reached in and handed her a box wrapped in beautiful pink paper with a huge snowy white ribbon on top. "This is from Andy and Kyle. She made me promise you would open hers first."

Grier felt a little tug of love for the teenage girl she had come to think of as the daughter she had never had. She tore away the wrapping to find a simple white box with the name of her favorite jewelry store on the lid. She opened it up and inside was a sterling silver charm bracelet with two charms: a Hound and a small fluffy dog. "Flo and Sebbie," she said.

"I think Andy was pretty proud of herself for having found their look-alikes."

"I love it," Grier said. "Will you hook it for me?"

He draped it across her wrist and secured the hook. "Perfect."

"And speaking of those two, here's a little something from the ones who rule our house." He pulled out another box, this one wrapped in paw print paper, and handed it to her.

Grier felt a knot begin to form in her throat and tears well in her eyes. "You do know how to make me love you more every day."

He watched while she opened the box. Inside she found two matching collars and leashes, one in Flo's size and one in Sebbie's. They were New York City fancy, dark leather with jewel insets. "Did they pick these out or did you?" she said, her voice raspy with emotion.

"I confess. I did."

She leaned over and kissed him on the cheek. "They're beautiful. Thank you."

"You're very welcome."

"Did Flo approve?"

"If Sebbie's for it, you know she's for it."

"They are a pair, aren't they?"

"Not sure how they ever lived without each other." He

reached back in the bag and pulled out another package. "This is from Hatcher."

She pulled the paper from the present and found a beautiful Mediterranean cookbook inside. She opened the cover, and in the older man's less-than-steady handwriting, read:

To my friends, Grier and Bobby Jack. When you get home, I'll use this book to cook up memories of your trip. May it be as wonderful as the two of you.

"Lucky for us, he lives in our house," Bobby Jack said. "Although if we keep letting him do the cooking, I'm going to have to take up distance running."

Grier smiled and felt an instant lump in her throat. Hatcher's gratitude humbled her. But the truth was she felt indebted to him. Through Hatcher, she had come to learn a great deal about her mother. He spoke of her with such fondness that his recollections had softened the edges of Grier's own memories. She was grateful to him for that.

"It's like he has a new life," she said softly, running her hand across the book's cover. "I'm not sure you realize how much it means to him when you take him out to job sites with you."

"I enjoy having him with me," he said. "He knows a lot of stuff."

She looped her arm around his neck and kissed him full on the mouth. "Thank you for being you. And for bringing these presents."

"You're welcome. But there's something else in the bag."

"Oh?"

"Yeah," he said, reaching in and pulling out a small box wrapped in silver paper with a red bow. "For you, my love."

"What have you done?"

"Open it and see."

She pulled the ribbon and untied the bow. The paper came next, and then she lifted the lid. A small black box sat nestled inside. She opened it, carefully, and then stared at the beautiful diamond earrings inside. "Bobby Jack. You shouldn't have done this."

"You like?"

She carefully loosened one and took it out. "I love."

"Good," he said, looking pleased.

She put one in her ear and then the other.

She sat up and then slid onto his lap, the white sheet dropping away from her.

"Stunning," he said.

He reached up and smoothed his thumbs across the diamonds in her ears, then traced a path down each side of her neck and the curve of her breasts. "You. Are. So. Incredibly. Lovely."

She leaned down. Kissed him with an instant igniting of desire. His hands anchored at her waist and then in one fluid motion, slipped her under him. He held her wrists above her head, waking her body to his once more.

"We should probably see something of the town today. In case anyone asks us what we thought of it," she said.

"We probably should," he said, kissing her then, a slow, lengthy, purposeful kiss.

"Later?" she said.

"Much," he said.

More Books by Inglath Cooper

Swerve

The Heart That Breaks

My Italian Lover

Fences – Book Three – Smith Mountain Lake Series

Dragonfly Summer – Book Two – Smith Mountain
Lake Series

Blue Wide Sky – Book One – Smith Mountain Lake
Series

That Month in Tuscany

And Then You Loved Me

Down a Country Road

Good Guys Love Dogs

Truths and Roses

Nashville – Part Ten – Not Without You

Nashville – Book Nine – You, Me and a Palm Tree

Nashville – Book Eight – R U Serious

Nashville – Book Seven – Commit

Nashville – Book Six – Sweet Tea and Me

Nashville – Book Five – Amazed
Nashville – Book Four – Pleasure in the Rain
Nashville – Book Three – What We Feel
Nashville – Book Two – Hammer and a Song
Nashville – Book One – Ready to Reach
On Angel's Wings
A Gift of Grace
RITA® Award Winner John Riley's Girl
A Woman With Secrets
Unfinished Business
A Woman Like Annie
The Lost Daughter of Pigeon Hollow
A Year and a Day

Dear Reader,

I would like to thank you for taking the time to read my story. There are so many wonderful books to choose from these days, and I am hugely appreciative that you chose mine.

Come check out my Facebook page for postings on books, dogs and things that make life good! www.facebook.com/inglathcooperbooks

Wishing you many great escapes!

Inglath

About Inglath Cooper

RITA® Award-winning author Inglath Cooper was born in Virginia. She is a graduate of Virginia Tech with a degree in English. She fell in love with books as soon as she learned how to read. "My mom read to us before bed, and I think that's how I started to love stories. It was like a little mini-vacation we looked forward to every night before going to sleep. I think I eventually read most of the books in my elementary school library."

That love for books translated into a natural love for writing and a desire to create stories that other readers could get lost in, just as she had gotten lost in her favorite books. Her stories focus on the dynamics of relationships, those between a man and a woman, mother and daughter, sisters, friends. They most often take place in small Virginia towns very much like the one where she grew up and are peopled with characters who reflect those values and traditions.

"There's something about small-town life that's just

part of who I am. I've had the desire to live in other places, wondered what it would be like to be a true Manhattanite, but the thing I know I would miss is the familiarity of faces everywhere I go. There's a lot to be said for going in the grocery store and seeing ten people you know!"

Inglath Cooper is an avid supporter of companion animal rescue and is a volunteer and donor for the Franklin County Humane Society. She and her family have fostered many dogs and cats that have gone on to be adopted by other families. "The rewards are endless. It's an eye-opening moment to realize that what one person throws away can fill another person's life with love and joy."

Follow Inglath on Facebook
at www.facebook.com/inglathcooperbooks

Join her mailing list for news of new releases and giveaways at www.inglathcooper.com

Get in Touch With Inglath Cooper

Email: inglathcooper@gmail.com

   Facebook – Inglath Cooper Books

   Instagram – inglath.cooper.books

   Pinterest – Inglath Cooper Books

   Twitter – InglathCooper

   Join Inglath Cooper's Mailing List and get a FREE ebook! Good Guys Love Dogs!

Made in the USA
Middletown, DE
29 August 2019